More Praise for
Gun Dealers' Daughter

"[Soledad] holds our attention to the last word with what is almost, yes, a writer's sensibility and style. . . . It's as deft a sketch as something from Fitzgerald, and the happy accident of the able storyteller is contrived with so much greater grace than in too many new books. . . . A *tour de force* tale about late 20th century Manila, but . . . also a book for our times."   —Brian Collins,
Los Angeles Review of Books

"A daring fever dream of a novel."   —Alex Gilvarry,
author of *From the Memoirs of a Non-Enemy Combatant*

"A stunning novel of the Marcos-era Philippines. . . . [Sol's] telling and retelling and editing and tweaking of her own history . . . ultimately proves to be one of the most successful aspects of Apostol's creation; the technique invites readers into the very core of Sol's experience. . . . Readers are treated to a captivating look into this period of Philippine history and the gripping story of one girl's struggles to find her place in the world."   —Kerry McHugh,
Shelf Awareness

"A stunning and lyrical word-portrait of a 'martial-law baby' whose story of teenage romance and rebellion allows Apostol to braid together a wider set of issues: memory, history, language, nationalism, exile, and revolution. These may be familiar themes in post-colonial fiction and Philippine literature, but they gain a renewed significance in Apostol's hands. . . . *Gun Dealers' Daughter* is an engrossing if challenging read not only because of its complex narrative structure but also because it asks hard questions about the possibility of revolution."   —Paul Nadal, *Public Books*

"[The] complex narration is, in fact, one of the major strengths of this classic example of madness and trauma, repression and guilt. . . . [H]aunting."   —Charles R. Larson, *Counterpunch*

"Vertiginous. . . . Poetically told through the shattered prism of Sol's memory. . . . Apostol (*Bibliolepsy*) offers an intriguing and significant view of Marcos-era Philippines in this complex and feverish novel."   —*Publishers Weekly*

"Rich with emotion, reflection, and fervor, the story takes on an added element of revealing the struggles of Filipinos and women. While the narrative is strong, Apostol's writing style—simple, poetic, and captivating at every point of Soledad's journey—is the real draw. . . . Reminiscent of Toni Morrison's *Paradise* and Melissa P.'s *The Scent of Your Breath*, this book will appeal to readers of literary fiction."   —Ashanti L. White, *Library Journal*

Gun
Dealers'
Daughter

Gun
Dealers'
Daughter

A NOVEL

GINA APOSTOL

W. W. NORTON & COMPANY

NEW YORK · LONDON

FOR ARNE

For information about permission to reproduce selections from this book,
write to Permissions, W. W. Norton & Company, Inc.,
500 Fifth Avenue, New York, NY 10110

For information about special discounts for bulk purchases, please contact
W. W. Norton Special Sales at specialsales@wwnorton.com or 800-233-4830

Manufacturing by Courier Westford
Book design by Ellen Cipriano
Production manager: Louise Mattarelliano

Library of Congress Cataloging-in-Publication Data

Apostol, Gina.
Gun dealers' daughter : a novel / Gina Apostol. — 1st American ed.
p. cm.
Originally published: Manila : Published and exclusively
distributed by Anvil Pub., c c2010.
ISBN 978-0-393-06294-6 (hardcover)
1. Amnesiacs—New York (State)—New York—Fiction.
2. Women revolutionaries—Philippines—Fiction. 3. Philippines—
History—1946–1986—Fiction. I. Title.
PR9550.9.A66G86 2012
823'.914–dc23
                            2011049404
ISBN 978-0-393-34948-1 pbk.

W. W. Norton & Company, Inc.
500 Fifth Avenue, New York, N.Y. 10110
www.wwnorton.com

W. W. Norton & Company Ltd.
Castle House, 75/76 Wells Street, London W1T 3QT

1 2 3 4 5 6 7 8 9 0

Part I

1

UNCLE GIANNI MET the girl at Nice Airport. He held her by the hand as lightbulbs flashed. Revise that: not hand. By the sleeve. He held me by the sleeve, gently. There was something awkward about my arrival.

My stooped, discordant figure—my bandaged, gauzed lump of hands.

A cordon held curious onlookers at bay, and a film crew, Gallic and impervious, skinny, tilting men in black, strode about my cleared path. I moved along the cleared-up space of an orchestrated welcome, following the straight line of a utility rope. I stumbled. I kicked the shin of a blond gaffer on bent knee, a gofer pulling tape from the floor. "A commercial," Uncle Gianni muttered. I shivered as a door blew open. A lightbulb blinded me. I felt someone rushing behind me—a lady walking a dog? A cripple with a parasol. My suddenly myopic eyes distinguished a lame man's fleshy elbows, or was it a leash? Uncle Gianni tightened his grip and, almost dragging me by an armpit, moved me quickly along.

And in a cutting room somewhere, freeze-framed, on the margins of that black-clad crowd posing to sell condoms or perfume, a girl's stricken face—my gaze—looks down, denying evidence of its arrival, gaunt-cheeked and hollow-eyed.

No QUESTIONS ASKED, no thoughts pursued. The days in a winter town, in the south of France, were a blur of boats. Medicated recall. My bandaged hands held me back, a drugged drag. I watched the gauze on my wrists fray, a gray, wispy itch.

By the look of our lodgings, it had not been planned: the place was not worthy of Uncle Gianni. Uncovered beams, rough wood. This cramped place by the water in a narrow street overlooking a threaded sea was, I thought, pretty. But Uncle Gianni raised an eyebrow at its crude renovation. The room was whitewashed: brown timber framed the paint. Sometimes, the white walls seemed to reflect the silver sea, its glints, its undulating glare. You could see the boats from a window, cutouts in a livid blue.

Uncle Gianni ordered lunch at the square, near the carousel. I gave the man the merry-go-round ticket, a neon-colored heart, and rode the horse, a slow reverie of motion. Up the rue du Haut Castelet, a writer had pursued a novel in exile, and now it contained a memory of his name, hidden in bougainvillea. A one-eyed dog, its absurd body stunted by heedless breeding, shat on the cobbles as its patient owner watched, while the French diners drank their anise, and I wished to retch.

I watched the angled play of masts, the modest geometries of massive hulls waiting for domestic ghosts. Winter boats moored for pleasure. Wrinkled caretakers appeared amidship, smoking joints and dragging rope. I noted names and origins, boats from Guernsey and Oporto. None of the names struck my fancy, though one was a namesake: blue and sunless *Sol*, a gloomy sloop, dingy dinghy. Unappetizing clothes—denims, a hat, underwear—flapped, drying, on her deck.

When Uncle Gianni learned from one of the caretakers, a youngish sailor with receding hair, that I wished to know, in broken French, how my services could be of use, laundering or scrubbing, not for pay, just for board, once the yacht left the marina, Uncle Gianni took me away. First we had that scene, the drama on the jetty.

UNCLE GIANNI HAD been walking along the stones, the lank seaweeds, and there I walked beyond him. He couldn't see; he was looking at the horizon, at the green, jutting rocks. I walked until I reached the end. And in a muddled move—I made this leap. A deep, chilling immersion.

I tried to sink in the Mediterranean, which was hard to do.

I am no Ophelia.

I'm a floater.

It was my second escape.

I had tried it in Manila. With broad, stupid knives. Big, messy gashes, a knotted misery in my wrists. Hullaballoo in the hallway. It was the maids who saved me, a stampede from the kitchen. Hard to die in a house of servants. All I have to show for my remorse, my dead feelings—this shallow well of scars.

I tried to sink.

But the calm ice waters of the Mediterranean buoyed me up, as if I were light-born. The sea kept lifting me toward the light. The chilly waves gently lofted me.

And then I froze.

I panicked. Awash in that chilly, wide, engulfing sea, I felt myself sinking. The ice-waves rolled over me, a heavy rush thrusting me underwater. My legs locked, my limbs froze. I couldn't move.

Once more the sea rolled over me.

I wished to live.

I struggled. I gasped for air. As I did, I saw my final images: a green-veined hand, a rock in the distance, a stern, unforgettable sky. I saw two goons in starched blue Makati security guard uniforms, smiling and interrogating me, one holding a stuffed animal, "Ali Babar? Ali Babar?" Then they were holding on to my shins, dragging me down. In incoherent, sputtering flashes.

Brown-dotted seashells, like turtle's backs. Scuttling across the floors of silent seas. An infinite array of books.

Jed holding a banner, a look in his eye that was not comfort or appeasement. A strange absent tenderness—a hand against barnacled rock.

A wave spun me. I reached for the rock. Visions rolled as I met the sky. Rain, sleet and snow, heavy, fat and diabolical. The weight of sand and rocks and that volumed, fickle water, and I sank, losing ground, losing the features of my dull face; the pull of my heavy, tenacious hair; and Manong Babe, his belly slack and his shoes shined, holding a baseball bat in my old garden, smiling at me while I drowned.

A STICK FIGURE ON the stones: Uncle Gianni. A quick splash. As he swam closer, he seemed to slow to an excruciating, meditative, languorous crawl, then to a towering grin as he held me, my thrashing legs against the rock, my floating, freezing tears.

OLIVE GROVES ARE medicinal. That was the verdict of the new place's founders, who lined the path to the clinic with spare, gray-green trees, a view that was not optional. Stiff white sheets in an austere room, padded with those strange, sausage French pillows, uncomfortable and almost demeaning, as if I were not some human but a creature who thrashed against a cage. There was a crucifix on the whitewashed wall. That, too, was implacable: the corners of the cross were nailed fast, in anticipation of heretical moves. Trim French nurses guarded me, mild-faced orderlies with bronzed skins. In the chapel, Baroque music played from invisible speakers, and the haunting tones of a sourceless cantata convinced me momentarily of the presence of God. He was there in the screen. I cowered miserably before it. God spoke English with an accent. I didn't speak. I looked God wanly in the eye and didn't blink. My sobs echoed in the chapel, and God in hiding had nothing to say.

I planted tulip bulbs in a shady part of the garden, moving timidly with other patients, all of us passive and not meeting other eyes, afraid to be caught in each other's company, wearing our white uniforms with blue sashes. As I knelt, I tucked the skirt's folds through my knees in a perverse, modest way: as if the skirt were fastened in my crotch, in tune with ancient convent-bred women, Lola Felma, for instance, my grandmother frozen in childhood, squatting just so, folding her skirt between her thighs, so that her underwear did not peep through.

Vague things came back as I smoothed the earth, distant, trivial things: this same white and blue outfit, worn in Manila a long time ago (the uniform of Our Lady of Lourdes); a little girl with desperate eyes and sausage curls; a refrigerator magnet I once bought in Boston. The white poster of a headless woman. An orphan and a giant peach, maybe a guava. And then I thought of a body in the dirt, a head buried like this tulip, just so.

A cry like a relapse. Turning earth. I am pounding my fist into the soil, pounding the tulip bulb into a pulp. I am drumming earth against unyielding ground.

I am carried, kicking, away. I am not allowed out of my room. Once again. I watch the other patients from the window, walking obediently, sedately amid the olive trees. It was good to handle the earth, to be outside. A good thing: it was material things that I recalled, neutral matters: the soft fist of the fetal flower that I buried in the cold ground was the damp skin of a doll I once owned, a dimply marvel with a digestive tract. The wet smell of the earth revived, strangely, the smell of a book: what was its title? I sifted through the black film of earth, patting the tender tulip in, a fuzzy top, a creature burrowing softly in the ground. Though I could recall that I had read that book first in Brussels, or maybe Boston, then continued it on a train into Amherst, or maybe Antwerp, and finished it in Manila, or maybe Maryland—I couldn't remember the book's title. It had smelled always, whenever I opened it, of some kind of dankness, a mixture of pulp, offal and enclosed air—the mixed smells of the smooth, black soil. Then it came to me. Evelyn, Edward, William, Waugh. A book in green binding.

Brideshead Revisited.

Insipid, detail-filled days like this. Life was this multiplication of things, actions, trivial gestures. That had always been the case, and one is meant to accept this, the successive production of wasteful days. To seek this replication, to fertilize and shelter it. One is meant to *prolong*.

At the clinic, my problem was finding the right angularity of things.

The efforts I made so as not to bump against swollen objects were tiring. At first, merely moving an inch or two required supreme lucidity. The wingbacks of armchairs swelled into unnecessary flight. It took time for things to discover their integrity, turn into matters I could grasp.

Worse was my recurring, miserable dysgraphia, a slip-sliding dementia of letters, an almost untenable mental pit. I could write, if I wished, bleak, simple sentences, many of them at a time, and it became my hobby, my way of staring at things, trying to get them right. But then I would unravel like a wobbly top, a reeling, slow yo-yo: my brain was a clumsy, badly made toy.

Sometimes, I was fine, as in that morning looking at the Alpilles, when I wrote a letter to a person named Vita, though I couldn't place her face; I told her about the hesitant, nail-shaving-like sprouts of herbs: thyme, rosemary and mint. Their smells developed before their bodies did. The nurse, on reading it, said that was

because the earth remembered its old souls. "Good girl," she said,
perhaps. She spoke French without apology. Humbly, joyfully, I
acknowledged her praise, without language of my own.

It was troubling that, while at times offhand words recalled
subtle sensations, banal facts resisted my net. Before the moose-like
overbite of the gentle doctor, I called back the layout of my rooms in
Manila, a mental furbishing: the book-lined wall left of my bed, the
connecting door, and somewhere a poet's floating ghost, her kerchief dress. I put the intercom in the wrong place, by the left side
with all the books; but what was on the right side of the room? The
doctor waited. It was blank, a terrifying, effaced, empty portion of
my brain; and it began to fill with the same old demons, the little
girl with the sausage curls staring at me in despair, her guts
impaled—in ludicrous, steady motions—by tridents, which my
father himself held, like a serene scepter in his hand, but it was only
his cigarette holder, a shining, ephemeral piece of ivory, and then,
like a fast shuffle of cards, Jed, looking at me with a cigarette;
together, in a haze, we soothed an inert creature, a fire ant, a spider,
with a lighter made of ebony. The spider turned its face to look at me—

And then it occurred to me: Yes. The connecting door to a gym,
my spoliarium. A sunroom. That had been to the right of my bed.

The doctor nodded approvingly, *Bon*, and snapped his notebook shut.

2

I MET MY PARENTS finally in New York.

A day of rain, the mild bleakness of months away; or had it been a year, or two dozen months?

In Europe, I had acquired pallor and an incoherent sense of time. Even my old, flexed muscles were gone, and when I lifted my hands to wave at Frankie and Reina Elena, my parents at the gate, I felt the soft prefix of flab, my substitute triceps, sadly dangle in the air.

They had not been allowed to visit—*for your own piss of mind*, the doctor said, *it is best for not to have perturbation*; and instead an entourage of nurses had followed me across the ocean, a flock of pensive chain-smokers and tender crossword puzzle addicts. When I embraced my mother, then my father, my flattish, soft body suggested welcome as well as it could, but even that was sluggish. In turn, my parents seemed to be this dull, tentative grouping, a woozy arrangement of flesh.

The nurses huddled with my parents, clogging up the welcome line.

I had left part of myself behind somewhere. In vagabond Europe? In even vaguer Manila? When I lifted my bags and felt their heavyweight adventure, their packed solid matter, I knew I had misplaced some important item, an organ—someplace. Everything else was full and intact, my luggage, the city, its traffic, the bauble of a home that we swerved into, full of itself, a shambling mansion sprawled out for my inspection, familiar, monstrous, and complete. Everything else was whole except for me: something had fallen behind, and was that a habit or an accusation?

But i couldn't tell where it had been lost, or which part or what limb, because no one in America asked. In those early days in New York, my parents moved around me, circumspect, as if I were some totem in danger of toppling. Oh, they looked concerned, of course—my father in particular had a wistful address, as if he wished to say something he had no language for. But nothing was remarked upon: thus, parts of my life were closed, like a remaindered book.

When things are not named, do they disappear? I settled in this throbbing place, and for a while the largeness of things alarmed me, the sofas plump like sideways, floating baobabs, and the cabinets and bookcases leering at me from a height, steadily rising with the curving ceilings. My doctor in France was wrong, wrong, wrong: all was not *bon*. In New York, I was not well.

The postman reproved my crimes. I would scribble addresses on envelopes, and they would come back; I would note my returned-to-sender scrawl, my mad, syllabic combinations. I would stare at them, the unpronounceable syllables and consonants in my neat unbandaged hand, as if they were badly behaving atoms of my

extended flesh, inhabiting a void I had conjured but did not understand. I would slap my lame wrist and begin writing, again.

Who was it for, the struggle to write, my unrequited mail?
Deposited here, installed with my parents whose guarded, sympa-
thetic eyes soon stopped following me around, who soon began to
talk in normal tones before me, easily at ease in the world, as they
were, I wrote at first out of some attempt to practice.

I wished to be good; I wished the nurses to say, *bon, bon*: though
now my assistants were rabbity men with smoker's cough and
women who spoke in a vacant singsong drawl. I began to scrawl
effortlessly, absentmindedly, words that came to me from thin air.
Pendulously. Ruminant. Versification. Things I snatched from the
window breeze. *Scrofulous. Milieu. Duchess of Malfi.* I found delight
simply in listing words down. I spent hours at it. I began to write
letters, to strangers and made-up emancipated people, those in the
world outside. Letters to Simoun and Kandinsky. To Ed, Fred and
Jed. To Ching Byun Co. Chin Ming Boo. To the Big Friendly Giant,
to Winnie the Pooh. An airy raft of names.

Names were the least demanding of words. So it was upsetting
and weakening to find them returning, my sudden dysgraphic
bouts, the awry stuff of language, which hounded me, on and off, as
I tried to move on.

3

MY DOCTORS SAY (they're a bit cuckoo, I'll admit, one of them fairly rundown himself) that cases of anterograde amnesia are common in traumatic instances. A senile diagnosis. How can it be amnesia if one remembers even the terms for herbs or the shine of someone's shoes? But this is my case, the doctors say: I carry phantom mnemonic cargo, nauseous waves of memory. I shore them up by words. I've been given the medical term for intermittent clarity, these strikes of lucidity upon which memory invokes its pathetic fallacies: hyperthymestic scenes, with lacunar phases. The mind at the best of times is a ruinous house, with traps.

Language plays its part, the doctors say: above all, words are symptoms. I must be alert. Even one's vocabulary could be a crime. The way sounds repeat themselves. Assonance. Odd lines in slant rimes. Repetition: the site of trauma. *Repetition is the site of trauma*, the doctors repeat. Beware the Asian mariner, the lady with the albatross. Words have their own way with you: be careful. Allusion, ditto. Consonance, epistrophe, chiasma, miasma. Ditto, ditto, ditto, ditto.

But I kept practicing, and sometimes I felt I could become whole. Words were everyone's crutch, anyone's accomplice. I told the aging quack doctor—*is it not so, that it is language that will save me?* This work I am doing right now could become a hesitant, crepitating—*talambuhay?* A reckoning. A confession. The doctor just kept coughing, looking for something, a slipper, the cat that got his tongue, hiding under a rug. Bunch of useless geriatrics. True, he could be right. "Reckoning" may be too strong a word. And to what was I confessing? Who was to blame? The doctor kept scratching at his throat, coaxing out with scrawny fingers his furtive phlegm.

The strange thing was, when the day came that I could write whole paragraphs, tentative, one-storied stories, linked sentences in a coherent void, my vertigo stopped. Rooms stabilized, objects stayed in place.

My parents soon returned to Manila. I understood that Frankie and Reina Elena, founders of Soliman y Kierulf Import-Export Emporium, Inc., were building a new palace. They had a business that required their presence all over the world, from Ankara to Zamboanga. Their lackeys remained: comforting stooges with graduate degrees. They were harmless, but I kept away from them nonetheless.

Intermittently, my parents would telephone. But since it became increasingly clear we had nothing much to relay to each other, even these halfhearted acts diminished. One must forgive them. They were dealing with architects, feng shui advisors, visionary salesmen of their new order. They were carrying an empire into a new world. And in the meantime, I was gathering a sense of self without a designer to keep me informed of my errors. My days were subsequently taken up by my disasters.

To be honest, the early days in this precarious mansion had a calm sense of emptiness that might translate, if I bothered to name it, into a kind of peace.

So MAYBE MY discovery of that oriel window was unfortunate. I do not know how long I meandered along my allotted portion of the house, like an obedient child, with the gym to the west and the balcony facing the river, so that some phantom of beauty always hovered about my vision wherever I turned.

That day, I was done with lunch, and with guilt I had left unopened the canopied silver of the usual canapés—Reina Elena had left behind a new chef, a shy girl named Eremita. Victoria Eremita. When I was done with all my meals, Eremita, who looked only a bit older than I, a slim girl in her twenties, always lifted the covers of the dishes in my presence, to check my appetite for her budding art.

Another servant, some dwarf apprentice, a little man in grown-up clothes, also looked at the dishes in reproof. In this way, I learned that dawdling after lunch was impossible: I would witness Eremita's disappointment as she left the room with the laden plates. At first, I felt the need to reassure the girl by biting into each cake and pudding and casserole, flattering her good intentions. Then I took to wandering the hallways and stairwells to escape her return.

As I said, the house in New York was familiar, but surprising. It had lacunar themes—sculpted vaults and scalloped corners. Bootlegger Baroque, Uncle Gianni would call it. I wound up, then down, its marble staircase, knowing someone's steps might follow. Shadows were everywhere amid the Brahmin brocades. But everyone was discreet. Down in the basement, I found a broken bowling alley in a mysterious labyrinth reeking of ancient steam. It was spooky. I rushed up the marble staircase, happy to see a fleeing figure, an orderly with a notepad in his hand, pretending to be a writer, dispelling ghosts.

Back in the house's main rooms, I found myself in the second-floor hallway, where I avoided my image, a serial loiterer against mirrored walls. I escaped into a passage. To my surprise, it opened onto an outdoor ledge, full of ladybugs: a flimsy path, a vertiginous virgin walk. Mine were the first footsteps in ages on its dust. If I reached out, I could grasp the house's buttresses. If I looked down, I would fall.

The best thing about it was no one would follow.

It was this path that led to the oriel window. The window jutted toward the river. I hung upon the window's travertine and peeked into my home's reflection.

At first, all I saw was my face, peering at me in illusion, a figure hanging from a ledge as if seeking refuge from bad weather. The river and the trees behind me framed my dark hair, a graded mesh of black, and a halo of light from the horizon tricked my blinded eye. Gradually, I glimpsed bits and pieces of the benighted room.

It was easy enough to jimmy the window open and enter through the unscreened casement. Moths, cobwebs, a host of ladybugs and gentle pests. I had seen it, an old door, reflected from the window. A massive mahogany vault, with an unaccountable lunette: a peephole of darkness framed in antique stencil.

I walked across the room's dizzy floor, a trippy tortoiseshell motif with an oleaginous layer, a syrup sheen. Everything was dusted and polished, but untouched. The door itself was unlocked, like the rest of the house's rooms. Why lock up a place in which no one ever stepped foot?

I looked out from where I had come. I had a clear view of the silver river. A twin tableau, a pair of stucco pomegranates or concrete figs, framed a vanishing point in my vision, toward the water.

I walked about the cluttered room. I found portraits lined like suspects against the walls. I vaguely recollected them. Solemn pictures of morbid women. A scary child in sausage curls. Watercolors of French cypresses and wheat fields by someone who was not Van Gogh.

A life-size picture, framed in gold.

A diving sensation in my chest. A kind of heated swarming. Pink and blue gases colored the monstrous frame. I heaved. I thought I would vomit, but my throat was dry. My body jerked in convulsions, I was shaking as if poisoned: though I had left Eremita's tiramisu untouched, and my insides, in fact, were empty.

4

I ADMIT THAT I had liked the experience—of sitting still in Manila's torpor while she had painted in our living room. I had liked the pleasant effort of repose, a kind of introspective challenge. My mother, posing stiff-backed beside me, kept lapsing into her hostess-fluttering, offering cakes and juices to the artist as she worked, though Madame Vera barely answered, speaking only to correct our poses.

Madame Vera was an emaciated Spaniard of a remarkable hue—stale, dry glue comes close to her pallor: a glutinous texture of gray. On the first day, she had appeared at our doorway in Makati in fur and a venerable silk suit, a corrugated glistening that trailed the musty smell and mothball stench of some theatrical company's dank costume department; everyday she wore the same kind of suit, like some outlaw from an ancient dry cleaner's.

I watched her pull off her gloves while the maid buzzed my mother. Madame Vera's rings supported her fingers rather than the other way around: it seemed to me the rings kept her flesh in place. I imagined that her entire body was precariously meshed, held together by the same miserable flesh that one saw on her freed hands—a veined, brittle hide in an advanced stage of molting. Waiting with her in the living room, I imagined, as she pulled off a late glove, that if one pulled hard enough, one could rip her skin off, and she'd emerge from the shell of her body, like a cicada.

She did not look at me but at the furnishings of our house. She stood up to examine the Amorsolo: rose-cheeked women selling flowers in a fresh-meat market. She muttered, I suppose to me: "Nnguhh. This picture is nothing; just wait till you see mine. Nngoohh." She had a gargling, nasal accent, but I believe she spoke in English: I'm not so sure of what she said.

As I said, it was pleasing to sit for a portrait, as if I were giving up my duties to someone else, some obligation. The obligation of self-study, one might put it. I delegated so much of my daily existence—there was always a personal servant, a driver, cook, baker, gardener, floral designer, including a personal dog groomer, who used to come on scheduled visits to redecorate my pets, a sweet pair of Alpine pinschers, now dead, victims of some rank methane plague (their mystifying gassiness expelled them from paradise, and I sobbed over their loss). So it was no giant step to surrender my idea of myself to someone else's expertise. Even my mother relaxed, silent, forgetting her posture so often that Madame Vera barked "*Sientate!*" My mother would apologize, sitting up.

In fact, my mother had been in Madame Vera's thrall. I couldn't explain it. At first, I resented my mother's obedience to this hag of a Picasso. My mother was often prey to a procession of hacks, foreigners whom Manila attracted the way the wet season draws moths indoors. That's how she almost had our entire garden replanted, to put blocking wind trees in the appropriate spiritual corners upon the advice of a lightweight Westerner, whom Mr. Kow Lung, the rightful feng shui master, denounced when he came back from Hong Kong. That's how we acquired gigantic gold-leaf murals in the private den, when she fell to the folly of a debonair Frenchman, a passing interior decorator, who soon after romped off with someone's bank account and teenage child. That's how we got our portraits painted, a frothy extravaganza of Fragonard wisps and the hazy perspective, in the background, of what seemed like a miniature palace, a schematic design Madame Vera had already practiced for her previous clients, a fantastic couple in delusional clouds. That's how, in the frozen eternity of oils, I miraculously acquired prominent cheekbones and, most wondrously, a chin. And my mom gained the height of Venus de Milo rising from a cowrie shell.

Madame Vera had painted us with the most awkward clairvoyance—sketching what she sensed our fantasies to be, an embarrassing wish fulfillment. I understand that to one lady's furnishings, she had added the lion's emblem of the old viceroy of Mexico, though the only viceregal things about the subject were her vacant eyes. She looked like a blind pug going up in smoke. For the portrait of the couple, her biggest patrons, Madame Vera had added the mythic complications of tropical genesis—brown Adam and Eve rising to pink and blue clouds from split bamboo. She had smoothed the man's lupus into a lapidary plumpness and had restored to the other her winsome youth. In my opinion, in Madame Vera's heaven they seemed to wallow, like my unfortunate dogs, in some hissy, flatulent eternity. Madame Vera was not so much a painter as a pander: in the *Inferno*, easily she'd be a sinner in lower hell, condemned to eternal lashings from horned demons. In Manila she had found an ideal world for her talent.

When I saw the painting, I knew I had been right to fear for my mother's goodwill—that some awful discovery of bad taste would come about from this misguided aesthetic project. When Madame Vera unveiled her prize (she hadn't allowed us to see the piece in progress, and I for one never looked), I felt as if I had been smacked: caught in an insult. My cheeks burned as I looked at my unrecognizable self, my smoothed-out nose, my pink, sculpted cheeks, and most of all my blameless chin: I was caught out in my hideous dream of perfectly symmetrical beauty. Madame Vera was standing in a corner, watching us. She still clutched pieces of the frame's wrapping in her avian arms. I imagined she was leering at us, in the beaky way of an unevolved creature, a vertical pterodactyl, some *ave de rapiña*. I felt sodden, spit-upon. As my mother came closer to look at the painting, I stepped forward, as if to shield her from the insult.

My mother took a breath.

"Vera, what can I say?" my mother said.

I knew she was going to speak it: my anger and embarrassment at the painter's dishonesty.

"It's marvelous," my mother continued. "You captured my Sol at just the right angle, finding her beauties so wonderfully—that mold of your chin, darling: she did it so well. Look. And I can't say that you didn't do so badly with my own self. I do like the coloring: it's so—lifelike. I can't wait to show it to Frankie."

Madame Vera clapped her hands at this, rattling her rings: "Ah, hush, hush, Queenie—it's all in the subject. I just draw. I'm a vessel."

I looked at both of them. I looked back at the painting, at my mother.

Madame Vera showed us where she thought she could do some

last revisions—in the refined shadowing of an ear, the adjustment of light about a head. And that was that. She asked permission to exhibit the work in her show that year, 1980. It took the capital by storm, as the papers liked to say. The last I knew, the picture had been installed on the mezzanine, a reception hall in the house in Makati—the house my parents were dismantling right now, as they set their bright hopes for a new life in the oasis they were building in Alabang.

5

Henry hudson had sought China but instead found Albany. Ferdinand Magellan found Manila and was disconcerted by geography. He came by accident upon the Philippine islands and was, as they say, disarmed. I transferred my notes and manuscripts to the oriel room. I continued my writing exercises there, gathering bits and pieces of time, keeping occupied. Its view satisfied me. Sometimes, looking down from the balcony into the distance, the long, tree-lined road, I felt a thrill of solitude, as if I were Antonio Pigafetta, the ancient chronicler, seeing a primordial wasteland—the greenery of old Manila, say, before the arrival of the pirates and the pillagers. I was a discoverer. I was getting better. They say this part of the river leads to some salt waterway where the Mohicans used to pray, before the advent of the casinos. The shadow of Native American wilderness, the survey of sedge and sediment on this winding drive may not be so different from old Manila. Both islands reek from the salt of ancient error. The resemblance was a trick of my downcast homesick angle, anomalous mist of monsoon-like rains, the bent, gray sky and low tree limbs, spent autumn brown leaves curled and cankered.

I kept seeing Roxas Boulevard at a narrow glance—I closed my eyes and smelled it: the smell of shrimp, evening dinners and wet trees. Moist heat. Palms. Ruined iron-trellised houses. Low bungalows against bright green lawns facing the open sea.

I heard the dish carts trundling down the hallway into the service elevator. Garlic smells. Then the clanging of the elevator's ancient shaft. Rumbling shut. Then the wily creak of its creepy descent, Eremita's daily freight.

I kept writing.

It is easy to like New York, from this quiet quietus—the soft butt-end of the Hudson's light as I write. A sense of doubling persists, a shaky orientation. But always, the sight of water renews. I hope to find footholds, after all. To remain well, I must find ways to feel at ease. *Live in the moment.* A corny slogan I gather from my doctors. An octogenarian chorus bleats in my brain. Recovery, they say, means learning to exist in the present tense.

It is a delusion of my memory that my past exists at all. When was that concert, for instance—that birthday concert for the president? The midterm of the eighties? The finals of the seventies? I know that incident, a gathering of identities within a single event, has perhaps only an apocryphal significance, but I keep recalling it nevertheless—that limousine taking a swift turn, heading for Manila Bay.

6

IT MUST HAVE been Manong Babe who drove us to that entrance facing the water. Already you could see it—the tale of a different city beyond the bleakness of scheduled failure: we passed the blackouts of Manila's streets, a regulated system of select disrepair. By the water, gowned, crowned women were alighting from their cars, sweeping onto the sidewalk. Even if it was easier to park first and walk across the street, no one bothered. Limousines waited in line by the sidewalk, drivers idling as all the idle matrons of Manila disembarked.

Ladies in Manila do not walk. I have never seen my mother, Reina Elena Soliman, the former Queenie Kierulf, cross a street.

I recognized Mrs. Esdrújula, the stateliest lady in society, emerging from a car a few feet away. She was wearing her single-lined blue tiara. She had begun to wear it ever since she had been knighted by the pope. It was a sweet indulgence, granted for her gifts of new money to old charities. In return for her saintliness, she got to wear a crown of her own design, with subtle celestial symbols and utterly terrestrial stones.

"Dear Bumbum," my mother murmured as she spied her old friend. Manong Babe got out to open my mother's door. "Doesn't she look so saintly, just like Saint Catherine of Siena!"

I did not remind my mother of the actual fate of her worshiped and beheaded saint: we had seen it one summer on a trip—a face visibly decaying against sweating glass. My mother had shrieked in the cathedral: *Oh my God, inday, the saint is ROTTING!*

A guard had shushed her in Italian.

Annabelle "Bumbum" Esdrújula, obviously much better preserved than her patron saint (her legendary slanting cat's eyes could be duplicated by no amount of surgery), approached us with her retinue. Guards with guns preceded her, and guards with rifles marked her egress. A maid walked behind her, carrying her towels.

In only one thing was Madame Bumbum Esdrújula unfortunate—she was always perspiring like a pig, a porous animal—the single miserable aspect of her genes, her Basque pedigree—or was it Alsatian? Her origins, in fact, were inscrutable, though impeccable. Her malady required a ritual of prevention—this tidy, ingenious parade, with towels and a maid.

It was a curious thing to see this magnificent woman followed everywhere by the white-uniformed girl, who bore white, folded, monogrammed towels, three at a time, like some latter-day midget-page in Francisco Goya. Sometimes this maid, forgetting the occasion, would go about in rubber slippers, flip-flopping, adding to a glamorous event a comic genius.

When Mrs. Esdrújula stopped in progress, the maid knew what to do. She came up and swiped at the famous clavicle while Mrs. Esdrújula bent to her delicate ablutions. The process of guards also stopped to watch. This expert procedure required the maid's ginger knowledge of the limits of foundation cream and how to dab precisely at fine, etiolated, clammy skin.

My mother tiptoed to kiss Bumbum on the cheek, *beso-beso*, left and right. These rituals were not useless—they made a public comment without need for words, expressing personal regard with due restraint and, in some cases, contempt without bloodshed.

I followed my mother out of the car. Manong Babe held the door open, winking at me.

"What is it, Babe?" Ma said to him, turning back to look at us: "Are you ill?"

She was sharp-eyed, my mom. Nothing missed her evil eye. Manong Babe climbed back into the car. Ma introduced me again to Mrs. Esdrújula. I was, in fact, several inches taller than she was; I calculated that, barefoot, Mrs. Esdrújula was really only slightly taller than my mother, who was not quite five feet in her heels. That must be the mark of these ladies' stature, I thought, as I kissed her moist face: Madame Bumbum was not quite life-size, but she could fake it.

Mrs. Esdrújula barely touched my cheek, and I inhaled her fragrance as she turned away.

"Ah, *chica*, you are now so—large. Queenie: how scary. Your daughter is a lady now." She said this to the air, to a portion of Manila Bay, while she tenderly touched a part of her cheek, as if to make sure it was still there, uncorrupted by affection.

We walked toward my father on the sidewalk. He was chatting with Mrs. Esdrújula's husband, a nondescript bald man.

Mr. Esdrújula outsmarted God by his plainness. A minister without portfolio, the Secretary, as he was called, was a man whose face you never remembered. The incredible ordinariness of the Secretary's face, the dull features that lent itself to no caricaturist's wit, the extreme cipherly quality of his presence—clearly, birth had given him an advanced ticket for oblivion. No one knew who he was except the shrewdest of operators.

There were rumors, of course, but in such a minor key one never thought of them twice—that he was the biggest gun dealer in the country; that he whispered in the leader's ear the occult plans for years of ruthless rule; that he was a foundling child, an orphan with a bloodlust—or was he the bastard son of a basket case? It was not clear. The mumbo jumbo of the times. What I knew was that he was the same age as my father. They had gone to school together.

As a child, I called him Uncle.

I used to interview him for social studies reports and once for an English assignment based on Studs Terkel's book *Working*. He gave me a firsthand account of what he did day to day, just like the bank clerks and the bellhops in the book. He drank milk, signed forms, took naps. The fateful trip that Pa had taken, to scout the environs around San Juanico Strait, where Pa had first lain eyes on Queenie Kierulf, the rose-seller's daughter, a sprite in a garden that was soon to be bulldozed for history, to make way for the "Longest Bridge in Asia!"—that trip had the mark of the Secretary on it. Not the least of the projects of the least of the provinces in the Republic of the Philippines did not know the cool, dry handshake of this nondescript man, the exact features of whose face already escape me: a clean, mild-mannered blur in the night.

7

ALONG ROXAS BOULEVARD, the women continued toward the concert hall, white-lit; I recognized them from my parents' eternal dinner parties, from celebrity photographs in my mother's magazines. They wobbled in tight *ternos*, butterfly sleeves sagging from the weight of stones. Powdered hags in satin, their foundation running. No one, not even the gods, could escape the ravages of Manila's heat. The night moved quietly, the wind softly handled our stiff satin skirts. I noticed this red-haired lady—in tulle and jewels, she looked like a miscast ballerina, her tanned inordinate breasts bursting from her corset's lace. With that skirt and her bust, she looked a bit like the letter *R*. Heaving, not rolling. She walked beside a man I recognized.

Jed's father, the *katsila* Don Mariano Morga.

"Pa, that's not Mrs. Morga, is it?"

"Of course not, darling, unless Prima De Rivera shrank and became a turd."

My father swept forward on his lump of wit.

"Poor Prima," whispered my mom. "No. That's the newest one.

You don't know that one? Good—never listen to gossip, inday. I don't understand Don Mariano. I mean, Prima De Rivera was Miss Spain—or was she Miss Shellane Propane? Anyway, she was a beauty queen. While that girl—that girl looks like a salesgirl from Shoemart—"

"Is she?"

"No. She's the ex-mistress of the ex-mayor of the ex-capital of Bulacan. That's what the gossip Zubiri de Zoroastre says in his column. Ha-ha. You know people won't have his women in their homes, so instead they come to these events."

She smiled brightly at them as they looked our way. Don Mariano Morga beckoned us to his group.

I waved to someone by the ticket booth. Mrs. Llano. Plump and amiable in her robes, she looked like a doleful, extralarge version of the Holy Child of Prague. She was gesturing to my mother, her old childhood friend. Tonight Reina Elena Soliman *née* Kierulf looked like the ethnic version of her namesake, the queen of Constantinople, Queen Helena of Byzantium herself, seeker of the Holy Cross. It was native costume night—originally plain, pliant dresses recast in rhinestone. My mother's native *camisa* was devoid of décor, except for her jewels. She walked ahead of us. Lights warped under her glitter.

I saw Mrs. Llano's welcoming smile freeze as my mother turned away.

Mrs. Llano used to visit our home in Makati. She always came with a church group to sing Christmas carols and ask for money for her causes. What a surprise and clamor whenever they saw each other, long-lost high school classmates. And now my mother walked straight ahead, without even bowing her head. I saw Mrs. Llano take her fan vigorously, stung into animated talk with the woman beside her, a tranquil nun who held her concert tickets tightly in her fingers while she beamed mutely at the world.

I turned away, following my mother.

Reina Elena had found her center, the group for which she reserved her charms. I recognized some people: politicians, a man who controlled an agrarian monopoly—pineapples or peanuts—a few choice foreign businessmen, diplomats, and generals. Don Mariano and his corseted lady were among them. I moved to hide behind my mother, but she introduced me once again to everyone.

A lady gushed, the wife of a purveyor of palm products: "I recognize your daughter exactly from her portrait in the exhibit: Madame Vera, you did an excellent job. What a likeness."

I tried to ignore Madame Vera, who was dressed in dramatic scarf and matching Moorish robes, gurgling her usual gnomic curses like some zombie from nomad land.

Creeping away from the sight, I bumped into Don Mariano.

"Ah, *hija*: so how is university life?"

This man, Don Mariano Morga, always looked happy. I had last seen him at my dorm when my parents had registered me on that first day: no matter where he was, he charmed—at a residence hall or a society banquet, he had a knack for making you feel he had just been thinking about you.

"Have you seen my son?" Don Mariano asked.

I looked around, surprised: "Is Jed at the concert?"

"No, no," he said hastily. "I mean, at your college. Haven't you seen him at college?"

"No. I mean, yes, he's in my dorm. I—yes, I've met him."

"Jed is his own person," he said, almost wistfully. I kept noticing the chatter of the woman by his side—a low, lazy voice talking about clothes. "But he has a good heart," Don Mariano said.

I wondered what exactly Don Mariano knew about me and Jed. I stared at him, daring him to tip his hand, to reveal his spies and sources.

I had no illusions that Jed would speak to his father about me.

Don Mariano continued: "I only wish him to be happy: do you think he's happy?"

I thought it was a strange question, given the circumstances. I listened to the drone of Don Mariano's mistress, nattering on about shopping like an empty-headed wife in her own right. "I very rarely see him," said Don Mariano. "He's so busy with his studies, you know. He was at the top of his class at the American School. But of course, you know that: you were at his high school, isn't that right, *hija*? He's a reader; he takes after me. But I'm a boastful man, am I not? When I talk about my son, it's just to talk about myself. Jed is always telling me that. Anyway, come, let's join the party. Have you met Colonel Grier?"

Don Mariano patted the arm of the man standing next to him: "He's a soldier and a scholar."

My mother had caught up with us: "Yes, darling, I told the Colonel: my daughter would love to meet you. He's an expert on Roman stamps, darling. And Philippine historiographics. How eccentric, don't you think?"

"Yes, very eclectic," my father intoned. He liked to correct my mother, though he, too, had dropped out of college at the right age.

Ma pouted and wrinkled her perfect nose, making her small, heart face seem even smaller. Next, I knew, my father would touch her button nose and laugh. It was their trademark exchange.

They had found their man. It was a family business, our friendly art. I knew, on these occasions, they always had a specific target. Ma and Pa fluttered from one person to the next, as if to allow some time for their prey to relax and think itself out of danger.

"Coins, actually," said the American. He was very bald; a chandelier shone on him with unadvised relish. He was fidgety in his barong, a gossamer shirt in tune with the occasion, appropriately appliquéd with insect wings.

"From Connecticut or Colorado," Don Mariano intoned.

The Colonel's taut, pink-skinned body, like a sorry piglet in piña fiber, uneasily filled his dress shirt's transparent gauze. I was afraid the piña would split, destroying the shirt's fine filigree.

"Byzantine coins, really," he said. And he bowed his head at us, looking briefly at my mother, and, I don't know if I imagined this: as if with a look of loathing. But he introduced us to the lady beside him, his wife, as they waited for us to move ahead.

My mother wouldn't budge. She nudged me.

"Do you collect them?" I asked. "Solidi, I mean. Pardon: is that the plural form of the word?"

I noticed the young wife looking away; I thought she was not that much older than I, except that, if you looked again, you'd notice the waist and arms of a woman who had just had a child—a wide-eyed blonde thickening into womanhood. Her face was red from the heat, and she looked, in her wrinkled linen clothing, as if she had just come from a swamp, already sweating before the evening had begun, and without even a maid to wipe off the calamity. She was wearing the wrong clothes: linen wrinkled easily, and its creases caught sweat. She had not gotten the memo about Filipino dress.

Colonel Grier, when you glanced more closely at him, had a formidable presence, despite his smallish height. He had a frame like a shuttered bungalow—a rectangular bulk with massive shoulders. He looked as if his body had armor plate. His arms were crossed against his chest.

I couldn't help it: I stared.

His gauzy barong revealed a crisscross of keloids, a jungle of scars all along his biceps' raw length.

I looked at his face: "I suppose the most common coins might come from the time of Anna Comemna, during the reign of her father Alexius I. He changed the Eastern monetary system, I believe."

"You're talking about Late Byzantium," he said. "You're right." The Colonel looked surprised, as well he might. I always thought my forms of knowledge were a kind of autism, the sign of my indifference to more important things. I collected bits and pieces of useless information: biblical parables, grammatical games, a flotsam of historic details, a rattling can of artistic arcana. It endeared me to no one. He leaned toward me: his round pink nose was inches from my face. The impression of his power began in the shoulders—a broad box of constrained muscle. His stolid body did not match his glance: a whiskeyed softness of the features, especially around his bulb-like nose. He had sad eyes.

His physical parts began to cohere, but the tenor of his interests confused me.

"You know your history, I see. Are you one of those feminists who wants to raise Anna Comemna from the grave?"

"Oh, no, sir, I am not," I said. "I am researching the Byzantines. For a project in history. I've always liked them. They're weird."

"Well, that's too bad," he said, straightening up. "I like Anna Comemna. Have you read the *Alexiad*? No—my coins are not as valuable as that."

"From the reign of the Asiatic emperor, the child-king? Elagabalus?"

"Oh, no, no, no," said the Colonel. "No coins from Elagabalus: I'll have nothing to do with Oriental freaks." He smiled. "Anyway, I'd need to quit my job if I got one of those—"

"What a shame that would be," said my mother, "you have just taken up an excellent position here in Manila. Inday, he's with Tom at LOTUS. With our own General Tom."

"—it would be a full-time job guarding a rarity like that," the Colonel continued. "So—you have a mind for ancient history."

"Only pieces of ancient history, I'm afraid," I said. "Obscure little things. Useless knowledge."

In the humid heat, amid the masses straining to get into the concert, I was beginning to feel withered myself—my usual sense of suffocation.

"Oh, you don't know my daughter, Colonel Grier: she wants to be a historical scholar, would you believe," said my mom.

She took my shoulders and held me before her, so that I was walking beside the Colonel like a puppet being moved, and I let her. For a minute I was pleased to lean against my mother's firm hands.

As if at a signal, the gowns and diamonds rustled toward the concert hall in reluctant clusters. The interlude before the show, when one stands for public inspection in the spotlight of the lobby, seems to be the heart of the occasion—the reason for coming. It's disheartening, after all, to be in full-jeweled array and have to sit in the dark, permitting someone else to take the spotlight, usually a plebeian, some artist who sings for her supper. On this occasion, it was a Visayan, a pianist. The concert was his debut at home after winning an award abroad. To honor his talent, he got to be the star at the birthday concert for the dictator, organized by the dictator's loving wife.

People had been waiting for something. By the bulge of the crowd in the far corner of the lobby—a kind of rippling that predicted a greater requirement of space somewhere else—you could tell that it had finally arrived.

"Well, the band's all here," said Colonel Grier. "Shall we move on?"

And in the mob of bodies, I believe I gathered his version of history.

"It's not useless knowledge," he said. "You never know what one can do with knowledge of the past, given the chance. As a prisoner in Vietnam, I can tell you I used it to my advantage. My knowledge of history. I can show you my collection. I have many Filipino coins. I studied it, you know, your history. The Philippine insurrection against the Americans. An interesting affair."

"You mean the tail end of our revolution, the Filipino-American War, in 1899," I said.

"Correct," he smiled. "That small matter in the Spanish-American War. A side dish, you might say, to a more significant feast."

His ironic salute melds into a stereographic double of iconic Americans in my academic memory: governor-general of Manila, Arthur MacArthur, and his returning swashbuckling son, General Douglas; William Howard Taft, the first and fattest *gringo* governor of the Philippine islands; William McKinley, presider over the American invasion, aptly assassinated by anarchists.

The American provoked me into pedantry, and I found a tone in my voice that I hated in others.

"That was no insurrection, Colonel," I answered. "We were fighting a war against your enemy. You said you came to help us. In the name of democracy—to free ourselves from tyrannical Spain. Instead, you invaded. In the Treaty of Paris you paid twenty million dollars to buy our islands from the already vanquished Spain. We resisted you. Your army killed six hundred thousand Filipinos from 1899 to 1902, a war worse than Vietnam. That was no insurrection, Colonel. That was our war of independence."

"Which you lost," the man grinned at me. "We won. You forget that point."

And the American moved on before I could gather the wit to reply.

My mother's hands on my shoulders steadied me where I was. I was trembling. We were positioned to be in full view of the arrivals, but Colonel Grier was already proceeding toward the doors. My mother was divided between following him and greeting her compatriot.

The wave bulged deeper and reached us. They came: security men in blue shirts, a flurry of mean-looking people with walkie-talkies. The security men had pitted faces, as if chosen for their physical defects, so that the terrors of acne acquired deep meanings in a debased society. And then came the celebrants themselves. It was almost too late to follow Colonel Grier and his wife. My mother was beside herself, standing her ground amid the leaning bodies in order to greet the arriving pair, do the cheeks, *beso-beso*, but at the same time she was also anxious not to lose her man.

The tension of state procession is heady, a sharp, combustible affair. The couple proceeded in glacial motion, like the Israelites before Moses' parted waters. Even without signals from the guards, people stepped back to create a path, an invisible cordon of their awe. The couple came closer, the slow, shorter one first in his everyday heels, white heavyweight platforms; he was dressed all in white, with his dull upswept gleam of hair. I was always surprised at how red-cheeked the president was, as if someone had vigorously scrubbed his face before he came into view. I had been told it was the steroids, or whatever nourished the systemic incubus, his disordered kidney and wasted spleen. People in the know said that a machine in the Palace kept him alive (my dad, in public, kept refuting this vile gossip, though in private, he shook his head over its damnable truth), so that in effect the country was becoming a lupus archipelago, a codependent in synch with the man's gradual demise.

Then came the woman, sailing behind like a *vinta*—a brilliant coloring of Islamic silks (the war in the south was on everyone's mind).

The Lady approached us.

My mother stepped forward, as if to offer her sweet cheek. Her patroness walked right past. I felt—I did not see—my mom's frozen smile. The Lady barely nodded her head at Reina Elena Soliman *neé* Kierulf, moving on as if brushing off some crumpled moth. The last time I had seen them, they had kissed each other in an affecting reunion. The Lady had eaten *churros* and drunk *chocolate* at the house in one of those midnight revelries that do not make the papers. They had danced and squawked together, old high school classmates, a pair of genuine warmhearted Warays.

This time, the Lady floated straight into the theater, a giddy mast with a ballast of hair. At that point, I saw Mrs. Llano amid the surge of people who had stepped back to let the couple pass. The towering, powdered *vinta* stopped and waved at Mrs. Llano, her high school classmate, amid the masses.

She was, after all, the First Lady of the people.

Realizing she had been singled out, Mrs. Llano gave a curtsy, smiling broadly. People stared at Mrs. Llano, who started to fan herself, the fan saying, "Yes, yes, uhum, we are bosom friends."

Beside me, I saw my mother's lip curl. But it was all Queenie Kierulf could do.

After this, people started milling in, and my mother and I barely avoided being swept away from the doorway into Manila's humid dusk.

We found my father already standing beside Don Mariano. Colonel Grier had gone to a front-row seat. He and his wife were standing beside his general.

General Tom was a large-nosed man with an iron lung, or plaster heart—I never got that right. It was he who was my parents' old friend. He had wires attached to his body to keep him alive, but he was still the head of the American government outfit LOTUS. He had always been this fleshy man with sketchy features—this impression of an unfinished brow, of a face drawn badly from memory. But with his recent illness, a mild stroke, the subtle vapidness about his mouth was exaggerated. The right side of his face had this local morbidity, a paralytic tic.

With other foreigners in Filipino dress, the American officers stood to wait for the couple to take their seats; then the American general sat beside the president, and Colonel Grier took his place beside the Lady. Her über-hairdo, a hive without the honey, gave the ceremony its loud important spell. I stood beside Don Mariano while my mother took the place beside my father. Before me was Bumbum Esdrújula, that paragon of style. Fortunately, I was a full head taller than her exquisite coif. The band struck the notes of the national anthem, and people around me followed their leader's example, right hand on the heart. If you could sing with a high, lasting tremolo, so much the better; if you could do second *voce*, skimming the notes of the melody with artful dissonance, that was okay, too. Unluckily for the maid beside Madame Bumbum, she had to hold the towels. Bumbum's musical exertions were genteel but prodigious, and the maid kept making her patriotic efforts as best as she could, dabbing at Madame Bumbum until the end of the stirring song.

AFTER THE FINALE, roused from the coughing that had plagued them while the pianist embarked on a complicated composition by an unfamiliar Slavic name—where was their Mozart, their Rachmaninoff, even a Chopin of some sort—cough, cough—(the theater had been enflamed with a whooping disease, an aggrieved contagion, during the prolonged unfamiliarity of the difficult composer's piece, accompanying the bell-jar cacophony of my numb sensations), the people loudly asked for an encore. After all, they were sophisticates—some woke up, instantly clapping: what a beautiful tune by that composer—what was his name?

The garland of roses came on stage, a funereal wreath. A minion, equally dressed up but doomed to remain unnamed, brought it up, and then came the loud cheering for the Lady. The lady, the lady! The clapping grew louder; she rose from the depths; she walked up the steps; she came onto the stage. She took the bouquet of flowers. She made a low, meaningful bow to the pianist, reappearing from the wing, now suitably irrelevant. Then she offered the roses to the man of the hour.

"Oh, *mahal*, you see what a Filipino can do? He is a talented boy, and I always knew if we helped him it would happen. He would reap rewards. My people, I always say this to the president: if we have the right weather, we can build swimming pools in two days. With the right talent, we can be famous around the world."

Her tongue was tainted with that accent that still lulled me to sleep, my mother's perfectly embalmed Waray—their language clung to their tongues like the formalin that kept skeletons intact.

The audience roared its deep wave of praise.

Then the pianist sat down; he signaled the page-turner to leave the stage; all alone, he flexed his fingers over the piano; he started trilling, his fingers weaving a wild storm. Through the thunder of his display, the audience found the sweet melody. How proud and pleased everyone was. His fingers turned the old Visayan drinking song, the light Waray tune, into an elaborate tribute. The ladies in their gowns were nodding their heads, jeweled combs were wobbling. A Filipino talent! A success in Europe! Ah, this romantic throbbing, this delirious *Dandansoy*. As the clapping swelled, who was it who came up from the audience? People craned their necks to look, but in their hearts they guessed. She floated back onto the stage, the sails of her varicolored gown flying. She took the microphone from the far right end and began to trill the introductory words of the song, huskily. As if she were shy.

The man in festive white, standing small in his platform heels, had a husband's look of repressed boredom, used to these domestic displays.

Dandansooooy, she began. And it became a medley, an unrehearsed piece of wit that everyone expected: she changed the tune to her signature song—

Because of you, she sang, *I wish to live.*

IT WAS ENOUGH to make one turn to revolution.

MR. ESDRÚJULA, THE Secretary, was the first on his feet, then the rest in the front row stood up. Only Colonel Grier remained seated, though his wife rose uncertainly, as if something were falling from her lap. Soon the entire hall was on its feet, clapping for the lady as she sang the song in increasingly dramatic vibrato. What a Filipino she was—what a woman of style. Greater than Maria Callas! Now even Colonel Grier stood up. I saw the Secretary look sideways at him, briefly, then resume his applause. The pianist did a last flourish, an exercise in digital flirtation. The jeweled crowd went mad.

A great concert, said everyone, especially those who had been coughing their heads off a few pieces ago, ready to wallop Shostakovich.

8

THE EARLIEST VOYAGERS had this insight: to keep Manila, all they needed was to gain its harbor. Historical demons knew that—all the Manila characters. Indentured sailors and boatbuilding men. Jesuit priests and Muslim sultans. Impecunious, cunning Miguel López de Legazpi, the first Spanish governor-general of Manila. Basque adventurers. Chinese pirates. Devilish, blue-eyed Dutch smugglers. Everyone took the harbor as prize. Otherwise the city is a disaster. It is muggy, its humidity is disorienting, it is susceptible to nervous illnesses, swamp fever, and dengue. A refuge of rascals. Prime real estate for amoks as well as prostitutes, scavengers and social climbers. Not too different, I guess, from the Hudson's ancient Mannahatta, lusty grave of the Algonquin nations. Like any old city, Manila has attracted a host of dissolutes and dreamers, with its old harbor and its sinking palisade, easily defended and easily betrayed.

The nurses, knowing my habits, now left me alone. When I opened the drawers in the library, somehow I knew what I would find: Aging music rolls for the Aeolian harp. Leftovers of the old mansion's gilded age. I remember as a kid wondering what they were for, these scrolls that in a certain light unfolded shadows punctured on my hand. On the mantelpiece, a redundant oleograph reproduced the room's view, but I had no memory of drawing my childish name on the cheap print. My signature spoiled its bottom right corner: a loop of *S*'s scratched the view of cows chewing cud and upset a pair of precisely drawn pigs.

My mom in her high heels click-clacking down the Grecian parquet, with the lady who had first enumerated the house's gifts. The secret doors for the servants, the rams' heads sculpted into cabinets. The lady's words were impressive: the Guastavino tiles, the Della Robbia graces, the porte-cochere. *The, the, the.* I noted how she introduced all the novelties with a definite article. She pointed out where we could put a trampoline in the music room and a playground on the lawn. I refused to ride the elevator, a creaky beast with an accordion mouth, like the contraption in that show I used to watch in America, *Get Smart*, about a dumb detective.

We must have lived here for a spell, deep in the seventies. When the country was in tumult, a new regime installed: after the awful pall of martial law in 1972. When the demand for their goods was at its height and the money came flowing in, my parents relocated to America until the mobs died down—the bleeding demonstrators on the streets. Down with the Dictator! Lap Dog! *Tuta!* Not that I could translate those words then. I was seven, eight? Bodies hunted down, radicals lynched, senators jailed, and farmers massacred as the military government clamped down on the storm. How was I to know? I was a baby. From the spoils of those bloody times, my parents purchased this gilded womb. I traced the fleur-de-lys reliefs inset in the fireplace: dimly I recognized the gesture, the way I had followed the gilt trim when I was a child.

I was a martial-law baby. A hyperactive bundle too quick for my yaya, Manang Maring, who seemed old even then. I tortured her on the double staircase—leaping down one side before she had the chance to climb up on the other, and doing it again before she could catch her breath. Now I know the entire house has a dizzying design—the staircase has a twin, and so does the oriel window, and the Grecian keys on one side of the room can be trusted to find themselves again on the other. As a child, I raced through the vaults and the niches and the fireplaces and the bays of this rambling ever-lasting hide-and-seek place, poking and giggling and running about, while the flustered servants called out my name. And in the meantime, on the other side of the mirror, my country raged.

I don't know exactly when we returned to the Philippines and my parents sent me back to school in Makati, but I know we came back here, to this mansion, off and on, for summer vacations, for trips with Uncle Gianni to visit museums, parks, and churches in the city. I know it was he who installed soccer posts parallel to the spiral driveway, and the ball would fall, as it would, into the flowers by the porte-cochere.

I imagine everything in the house must be as it was then: even the rusty goalposts must hang about, forlorn without their netting, if one peered beyond the Guastavino entrance, *the, the, the,* to the lawn enclosure rolling toward the street. But the house's vacancy disturbs me, its enormous solitude.

Why am I still here?

AFTER LUNCH, I peeped through the faint grisaille of the mahogany doorway's lunette, like a dumb detective. Not everything in the house rang a bell. My parents, hoarders and wasters both, seem to be storing keepsakes and curios from some disbanded utopia—*nuestro perdido Eden*. Who was this lady in a kerchief dress? A headless woman, all in white.

Emily Dickinson. A poster I had bought from the poet's house in Amherst.

I rifled through a boxful of gloves, tiny overcoats, galoshes — discarded winters of my mother's discontent (above all things in America she hates the cold, as if it were an affront to her affluence, the one thing she cannot control). A Pisan Pinocchio in limbo: tangled up in its own strings. Bundles of old wallpaper—Beatrix Potter prints and Roald Dahl figures—tightly raveled, unused.

Carefully, I smoothed out the scrim of the Roald Dahl wallpaper. It was Uncle Gianni who had helped plan the interior of my rooms in Makati, when we returned from America in the seventies. He was a fastidious looter, a keen-eyed man of art. He found copies of old Bauhaus typescript scrolls during a business tour of the Black Forest or White Mountains—had he flown in from Germany or New Hampshire? Wherever he was, he indulged my tastes. Like Magellan, his hero, he liked finding things. I guess I had a fixation for the Bauhaus then—their chromatic play, rigid lines. Obsessions overcame me, instant crazes, precious and obnoxious, but in the middle of a hobby, I'd find another horse, and in this way I filled my mind with passing knowledge, like those gold rings in transit in old-fashioned merry-go-rounds.

Did we see an exhibit somewhere in Copenhagen of some modernist memoirist? Aesthetes with a cause, Uncle Gianni laughed. The Bauhaus flouted the Nazis by fetishizing function: How German, he said. Anyhow he brought to Makati one day fine sketches

of interlocking *S*'s, providential initials of my name, and an ingenious printer from Bulacan fashioned the typescript into ribbons of
scenes from my favorite writer at the time, Roald Dahl. *Ciao,*
bellezza. Uncle Gianni presented my finished rooms with a flourish.
He liked to waste the frustrations of his artistry on me.

And when Jed and Soli had first seen my bedroom in Makati,
they had laughed. I didn't begrudge them their complicitous glance;
they were always acting like coconspirators anyhow, Trotsykites in
college drag.

Jed and Soli.

Jed and Soli.

Jed and Soli.

Jed and Soli.

My chest hurts.

Is it mere acid reflux, an unsettling in the gut, or is it a hypo-
chondriac twinge, an atherosclerotic pang or premature congestion
imagined in the heart? Something in that vein. A sense of decay, of
blockage. I will sit here and wait it out.

9

EVEN IN A freshman dorm full of Maoists, Marxist-Leninists, nat-dems, soc-dems, and plain god-dems, as Edwin Cardozo, a pervert in plainclothes, called the young Christian politicians who wanted a share of the campus election pie, Soli Soledad and Jed De Rivera Morga were a conspicuous pair.

You could say Jed and Soli were a monad-unit of basic class warfare simply by entering a room. And a downright theoretical contradiction when they entered hand in hand. Solidaridad Soledad was some kind of leader of campus demonstrations and midnight Mendiola rallies, a classic petty-bourgeois hell-raiser of our listless, insipid consciousnesses—while Jed was the avatar of all that she protested.

Soli was not, as she liked to boast, an aboriginal pygmy, but she had this deep sheen: the color of rare Philippine mahogany. For some reason, she smelled of butterscotch. Her caramel gleam, a dark brown smoothness of feature, complemented her elfin irony. From the first, to me she was riveting. Who knows where she was from—Albay or Albania. It's true, her ethereal quality belied her absolute allegiance to dialectical materialism; but of course, among kids at the university, that only added to her charms rather than subtracted. She carried her collegiate Maoism like a Joycean chalice, and in my memory, callow as my ideology, she lies in this fog of secular grace. In the end, I have no words, really, for my attraction. She never lectured me: but somehow whenever I was in her presence I knew my mere existence was a crime. At the very least, I understood I was a fraud.

To view my life through her empathy was like studying my nausea with a ready-made glossary—maybe I remember Soli so clearly because she gave names to my unease, though her doing so gave me no comfort. Exhibit A: Here are the Filipino people. You are the wicked witch beneath its wing. Exhibit B: To enter the gates of your country, give up your suite of custom-designed rooms and march.

So this campus radical's constant carrying on in the dorm with Don Mariano's son, my neighbor in Makati and like me an alumnus of that infernal American high school, haven of *bureaucrat-capitalists*, *imperialists*, and *feudal lords*, evil trinity of my country's didactic, dialectical griefs, as per Soli, was disconcerting.

Jed De Rivera Morga's fame had preceded his arrival at the dorm. I already knew that he had run away from his dad's home to live with his mother at her residence across the street from us in the Village, when Don Mariano refused to let him stay in Manila for college. Don Mariano wanted him to go abroad, like the rest of us. My mother retold in hushed tones the serial narrative of Jed's ridiculous rebellion against Princeton, Stanford and Cornell (oddly enough, when I got to the dorm, budding Marxists talked about him with the same deferential scorn). Ma rehashed each installment of Jed's anti–Ivy League capers in the way she always talked about the Morgas: as if they existed on another planet.

The fact was, for certain sections of Manila society—those who subscribed to the protocols of status and thus underscored, by their attention to its rigors, their own devout inferiority—the Morgas *were* from a different planet. As far as the evidence went, they were as likely descended from the Spanish-era *oidor* Antonio de Morga, who had written the history of the Philippines in 1602 as I was descended (according to my father) from Rajah Soliman, the vanquished sultan of pre-Hispanic Manila. Still, these twin legends kept each of our families' hired guns busy through several biographical volumes of sad veracity. Family book projects were a serial fad in Manila, gleaming coffee-table tomes called *Tides & Time (Volume 1: The Chinese Dynasty)* or *Modern Rajah: Kingdom Conquered to Kingdom Come*—vanity presses of fine megalomaniac proportions written with style by literary eunuchs. What separated the Morgas, of course, from my parents was that the Solimans and the Kierulfs were provincial upstarts whose genealogy was up for grabs; while Jed's people were old oligarchs who had owned the swamps of Manila when tamarin monkeys still lived in them. To its credit, Jed used to say, like primordial slime his family kept its grip on the land even now that different species of baboon held sway.

As Jed acted out his sophomoric dramas of privileged anarchy in Makati, my mother was already ordering the maids to start packing my bags in anticipation of my departure for some leafy arcadia in New England or New York—someplace new. Very few of my classmates chose college at home. But an infection that attacked me—a debilitating contraction of lungs, or esophagus, or ganglia— this withering in the loins kept me home instead of on my way to some hallowed ivy hall (a weakness, for some reason, strikes me at inconvenient times). It was that infection that reunited me, gratuitously, fortuitously, with the pale misanthrope, Joaquin Eduardo De Rivera Morga, aka Jed, gold-haired scion of Philippine gold and silver mines.

As if college in Manila were a form of convalescence, my parents allowed me to stay a term at the local university while I recovered. My mother kept saying, a bit doubtfully, "Well, if the Morgas are doing it——?" I guess if the Morgas did things, one did not have to finish one's sentences.

Anyway, I pointed out to my mom, I was not yet seventeen—everyone at the dorm would be my age. In Manila, high school ended two years earlier than ours at the American School, and at the American School, I had always been too young.

My mom, whose competitive streak was old-fashioned, as Uncle Gianni liked to say, loved to boast that in public school in America I had kept skipping grades—*inday, you were an advanced student!* She thought it was an advantage. As far as I could tell, at the American School it made me something of a dork (even in A.P. English). She liked to retell how I had begun reading at age three, was bored in school at five, and when I was seven tests in New York resolved the mystery of my moods—I had the vocabulary and comprehension level of a sullen ninth-grader. Now here I was, too sick to go abroad but just the right age for Manila. *Inday, it's ironic.* Precocity had given me leverage in the event of unforeseen disaster. She wrote my college to defer until January intersession; and after negotiations with the local university that made a fuss over some exam, she enrolled me in Manila that June.

I have a distinct, sunlit memory of passing Jed with Soli one sharp milky noon, there by the covered walk at the college. I remember that lost, malignant emptiness as I watched them, that wasteful coveting madness as I held a lunch tray (or was it a book) in my hand. Maybe it was an extension of my illness—a tardy canker— the shallow whinge of deflated gall—that occasioned the response I had at the sight of Jed with Soli. Did I love him even then? I had a dim notion I would get to know him in that ramshackle place they called a university dorm: after all, were we not high school cohorts (though in the early days he never remembered my name)? Did we not share the same road signs home, a pair of historic anachronisms saluting the wrong side of the revolution: Admiral George Dewey Drive, parallel to President McKinley Road?

No.

It was Soli's approval that I craved.

I had met Jed and his dad that first day at the dorm, and Jed was as grumpy and worthless as I remembered him, a beautiful creature wrapped up in vague martyrdoms. True, he had graduated valedictorian from my high school, a prize I had coveted, but I thought he had received it with rude grace, walking onstage in leather slip-ons and a t-shirt.

Jed was a millionaire who dressed like Saint Francis and acted like Saint Jerome; increasingly his temper was waspish and gloomy, as if he spent days starving himself in the desert, transcribing the words of the Lord. Everybody at the high school had adored him, his growing rage against the Philistines, and all the girls wanted to be his Mary Magdalene. When he spearheaded the food drives and the orphan visits, the boys on his soccer team went along, their hearts not quite bleeding; the girls on my soccer team were ready to anoint his cleats with oil, plus myrrh and frankincense. But when he made that speech at graduation, denouncing our imperial education to a crowd of imperial scum, no one was amused.

As I said, I did not begrudge Jed and Soli their conspiratorial gravity or cuckoo activism, as my dad had called Jed's evil valediction. In fact, Jed's meekness and modesty at the university dorm were new. From campus loudmouth, he became this mute nonentity, obscuring his beauty in red bandannas and hanging around with lumpen louts and morbid people, all similarly sandal-shod. Jed followed this girl around, that creamy betel nut of a radical, Solidaridad Soledad, my *tokayo*, my provocative eponym. He stood behind her at rallies and demonstrations, helping her organize late-night lectures, fetching chairs, lifting megaphones, and at the first event I went to, I saw him holding a banner over her head, like a matrimonial veil, at this farmers' strike to which Soli had made me tag along.

Yes, I know—I too became a recruit in Soli's student army. Don't ask me why or how. To put it in Soli's terms, I was just a well-mannered bourgeois with unspoken misgivings about my own desires. And yes, I'd be the first to say that recalling the idiocies of teenage days has the tinge, inescapably, of a young-adult novel—the irritatingly unexamined opinions of unlived lives. *Touché*.

In dumb pumps and op-art clothes, I looked radically ill advised, not chic. But even when I joined Soli and Jed on their rainy marches through the potholes of Manila's streets, I did have the feeling of being left out, though who knows if my sense of abandonment was my own fault.

It was hard in the early days not to feel, in Jed and Soli's presence, that the rest of us were out of the loop. In those first days he hung about her like an idiot Romeo, as if her every word were some

aphorism or lambent epigram, and his rapt look created the disturbing force field that foolish lovers make. To Soli's credit, she took it
like no Juliet. She was flattered but did not simper, amused, not
stupefied, by love. I admired her coolness, her romantic tact.

When they visited me that weekend in Makati, and they
grinned at my childish books (Winnie the Pooh, Willy Wonka)
among my Uncle Gianni's slew of other recommendations (Graham
Greene, Anthony Powell), I did not take their comradeship against
them. I was pleased they had dropped by.

"What are you doing here," I said.

"Just passing," Jed said, as if his neighborly visit were a habit. "I
told Soli you lived across the street from my mom's, probably home
on a weekend leave, and Soli insisted we stop by."

"Are your parents home?" Soli asked, looking around at the gilt
Versailles mirrors of the foyer. I thought she'd soon be choking on
some French pastry allusion or powdery Sun-King sally. "Can we
meet them?"

"They're at the Palace," I said to Jed. "Didn't your mom go?"

It was September, that day after the Manila Bay concert: the
president was celebrating his actual birthday with a bash my parents
never declined.

"I have no idea what you're talking about," Jed said.

I was sorry I said anything.

Prima De Rivera Morga, a former fixture at all functions my
parents attended, had gradually become that rare thing in Manila
society: a hermit. She'd stopped going out, and rumor had con-
cocted all sorts of despairs. Agoraphobic, alcoholic, anorexic; rumor
cooked a full menu of maladies, but she appeared in the society col-
umns always as "the lovely socialite." I hadn't seen her since she had

moved across the street after leaving her husband's home. When Jed moved into her home a few months later, ditching Princeton for the naked butt of the local university's Oblation, I'd occasionally see his proletarian bike propped against the bonsai, or glimpse a Rorschach shadow of his curls in a tinted car. But he, too, avoided my parents' company like the plague; and the sight of the recluse's glamorous son in our house, I knew, would be causing commotion among the maids.

I could see my driver Manong Babe, usually a man of decorum, gaping at Jed and Soli as they passed him picking his teeth discreetly by the stairs.

I sent them both straight up to my rooms.

Soli said she loved my wallpaper. What an ingenious design given the sad destinies of that orphan kid and his giant coconut. Jed found her view of Roald Dahl endearing. My own say in the matter, as the erstwhile curator of the room's motifs at age ten, was, I guess, moot.

"And look: my initials all over the wall," exclaimed Soli.

"It's a copy of a Bauhaus print," I said.

"What's Bauhaus again," Jed said. "Nazi narcissists?"

Soli laughed.

"No. The opposite," I said. "They were progressive. Designers and architects. Persecuted by the Nazis."

"And you have your own gym," Soli said. "And a spoliarium: cool."

"It's a solarium," I corrected.

"No," she said. "Spoliarium."

"That is the arena of gladiator corpses in ancient Rome," I corrected. "A solarium is a sunroom."

"The space of spolia," she appraised it. "Spoliarium."

I looked at Jed.

"Well, he has one, too, I bet. Bigger than mine," I said.

"And what did you think of the Colonel?" he asked.

"What?"

Jed repeated: "What did you think of the new man at LOTUS?"

"How did you know I met him?"

"My dad said you met him there."

"I have no idea what you're talking about."

"He's an interesting dude," said Jed. "That Colonel. He and your Uncle Gianni—Edwin tells me they're fascinating guys."

10

I MADE AN ERROR in that accounting: such things happen. Yes, right. Correct, erase, dismember. It is not true. Soli was not in my rooms with Jed that weekend of the concert by the Bay. A smell of gunsmoke and burning rubber—the sensational background of a New Year's wake, the day she visited me in Makati. The air stank of New Year's sulphur. No, this conversation happened months before, as I said: on the night of the president's Virgo bacchanal.

My parents were already at the Palace in their masks and decadent cheer, to sing ring-around-the-rosy about the dictator's dialysis machine. And I was not surprised by the arrival in my home of Jed and his sidekick, that invertebrate kid in a trench coat, Edwin Cardozo.

As tall as Jed but without his muscle, Edwin, in my memory, gives off the sense of someone unaccountably overlooked—a slightly mangled indistinct abstraction in an awkward draft that seeks the truth. Or maybe that is just the case of us all—what would I look like, to Edwin?

It's his fault. As far as I could tell, Edwin Cardozo was a wuss. Never quite part of the crowd, he failed to attend even the most innocuous protest marches (say, for the Education Act of 1980, a perfectly banal and proper cause); for the more dangerous ones, he cast us off as idiots, grinning as if he were some wise, ripened old Methuselah among an uncooked batch of juvenile Maos—though he looked younger than any of us, with his childish braces and baby fat. Bespectacled, his mouth pulled together by spidery webs, he leaned against a black umbrella most times, so that it seemed that he was kept upright and walking and talking mostly by metallic accessories, rather than by actual bones or spine. His main preoccupation was an endless game of chess with Jed, played in the dorm lobby.

Among all of the kids of those times, Edwin bugged me the most.

I'd go off to play soccer at the scraggly university fields, and I'd note Edwin in my sweaty vision seated in the crummy bleachers, scrunched with his sketchy umbrella amid the litter and the crabby grass. I'd browse through the secondhand books in the open-air labyrinths behind Vinzons Hall, and he'd be swatting at the flies on the tolerant dust as he read some bothersome science tome. True, Edwin and I had the same schedule, because we were block mates; and the university is a small-enough space for freshmen who are clumped together in limited spheres: lobby, library, Palma Hall— we'd barely get to the Annex, stuck as we were in our predestined ruts down the flame-tree road from class to dorm.

I recognized my relations with Jed and Soli and their group had begun deteriorating (one could put it that way) at some point in the detritus of that typhoon season—after the marches and the sit-ins and the countryside lectures, and the questions and the self-criticisms and the confessions. It was unnerving to keep finding Edwin Cardozo on the periphery of my lamest acts, burrowing in the library or brooding in a bookstall, as if killing time.

There is the impulse to gloss over, to wallpaper certain moments with creatures of my design. Edwin's flat face buried in a book at the British Council, sticking his nose in alphabetical savants—A. Brontë, C. Dickens, E. Forster—while I sat morose in a seat nearby. That library in New Manila became my particular obsession. I remember at one point I kept borrowing books that had the same incestuous signatures on the sign-out sleeves: and so it seemed inter-marriages of paired sensibilities could be graphed by the names on a book's stiff cards. Those odd couplings satisfied me.

When I kept bumping into Edwin Cardozo at the strangest places, even outside the university walls, I felt they were stalking me—the sons of the people whom I was shamefully escaping—even though reason told me that Edwin Cardozo, cowardly non-marcher, was not one of them. I remember once, when a shot rang through the dormitory lobby (it was only a drunken boy, breaking a bottle against a door's glass), it was Edwin who dropped instantly to the floor, cowering as if revolution had broken loose.

Coca-Cola philosopher, they called him. But the reason he never joined the marches was not just ideological. At heart, I thought, he was afraid.

The book cards told me that like me he was a restive reader. He read *Portrait of the Artist* before I did, but I had my hands first on *Sentimental Journey*. We read in tandem the twin dust covers of the library's duplicate copies of *A Handful of Dust*.

"WHAT ARE YOU doing here," I said.

If the maids had not been around, waiting at the doorway, I would have pushed the pair out of the house.

"Just passing," Jed said, as if his neighborly visit were a habit. "I told Edwin you lived across the street from my mom's, probably home on a weekend leave, and he insisted we stop by."

"Are your parents home?" Edwin asked, looking around at the gilt Versailles mirrors of the foyer. I could see he'd soon be choking on some French pastry allusion or powdery Sun-King sally. "Can we meet them?"

Edwin, as usual, was carrying his dumb black umbrella on his shoulder like a Garand rifle.

I stared at them from the staircase, unwilling to come down.

"They're at the Palace," I said. I looked at Jed: "Didn't your mom go?"

"I have no idea what you're talking about."

The maids were coming in and out, staring at their visitor, the reclusive beauty queen's son who hovered behind Edwin at the doorway, as if he, like me, wished only to escape.

Even my driver Manong Babe, usually a man of decorum, was gaping at the pair as he picked his teeth discreetly by the stairs.

I sent them both up to my rooms.

"What," grinned Edwin, "Juan and the humongous guava? What's with the orphan theme?"

"Those are scenes from Roald Dahl," I corrected.

"Your initials all over the wall," Ed smirked.

"They are copies of Bauhaus prints," I said.

"Nazi narcissists," murmured Jed.

"Quite the opposite," Edwin said. "They were progressive. Designers and architects. Persecuted by the Nazis. Ah. And you have your own gym. And a solarium: cool."

"A spoliarium," Jed said.

"That is the arena of gladiator corpses in ancient Rome," Edwin smirked.

"The space of spolia," said Jed.

I stared at him:

"Then you have one, too, I bet. Bigger than mine."

"And what did you think of the Colonel?" Jed asked.

"What?"

Jed repeated: "What did you think of the new man at LOTUS?"

"How did you know I met him?"

"I told him you would meet him there," Edwin said, head bent as he wandered about my room, checking out the books. He did not bother looking up: "I told Jed to go to the concert himself."

"I have no idea what you're talking about," I said.

"He's an interesting dude," said Jed. "That Colonel. He and your Uncle Gianni—fascinating guys, aren't they, Edwin?"

Edwin came up to us, holding a book.

"Can I borrow these," he said.

The Sickness unto Death. The Ordeal of Samar.

I stared at him.

11

MUCKING THROUGH THIS part of the story discourages me, but I might as well go through with it. I've been told Kierkegaard's sickness unto death is only a bodily malfunction, a glandular lack. Maybe this throb of incompleteness is the same. In my mind, the event has the anxious compass of something yet to be averted—a sordid, unsatisfying suspension. I keep pushing it down, stomping on it, this heft of my expectancy, my wish to resurrect him, again.

I had these jobs in Jed and Soli's group—we each played a role in our small ways. Mine was to collect copper five-centavo coins— solid centavos with a naked man on the obverse and a smoking volcano in the distance. I was a treasurer. I have no idea why we collected the five centavos—and not the pesos or the twenty-fives. They told me to collect them and I did. Every time I saw one, I'd put the coin in this rectangular tin of Fox's Glacier candy, a rattling can I carried around, like some beggar's bounty. Another of my jobs was to run errands, buy material for meetings, stuff like that. For instance, apart from the copper coins, I gathered goods for night ops. Of night operations, you saw the results every day, washed off then resurrected, painted over, painted back—red slogans on monuments and bridges.

It was my job to buy the Dutch Boy paint. Color: dripping blood, with a can of thinner to maximize our outlay. Other people, "warm bodies," cadaverous kids from the university belt, did the graffiti. My job was to get the cans and sometimes help mix the paint. Afterward, those of us left behind used to sit on a windowsill at the Annex. The domestic wreckage would lie before us, poster cloth, newspaper backdrops greasy with thinner droppings, brushes and rollers and someone's paint-splattered shirt on the floor. To relax, sometimes we'd walk over to the astronomer's tower. We took a beaten path beyond the Arts and Science buildings throttled by goats and wild grass. We'd go up and talk to the astronomer on duty. We pretended to recognize some constellations.

At the time, Jed was building some kind of fame in the narrow corridors of our imaginations.

Jed led lightning rallies—daredevil streaks after midnight. He looked for confrontations with police. He enjoyed the kinds of work, even drudgery, that led to danger. I'd go to the student council office at the Annex and note him among his insomniac pals, bony heirs of Bonifacio, tooling with their banners. He was an intense being with a dreamy look, a gaze skittish and grave at the same time. He and Soli were still a thing. I could not tell exactly how love happened among the radicals—they called courtship a *programa,* a romance of rules and guidelines the absurdities of which I failed to fathom. To be honest, at this point it did not look too different from love anywhere else. Soli complained Jed was impulsive and a narcissist, and Jed agreed so she would shut up.

Night ops, for instance, trivial as they were, appealed to Jed, though Soli pointed out they weren't his job. He'd come back from those chores looking drunk. The jobs gave him a rush, and when he returned, he had the irritable passion of a child. He couldn't sit still. He wouldn't return to the dorm. Instead he wandered around the campus with the stray dogs and the pensive goats. Once he slept by the tower.

The night I remember, the night-op painters had arrived, and Jed went with them. *Mob*, he liked to shout, organizing the kids like their boss—*let's mob! Mob* meant *mobilize*. He loved the jargon. I thought even the abbreviations gave him a hard-on, but he didn't mind it if people laughed. We liked to mimic him as he exited with his troops. The rest of us tramped to the tower. One by one, the group left, and I remained. I wound up alone, leaning against masonry; I sat there on the ground. When a shadow loomed, I jumped.

"Hello," Jed said, his white figure fluttering above me. I saw his face, his flickering teeth and incremental hair. I had only a faint light to snare him by: it was the earth that lit him up. He leaned against the masonry, his arm outstretched. "Where did the rest go?"

"Home."

"You're locked out," he said, looking at his blind watch. "The dorm's closed."

"You look strange," I said. "Are you drunk?"

"I don't drink. I don't even eat," he grinned.

"You also don't sleep," I said. "You have a red gash there. What's on your cheek?"

I touched the gore on his face. It was paint. But even when he brushed it off, his face remained ghoulish against the light—his cheeks an impertinent rash.

"You should have gone with us," he said. "It was fun."

No one was around. Even the astronomer was gone: his light was out. It was late. There were only stars, a new moon, and this weak phosphorescence on the grass, which seemed to illuminate Jed.

"Strange," I pointed out, "the grass is lit up."

"Glowworms," Jed said, settling on the grass. "They appear all over the jungles, you know. In my father's forests, they give off a greenish light."

"It's eerie."

I thought I heard a few birds, maybe an owl. Insects. The stealthy movements of a cat, a rat. I got up and walked around, pushed at leaves, a deserted snack bag.

"Sit down," he said. "What are you nervous about?"

I sat beside Jed.

"What fascinates about the sky's constellations?" I asked. "Why is it that people always look to the sky for signs, acting like people who are lost?"

"Is that what you do?"

"No."

"So what is it? Why are you still here?"

"I'm figuring that out."

OF COURSE, IT didn't happen like that: all of the above has an indulgent recall. Phosphorescent worms? That's a detail I gathered from this book, *The Ordeal of Samar*. Amid the narrative of a massacre of American soldiers by masked rebels in Samar in 1901, I found in me only a misplaced nostalgia, a sense of loss, in the American enemy's descriptions of the country's landscape, the wildlife I did not know—glassy fire ants, grassland moths, glowing phosphorescent worms. I imagine the illumination of the university's rural light in this lurid setting, a kind of tropical grandeur: when in fact, if I saw Jed's face, it was most probably by ordinary streetlight, if at all—a wan stippled glare. Maybe a few faint fireflies bustling about—and even that, though true, has the specious aura of art.

Memory *is* deception. There's a pall under which intentions lie, gross as an astrologer's ball. In fact, I don't remember that first time clearly, or even calmly. If I dig through it more deliberately, I come up with surprising blanks in my memory. I can't re-create the wetness of ground or measures of space, awkward movements or bend of light—specific facts elude my recall. Instead, fantastical, borrowed details recur—green, phosphorescent lies. Those offhand matters that should round off a significant moment with convincing clarity—these are jumbled, a general blur. Sharp grass, a cold nipple, clumsy pain, a stupid, blundering tongue. Pale generic claims, bones in my memory. I do remember strongly what I used to feel about Jed when he was impossible to get. For a time, the only woman he spoke to was Soli, and he barely remembered who I was. I have that distinct, sunlit memory of passing Jed with Soli one sharp, milk-eyed noon by the covered walk at the college. I remember that lost, malignant emptiness as I watched them, that wasteful coveting madness as I held up a lunch tray (or was it a book?) in my hand. A holograph: vacuum stasis of desire. But when I did eventually have him, memory falters. As if happiness, possession, were a blank, and only longing counts.

I HAVE HAD NIGHTMARES of interrogation, inflating my importance. In four-by-five, roach-scuttled rooms drenched with the smell
of piss, soldiers' cigarette and dry sweat. The smell of the low end of
human achievement: the ability to shit, spit, kill. The smell of vomit,
diuretic heat.

In one dream I confessed my actions, and I reported two things.

"Yes, yes. I painted signs on bridges!" I confessed.

"And number two?"

"I fucked the boyfriend of Saint Catherine of Siena!"

The prosecuting soldier, a well-shaved child, turned out to be,
of all things, a stucco Della Robbia angel, a naked Florentine figure
who laughed at me like nuts. Then I woke up. A stupid dream,
patched from the vague dregs of a vacation home.

But at the time I began going about with Jed, mucking around
near the astronomer's tower, where one can see Sirius the Dog-Star
in fitful spurts on clear evenings, in between the rustle of tall grass
and the anxious repositionings of one's weight, I thought nothing of
the affair. I do not believe I even had dreams. I stalked him by the
tower without guilt or illusion.

A night op was a kid's job. A rebellion without profit. Cadres
would not be caught dead painting slogans. A person like me, a
mere *sympa,* as they say, a sympathizer with dim potential, had no
business doing it either. Jed first drove me toward Kamias. It was
past midnight; the place was almost empty. Jed parked his car across
from a dull eatery; we moved into the shadows created by a nearby
building. Emptiness had transformed the street, and the city looked
disarmed. Traffic was its ugly armor, and without it, the city had all
the terror of a trashed cigarette pack. We saw people entering a cof-

fee shop across the street. At the next stoplight, a cigarette vendor lit up one of his goods. Near us, the cud of spit-upon stone, ragged edges of cheap road construction.

Jed walked before me, light brown hair obscuring his sight. He wore his leather Franciscan sandals and a white poet's shirt, with the string collar. In profile, his silence acquired an almost sweet tapered beauty. For his part, I believe Jed was pained by it, by the predictable reception his looks claimed. The cigarette vendor, wrapped in smoke, stared.

Jed had this gaze of ardor, a light-flecked cherub's brow, topped by golden curls and furrowed by his earnestness—he had a look of innocence, if you didn't think too much about it—and for this he got away with many things.

I walked behind, alert to dangerous sounds, surprises.

He chose a wall near the overpass.

We weren't organized—we didn't even divide by syllables. We acted on impulse and took each letter as it came. We aimed too high—when I stepped back to look at our work, the letters slanted unnecessarily, like mortal heart lines in a cardiograph. We were messy, uneven. The *M* in the word was Jed's height, the *R* in it was mine. I made a large, wet blob at a spot right before my temple. I was silent, jumpy. Sometimes Jed would paint with his body directly over mine: his arm outstretched against my chest, his breathing humid, disturbing. We began to paint in rhythm, fast, my hand with its paintbrush crossing over his sweaty sleeve. We finished a word. We had only begun the rising letters of the next when a car passed us with headlights full-blast.

The car stopped—and we abandoned our greasy cans. We ran. But it was just a motorist, coming home from workday stupor or carousing, blinding the world with his high beams. The man sped on. Jed cursed. Halfway to the car, we looked back. Our sign was ridiculous, an ad for the wrong thing, the opposite of our intentions—*Imperyalismo!* With the *I* in *ibagsak* acting as an exclamation point.

I'm embarrassed. It's true—our juvenilia were cast in communist red. I suppose it reveals what was most ridiculous about me. A neurotic adventure, an erotic ploy. We found spray paint and sometimes used that, but we liked best the gory texture of dripping red. Not only that. We'd plan ahead. Once, we did it at the wall by my house's Village, behind his mother's place—by the gas-station corner, near Ah Me! Kitchenette, where William McKinley trickled into a rut, a dirt road. Jed's elbow hit mine, and a bloody ghoulishness dripped on my breasts. He laughed. Later that night, he could not lick the bloody mess off, no matter how he tried, and for days my nipples ached, tender, from the comic stupor of his insistence, the pathetic rhythms of his obedient, ministering tongue.

We did it at Jed's dad's place, on James Buchanan Drive. The parking lot of the defunct American School at Roxas Boulevard. Our neighborhood playgrounds in Makati. The blind firewalls behind dead-end malls. We slathered our signs on the cemetery where I used to take walks as a kid, the beautified grounds of American dead. We made our marks, like peeing dogs, near the conquistador church where, two years apart, Jed and I were baptized. An emerging autobiography, our very own *talambuhay*, motives still uncast. We were exhibitionists, we were artists. We made infantile moves on elementary haunts. We could predict where our work would be slashed over, whitewashed and revised: the town of Makati was vengeful, self-policing, the city of Pasig not so much. We'd take a drive in the night to survey our bloody narration: proper red marks all over the city, preludes to other acts.

At first, we never had encounters. You had to find the trick to it—deserted leafy places, usually after midnight. You had to be ready to run. We had near-brushes. Silly, delirious moments, with my heart thumping so hard that I heard it in my hand, my brow, a loud, regular drill, my body like a drum. A rush in my cunt, a delicate throbbing. We were never caught.

We became quick, minimalists. We stuck to one phrase, monotonous but efficient.

Afterward, there were cheap motels, ruined places with awful smells. We barely noticed where we were. We noticed our bodies, like well-known parts of an alphabet. As for me, I keep remembering him in pieces. This fractured vision. To dwell on it, his body—I feel something in me unravel, like a loose string in the mind. Kneecap, square and a bit nubby, whitened by soccer scars. His funny widow's peak. Eyelashes, brown and whimsically long. Flat thumb and womanish calf. None of him comes together—a lewd, abstract recall. And then sometimes I remember some innocuous moment, like once when his stubbled hair chafed my chin and afterward the thin skin around my mouth was bruised, as if I had kissed gravel.

By day, JED was with Soli. Nights, we'd meet by the astronomer's tower, when the seers were asleep and the prophets had gone home. The group had a term for it, I forget, one of those abbreviations that truncated a radical's brains. S.O., D.A., F.U., C.K. Like the terms "adultery" or "bigamy" among canonical Catholics, our acts had terse definitions and legal consequences in the group's breviary, if anyone ever found out; the worst of it was, I would have nothing but my mind's dishevelment with which to refute its gloss. We stuck to the charade of our silly syllabus, *Imperyalismo, Ibagsak*, a tired rant we overplayed. These night-op duties, a sodden responsorial psalm, were mere preemptive strikes, I knew, a dilatory prequel. I only thought about the end, that dull apartment in New Manila, for instance, for which Jed somehow had found keys. He was a Morga, after all—he could have owned the whole street.

The thing was, Jed loved the cloak and dagger, but he always planned ahead.

As the final couplet in our repertoire, Room 1616 was an appropriate disaster, fully furnished in trite nationalist tropes. There were lampshades made of woven buri and a creaky rocking chair in abacá. Puka shell figures gathered dust on rattan side tables: and fat tropical ants scuttled upon the tawdry room's Manila hemp, oblivious of our devices. It occurs to me now as a twist of fate that the twined room's metaphor, a mirrored number, foretold some awful symmetry. Lying in the single bed, listening to the whistling susurrus of Jed's dreams while his broad wet arms lay warm upon me, I sometimes had this out-of-body feeling, as if I were not there, but someone was happy.

12

THAT LAST NIGHT, we had already done the job. We were about to throw away our paint cans. On a wall a few meters ahead, the man must have seen our mark, gleaming, still wet. I was horrified: I froze.

Jed barely looked at the policeman. It was as if he had long expected the scene, and he did the first take with cool self-control. He took the paint can and simply threw it in the bushes. Right in front of the policeman's car. Then Jed took the brushes from me and threw them away, too.

I did not move.

The man came out of his car, and long-lost fears arose, of blue-sleeved policemen on a street, clashing with a crowd, a long time ago when I was a child. Manong Babe kept driving through the crowd shouting silent taunts at the police, and I watched as a man battered a woman with his club, while I clutched my stuffed animal. Ali Babar. A purple elephant with a cloth crown.

The man in uniform spoke in Tagalog.

Jed mumbled a word I did not catch. Then Jed took something from his pocket.

He showed it to the man.

He took Jed's ID and peered at it with a flashlight. Even the cop's fingers, piggy and beringed, looked somehow consequential. His flashlight shifted, from Jed's ID to Jed's face, looking up at Jed's foreigner's mask, bloodless in the searchlight except for the scarlet darkness of his mouth. I was surprised by the man's gesture.

The policeman saluted Jed.

"Sorry, sir," he said. "Mr. Morga, sir. May I escort you home?"

"No," said Jed. "I have a car. Come."

Jed turned to me: "Let's go, Victoria Eremita. I'll take you home."

SHE CAME INTO the room, without knocking. Victoria Eremita had cooked a storm in the kitchen downstairs, from the looks of her traveling tray. As usual, the dwarfish boy, something of a good luck charm in the house, followed Eremita around, carrying extra cutlery and tablecloths. None of the servants who had stayed behind in New York walked about the house alone. Manang Lita and Manang Maring—the chief cook and the old caretaker—had not even bothered to come; they were home in Manila. Everyone wandered about the mansion in pairs or groups, as if solitude might curse them.

Eremita's pink-shirted page had a huge head, with a brow broader, I swear, than my limp thigh. But his face was very kind (though distorted, kind of funhouse-frozen): and I always felt, when it stared at me, that something tragic had occurred, but I did not know what.

How is it possible to be called Soledad and be granted absolutely no privacy at all? People followed me to bed and picked up my pajamas, they ran my bath and picked at my shirts, looking for missing buttons, if not missing persons. What were they guarding with such clueless care? At times, I imagine that if they could they would invade my damaged brain, with their soups and their ladles and their rice cakes, and somehow serve up my mysteries with clotted cream.

I smiled at Eremita and that stunted creature, who was not shy at all. For the life of me, I could not remember its name, right there on the tip of my tongue. It was in fact no infant. He, the juvenile dwarf, was coming into an awkward age: the kind of obese you could not put your finger on, only vaguely fat, a tween with incipient man-stink, and completely oblivious of his imploding glands. He clattered into the room with his utensils and smashed them onto a table, as if still practicing his gross motor skills. Someone had manicured his bitten fingernails.

"It's so dark, Ma'am Sol!" he exclaimed, in a surprisingly low voice. He always had this tone, addressed to me with his fingers in a formal pose, as if ready to chastise or pray—a tone of deep pity, but a look of awful respect.

Eremita, silent as always, flipped the switches.

"It's so dusty, Ma'am Sol!" he reproached. "You are not afraid of asthma?"

Eremita started vigorously on a table I had not even noticed, wiping in circles at its clean surface.

"It's okay, it's okay," I said, to both of them.

"The merienda is good," he pronounced, now staring straight at my arms.

And under his glare, I felt instinctively again for my wrists, their soft curdle and tumid scars.

"Does it still hurt," he said, as he always did, with that barefaced look of compassion, quite misplaced, I thought, for it was he who was a dwarf, and I who could silence him if I wished.

I smiled at him, trying to remember his name.

"No," I said. "I am healed."

"That is good!"

And he held up a thumb, for victory, before lumbering away with Eremita, trundling the wheeled tray back toward the hall, the trail of sweat and musk in their wake underlining the persistence of their humanity. I heard the elevator as they descended, an antique rumble, like a moan.

Inocentes.

That was his name. Born a week after my birthday, the winter solstice—Holy Innocents' Day—an orphan salvaged from a pile of castaways.

Edwin used to taunt me with my name. *Sol,* he said: *short for solipsism.*

"So you had a revelation," Edwin said. "Tell me about it."

He was sitting beside me, metal bit in his caged mouth, his fat glasses flattening his face. The effect of his late bloomer's braces was an awkward shower of spit, sometimes right smack on his lenses.

We were leafing through different issues of the same literary review. A dark wall of books framed the neat brick before us.

"I don't know. I'm trying to figure something out."

"You know that God spits out the lukewarm," he said, spewing out ungodly spit.

I felt alternately like cleaning up his glasses or waiting in fascination until his eyeballs drowned.

"But you've never even been. Not even close to ingestion."

Edwin turned the page, passing over a blind article on myopia.

"There's more to spit than meets the eye," he said.

"Beg your pardon," I said. "More to spit than what?"

"More to it, I said. Than meets the eye. Are you deaf?"

"I think I should quit," I said.

It seemed to me we spoke in code, maybe because it betrayed the absurdity of what we were doing if we actually divulged what it was.

"About time," he said, nodding. "You have discovered why you are with them, of course?"

"Of course not," I said. "I have not."

"Solipsism," he said. "Sol for solipsism."

Edwin opened up to a full-page ad for a bestselling book, about dreams or dentistry.

"I don't think so," I said.

"You're the worst kind of recruit."

"Thanks."

"You joined the group as a form of soul-searching, bogged down in existential depression over some Oedipal mess."

"Ha-ha."

"You want to find peace with your childhood, and once you do, when you return to the lap of luxury, radical action will look like a sport, an absurd, old-fashioned toy: when in fact, joining a Maoist study group, or whatever you prefer to call it, no matter how dumb your intentions, is the only thing you've ever done that grants you relevance."

"Thanks," I said.

"You're welcome," he said. "It's an old story," he mused, closing the now damp review upon the spine of his limp umbrella. "*L'education sentimentale*. Clearly. *Portrait of the Artist as a Young Man*. Arguably. Bertolucci, in his prime, beautifully. They played your movie last week at the Film Center. *Before the Revolution*. And then there's Simoun, in *El Filibusterismo*. Definitely."

"Simoun? What do you know about Simoun?" I demanded.

I should have known there was something suspicious about Ed. His snotty book reports were a goddamned pain in the ass.

"Simoun was the hero of Jose Rizal's second novel, *El Filibusterismo*. The *Fili*. The one after the *Noli*. Geez—haven't they lectured you on the country's history already? Isn't that the first thing the Maoists do—set you straight about the past in order to correct the future? Simoun's revolution was a failure, if you need to know. That's because Jose Rizal never understood Hegel. Not to mention Marx."

"Oh. You mean the work of fiction," I said, relieved.

"What else could I mean?" Ed said, laughing.

"You mean Simoun, the hero in that work, the novel of the national hero Rizal?"

"Yes."

And Edwin spouted on.

Coca-Cola philosopher.

Bla-bla blather.

"The plot of failed radicalism as doomed romantic fervor is so late-nineteenth-century. A populist fictional criticism not of revolution but of romance."

Bla-bla baloney.

"*Id est:* Nikolai Stavrogin in *The Devils.* Was Dostoyevski denouncing the Decembrists or denouncing Goethe?"

Bla-bla blowhard.

"For the world to progress, it is best to choose the latter. Solipsism has its uses, Sol, don't worry. Soul-searching is its good stepsister. But really, there are more interesting ways to save the country than marching in the streets."

13

WHAT WAS I thinking? I was unhealthy, recovering from a malignant internal tract, hepatitis E, F, or G, when I had arrived at the university during those June monsoons. The dorm was not what I expected, though granted, my hopes were uninformed. I met Don Mariano, a surreal figure in his Stetson hat, trying to keep face in the lobby while mosquitoes ransacked his ruddy cheeks. Flies crawled all over my rank, suffocating skin. A diseased organ, a distract gland, kept my head woozy but my sensibilities alert, and so when I met Soli that first day, I was both addled and hypersensitive, eager for novelty but frayed at the nerves. I felt alien. I felt lost. Even the language everyone spoke I understood in fragments, in unforgiving hallucinatory code. Like everyone else who had gone to school, I had grown up with English, and I had diligently studied French and Spanish and Italian, but of my own languages, my mother's Waray or my father's Tagalog, all I had were accidental bits, gaps and abominable indifference. I felt, in those first days, that I had betrayed someone, but I could not tell whom. It was awful to recognize that when Soli first addressed me I had no idea what she was talking about, and all she was saying was hello.

"I said, how are you," she said in English. "We're *tokayo*," she said.

"What?"

"*Tokayo!*" she shouted, as if I were deaf. She pointed to my name tag. She pointed to hers. "Same as mine."

"What?"

"Tokayo. We have the same name."

I looked at the tag.

"Ah. You're my eponym," I said, like an ass.

"No," she countered. "You are mine."

"Solidaridad Soledad," I read slowly.

"So-le-dad So-li-man," she mimicked. "We rhyme without reason, ha-ha."

I held out my hand.

"Sol," I said. "Just call me Sol."

She said something I could not understand. Then she said in English:

"Soli. As in the revolution. You know."

I had no clue what she was talking about.

"Soli, Noli, Fili. You know. The holy trinity. The sacred texts of the revolution. *La Solidaridad*, the journal of the propagandists of the 1880s. No? *Noli Me Tangere*? Rizal's first novel. *Fili* was the second. What? Does not ring a bell? You do not—?"

I shook my head again. I was feeling sick, and the letters of her winding name collapsed under my falling vision, a nonsensical repetition of syllables, *solosolosolosol,* and she was repeating a nonsensical rhyme, *filisillywillynilly,* like Humpty Dumpty, except that she looked like a dark polished legume with wild unlikely curls, not a cantilevered egg, and she was pointing a finger at me, pointing at my name, saying nothing.

I fell at Soli's feet.

I imagine that my parents were still talking to Don Mariano Morga—with his brown bulimic bimbo somewhere else—having found to their relief one of their own amid the crowd, and Manong Babe must have been putting my suitcases away in my blighted prison cell of a dorm room. No one was around to help. The surprise she must have felt when my weight descended, and then the disgust when I puked on her lap. It was the heat, the unfamiliar lack of air-conditioning, the dreadful dinginess of that pestilent place, the shrill and alien tongues, her good humor, my gradual horror. I don't know where it came from, my awful self-regard. Insects were buzzing at my lips before I even lost it, as if savoring my sickness in advance. I apologized; she was efficient; she led me to the bathroom. And in the Girls' Annex on the day I met her, I poured out my guts in front of Soli.

I WAS IGNORANT OF everything on that campus—the jokes, the allusions, even the forms of public transportation. I had never even ridden a jeepney, to my useless shame, and my mother threatened to keep Manong Babe and his limousine on campus for my disposal, until I told her I would never visit her again if she did. Still, I'd witness Manong Babe loitering about the university sometimes, trailing me in the limousine, on orders from my mother. It made me feel like a freak, and I pretended I had no idea who he was. But I admit sometimes I'd look out for him, for his familiar figure, his mole

distinct even at a distance. He'd weave by in the anomalous car as if
he'd just driven by in distraction. (I confess that I'd feel a rush of
childish emotion at the sight of Manong Babe, through the corner of
my eye, absently polishing his spit-clean shoes in the rain. He was a
neatnik and a worrywart, and sometimes I wanted to go up to him,
if only just to tease him, to say, hey, go away, I'm doing all right. I
never did, though I wish I had.)

I had grown up a stranger in my country, living in my parents'
landscaped cocoon in Makati since our return in the seventies from
America, and my discovery at the university of my potent and irre-
futable dislocation from it, when I could not respond to even the
most ordinary of moments in what should have been my native
tongue, sickened me. It sickened me even more, I thought, than my
lingering illness—or was it that the recidivism of my internal glands
was the abject correlative of my infirmity, my incurable sense of
who I am.

The state of the country was enough to condemn me, of course:
I did not need Soli's discourse to know that, under a military dictatorship, guns, goons and gold were not just tired devices in a slogan
but a percussive note that, in my case, dogged my every domestic
good—my books, my souvenirs, my clothes, my home. And it was
not the first time I had felt this nausea, an elemental eruption: this
split in my soul.

Part II

1

BARELY OUT OF puberty, with his voice acquiring subtle changes even as his old troop ship cruised along the Pacific, so that the experience of crossing the continents had about it the disconcerting sense of an inner demarcation, a bodily mutation, as much as a geographical change—Uncle Gianni's young father had shipped out to Leyte during the 1940s war and experienced adolescence in the jungle, and the island's unfinished landscape seemed to mirror his uncertain age. He saw boys who could make gadgets for every possible need, such as a contraption made of folding plywood and a handful of nails. He stared at it with an almost hair-raised terror, only to find it was a device for opening beer. Women smelled of oceans, and trees provided alcohol as well as leafy plates, hats, and rough-hewn flutes. Many children loved him. The boy soldier showed them his tricks with disappearing bullets. He made friends with a cow. Uncle Gianni's father, in his old age, mostly remembered the ordinary: a stretch of mangrove, alternately familiar and unreal; the tense look on the face of a child who, when the young GI saluted him, burst out in humiliating laughter; the framed, too-intimate view of jungle sky; and the sight and sound of a large, odd-billed bird in a thick tree.

Uncle Gianni's father had been planning a journey with old companions, a nostalgic trip cum tropical vacation, when he fell down dead a few weeks before his flight, on the carpet of his one-bedroom home in Lynn or Lexington, Massachusetts: and so it was that instead young Gianni, an orphan at loose ends, took his father's place for the celebratory occasion.

Uncle Gianni's father, by his son's account, had died a taciturn chemist, a discreet, conservatively suited servant of industry to the end. But he had this obscure notion of his prime time on the Philippine islands, a life he squinted at in his memory, his eyes narrowed, aiming at a better reception. Uncle Gianni, on the other hand, did not quite know what had taken him, a boy of nineteen, to Leyte, seeing as he had come to commemorate a war that was not his own.

A talented pianist with a bright future, Uncle Gianni had made the pilgrimage in the name of his father; but he finished it with a flourish of his own. The old soldiers on the stage in Tacloban made him play a song in honor of the Battle of Leyte Gulf, celebrating October 20, 1944, the day MacArthur fatefully returned after having abandoned us to the Japanese. The boy, who was still unclear why anyone would return to this backwater in particular, obliged.

And it was there on the stage, playing Verdi with feeling, that my parents and the townspeople first saw Uncle Gianni, a lean figure slanted passionately over a piano. He baffled them with the strains of the march people in Tacloban played only at graduations. The wedding march from *Aida*, his late father's favorite opera.

Then he had pleased people by staying. He dazzled everyone with his correct manners, his elaborate fashion sense, his ability to speak two languages, English and American-twanged Italian, and then Waray with a musician's magic way with sounds, as if playing a tune by ear: with disarming errors and confident, charming improvisations. He fell in love with several women. He was invited to everyone's home. Hostesses fought over him. He became my father's friend.

By then Uncle Gianni had decided to give up music, not even bothering with the occasional seduction of *Traumerei* upon impressionable girls; he was growing to be a man, beyond the stage of mere artistry. And unlike my father, who was a full decade older, Uncle Gianni had more than bravado and luck: he had vision. He knew people of industry in Massachusetts, he said. My parents, for their part, knew people in power.

This is my father's version of Uncle Gianni. His fondness for his friend is rooted in my godfather's youthful clairvoyance. Uncle Gianni's own telling of this matter ends in more piano-playing, riffs from pieces he's long unlearned to play in their completeness—a bright tune here and there, like colored feathers drifting off from an impatient bird.

One must imagine the trio's tact. It was a carefully orchestrated chain; a little syncopation and the deals were off. But my mother had this advantage: she spoke the language of power, Imelda's mournful Waray. My mother knew the nuances of dirt-floor debuts, flowers on birthdays, the paraphernalia of longing in the town she and the First Lady shared. She knew the topography of small-town desires, the soft spots where the rose thorns pricked, over and over again. She could tell the balm for ancient bruises: the devils' forks of mangled, unacceptable pasts. She knew the demons and the pleasures that most taunted and tricked, right down to the tender turn of the foot's naked arch, that hit the spot: the bull's-eye of loss, of abandonment.

The art of a trader is the careful science of empathy, intimacy's terrible skill.

Or so I must surmise.

But to be honest, it could have been quite simple. My mother had the goods—the best she could get. This is true. Uncle Gianni saw to that.

2

I SAW THE BLOOD dripping from my thighs, thick like wax. I discovered the blood in the bathroom. Before I did anything, I watched to see how far the blood would drip, down from the pubis, through the thigh, veering over flesh to run crooked above the knee, thinning and grinning about the kneecap, then in a bright vein narrowing to a hair-width, which trickled down my calf. It didn't quite reach the ankle.

"Hang yourself, you will regret it; do not hang yourself, you will also regret that."

It was a calm violence, and I giggled, already lightheaded, at the sight of my fresh blood. In the living room, I had left five of my mother's dinner guests. Three of them I had known from childhood, my parents' old colleagues, Uncle Fred, Uncle Emmanuel, and my godfather, Uncle Gianni.

That evening, Uncle Gianni had saluted me in the entryway.

"Ciao, bellezza."

I smiled and tiptoed to be kissed. I took the flowers and a wrapped gift.

"Volume Two? You found it?"

"I ordered it. So, where are those thugs?"

"In the living room. Uncle Fred is late. Ma's a mess."

"So what else is new?"

"She also mixed up her dates. So you're having dinner with my teachers."

"What?"

"She booked you and my teachers on the same date."

"Really?" Uncle Gianni fixed his Venetian tie clip in the mirror, a dolphin clip I had given him in deep blue Murano, or was it Burano, glass. I was the kind of tourist who always bought two of each. I had an identical dolphin—on a ring. "I get to have dinner with old ladies and talk about Levantine architecture in complex sentences. How horrible."

"They're both guys."

"Oh well, so I'll have to charm them with my brawn," he said, comically flexing his arms. "I need to talk to your dad. So Fred's not back yet? That's odd."

"No, he's not. Uncle Emmanuel's waiting for him in the sala. She tried to call them about it—my teachers. But they couldn't change their plans. I told her it was all right. Being salutatorian isn't so bad. I mean, I'm doing really well at school."

"You better stop that," he said. "That's so old-fashioned." And he touched my cheek with his livid hand—it smelled of alcohol and lemon.

Did I notice that he seemed leaner, aged, or was I more conscious of the body, now that my own seemed to be some mutant, morphing daily into a frightening thing? Uncle Gianni took my hand the way he had when I was little, and he paraded me into the living room. I always got dragged along by Uncle Gianni, all throughout my childhood—to soccer matches, communion rails, national parks, museums. Every summer I was in his hands, and I was happy.

Already, I felt better. In Uncle Gianni's world, nothing ever changed. I would always be a kid, his special harmless pet, not this hormonal monster molting putrid skin.

Did his flesh seem slack in his sleek suit—bonier, draped in it rather than fitting? We used to worry about what we called his noble qualities—a finicky attitude toward the world that none of us understood. Uncle Gianni, a slim man with a hound face, had the aspect of a starving gourmand, true, but it was only because the world as he knew it could never attain the perfection he demanded.

His skin was taut and smelled of citrus, a fading scent of cleanness. You could smell that all over Uncle Gianni: the masculine smell of fastidious men. He was not so much tanned but burnished, as if he had just spent days on a soccer field, soaking up Manila's sun, and he had this tendency, in drink anyway, to blush soul-deep, so that he gave the impression of giving his heart to you. I know it was something of a joke—how he always affected the dark silk suits, even in the heat, of a star in *La Dolce Vita*, like an anorexic Marcello, though to be honest Uncle Gianni had the voracity, the nervous curiosity of the other one, Paparazzo. On the inside he was not cool, like a hero, but nerdy, like a butler. I always thought anyway that Paparazzo was more likable than Marcello Mastroianni.

Uncle Gianni did have a thin sneer of a mouth, an upper lip that turned white or invisible in speech, so that my godfather at times seemed canine. And with that aristocratic nose, so admired by the maids and Manila's socialites, and the troubling thinness of his elegant bearing, my uncle did have the air of something mixed: of something maybe feral and human: a whippet, a wonderfully domesticated beast.

He already had that warm blush on his face, coming in as he did, whenever he was in town, from one dinner date to another. Entering the room, he went straight for his colleague.

Absent Uncle Fred was an old associate, a Brit with a snippy accent and a miner's complexion: sooty and sunless. He had two soccer-crazy boys, turnip-skinned and bracken-eyed, both with their dad's maniacal glint; he had a house with a manicured English garden and a wife who spent her time catering to irrigational systems on their property in Devonshire, fussing over her broom, her buttercups, and other Anglophiliac botanical things. I knew all about them, receiving their pale-faced Christmas cards every year, but I had never met them. Every time I saw him, Uncle Fred gave me a soccer ball; in his forgetful way, he showed affection. He had taught me the most useful thing I know—how to head the ball when it came at me from a certain angle, a trick that had endeared me to all my coaches.

But I liked best Uncle Gianni's game, running down the field with the ball at my feet. I liked the run of play, not my clunky attempts at goal, Uncle Fred's header.

I think now of those soccer tricks, how I used to play one-on-one with Uncle Gianni, his agitated, wiry legs absurdly bare, in his tight, old-fashioned shorts, and myself as a child: tentative and serious in the humid New England glare, amid the fainthearted green of summer grass (Uncle Gianni hated to mow his lawn: he was the enemy of his neighbors). And I watch myself circling in the festering light.

A childhood in charmed places—summers in Boston and springs in Bruges, wherever it was my parents held their meetings or met their globetrotting suppliers—this was the least of my rewards. As a child, I looked forward most to those pure days of pleasure when we met up with Uncle Gianni, in Venice, Dublin or Virginia. He had no children and had no clue how to raise me. He bought me masks scary enough to meet the Red Death there at the spotless atelier of a mustached mascarero above the Rialto. He haggled over the price of an Islamic prayer rug for my own amusement in Riyadh, and at the Grand Hotel in Rimini he offered me my first and only whiff of opium (a sickly sweetish stench that made me sleepy; I was eight). Everything was permitted: more gelato, more jewels, more shoes, more toys. When he wrapped me up, in that windy Oxford pontoon, prissily wiping off the splashing water from my summer calves; when he fussed over my Spanish mantilla before the march of the Feast of Fallas, one spring in Valencia, tightening the corset and smoothing the lace on my springtime chest; when he patted me on the head like a puppy, danced with me like a Gypsy, or put me to bed like my dad—I felt these odd sensations, of replenishment, of completion, of a confused sense of guilt and love.

I loved him with the absolute devotion of one who would always be loved back, no matter what she did.

Uncle Fred looked like the expansive one—stout, white-bearded, round-cheeked—and Uncle Gianni looked morose, with shadows about his cheeks like some archfiend in William Blake's depressing engravings of the *Inferno*. But it was the lean one who was jolly and the fat one who rarely spoke.

Uncle Fred was late.

Instead, my two teachers were seated on the couches, Mr. Fermi and Mr. Dreiser, science and English, respectively.

Between them, on the wicker seat, Uncle Emmanuel already sat. He was younger than the others, the upstart in the business, an Israeli who dressed like a New York banker; he always wore a Brooks Brothers suit, three-piece even in the tropics, with a dull tie. It was strange one evening to see him dancing the cha-cha with my mother, celebrating a deal, overdressed to kill. He was sweaty and red-faced when he danced; but he was always sweaty and red-faced.

At the time, it was my mother's policy to invite all my teachers every year, in one swoop, usually at Christmas. Her new campaign to make me middle school valedictorian had a hospitable side. She invited my teachers to our house as if to subdue them with the glory of our gilt mirrors, authentic chinoiserie, and melancholy carved mahogany screens—the usual cultural clutter the Makati matron favored. She was the kind of hostess who imported everything. Sweet potatoes, a basic root crop of the country, was shipped in canned from Ohio. Asparagus, plentiful in Baguio, was ordered from western Massachusetts. She'd serve Spam if it were expensive enough. For Uncle Fred, she always had the "pink paper," weekly football scores of the English First Division. To ingratiate herself with a spate of Indian teachers in my grade school, she once engaged a Bengalese dancer for the evening, so that the expatriates could witness the authentic gestures of a culture that wasn't, it turned out, their own: all the Indians were Catholics from Calcutta.

She had connections, associates in low and high places who could get her anything she needed. It was only a matter of timing and organization, she said, as if she were an overachieving secretary.

Dinner parties were the immediate expressions of her art. Every dish was a showcase, the way, at a Renaissance dinner, one could trace a ship's exotic route and a merchant's cleverness by the presence of certain side dishes at the table.

I had greeted my teachers and led them into the sala. I did see the surprise on their faces, their quick, serious look about the mirrors, the gigantic chandelier and towering vases.

Uncle Emmanuel was already in his chair, drinking his sherry.

It was a not so incongruous mix, if you think about it, three Americans, a Brit, and an Israeli. Allied citizens, a solid cold war front. In any case, no one would know my father's name unless you were some German operator on the military black market, a Pakistani with the right connections, or some American trader with a fetish for Third World wars.

I guess I should beat my breast, retreat into an ashram, join the crucifers of Pampanga and lash my body against a bloody cross, at the mere sound of my father's name. But as a lecturer in Soli's group had once denounced: I am a coward. I do not have the imagination to possess affection. To be honest, I have never been able to envision society as a creature with genuine warmth or pumping heart. I act by impulse, by the inarticulate suggestions of my errant sensations. I have a cadaverous soul. In short, I am a member of the damned *burgis*—in my case, the comprador bourgeoisie, with links to feudal lords, if you believe my father's claim that every Soliman is heir of the lost sultan long ago trounced by Spain. Whenever I think of my father's work, source of privilege and horror, I believe it is with conflicting purposes and incoherent intentions, when, in fact, I should never speak of it at all.

I didn't know what got into Mr. Fermi, usually soft-spoken and tolerant in class, even to Thornhilda Singh, my classmate who had steel wool for a brain—I don't know why he decided to get Uncle Emmanuel's goat.

Education is a banal thing; you receive no merit in your afterlife, and it gains only in inconsequence as you age. My schoolteachers, let's face it, were the trash bins of my self-regard. If not for this event, who knows if I would have managed to conjure the name or face of a single sorry adult from those obsolete times. Mr. Fermi may have been in his twenties, barely out of school, with a graduate degree in idealism. Mr. Dreiser was older: a celebrated being. His fame came from children's notions of adult mysteries, their terror about growing up. He looked like a fiftyish spinster, a prim adult of a Saxon hue. His face had a carnivore ruddiness. And though he had bland features and murky gray eyes, as if filmed with mucus and the cobwebs of his dreams, his face is imprinted in my mind. He had dry skin on top of his beefy complexion: he seemed ragged by some wilderness. But what most fascinated students was his mutable wig. It was a blatant cap of fiber and dried sweat, dull brown like a washed-out coin, plastered awkwardly to his head in an arbitrary wistfulness, a kind of sad accident. My classmates tittered when it waggled dangerously on his scalp, and then I would feel for my own hair, what I would look like when I grew old.

Uncle Gianni, sitting down, immediately began to speak, never at a loss for a topic, facing Mr. Dreiser, who even in class was partial to elegance—in manners, diction or fashion.

"Now think about it," said my uncle, hitching up his silken slacks. "America was discovered by accident. And Manhattan was Hudson's error—a funny thing that happened on the way to China.

What about Magellan—do you think he found the Philippines on purpose?"

"Does it matter?" murmured Mr. Dreiser. In class, his sounds had a smoker's tardiness, vague vacuoles in his speech, so that our lessons on Australopithecus or the Precambrian Age seemed to have appropriate, winded gaps.

"It does," nodded Uncle Gianni. "It does very much for Manila."

Mr. Dreiser's legs, pressed together with his hands between them, faced Uncle Gianni's fervor in demure passivity, and Mr. Dreiser was smiling at my uncle's polished profile with a benign, womanly admiration.

Uncle Gianni continued: "I think the Philippines was, unfortunately, founded on love. Yes, Magellan came upon these islands, and strangely, very sadly, as you know, fell in love. He had been here before."

"I read somewhere about that," said Mr. Dreiser, still murmuring. "That he had been to these parts even before. Under the rule of the Portuguese king."

"Yes, he had been to these parts before; certainly he had been in Sumatra, but maybe he had already known these other islands, with its painted chiefs and enchanted language, in an earlier trip. When his loyal friend, his slave Enrique, came out to meet the *pintados*, and he and the natives understood each other, it was then Magellan knew he had triumphed: that he had circumnavigated the world."

"You are wrong," Mr. Fermi, a precise scientist, was shaking his head. "Magellan had been to Indonesia, not the Philippines. Enrique, his slave, was not Filipino. He was Sumatran."

"Don't be a spoilsport, sir. Let's play this game with factless arguments. It's more fun." And he leaned toward Mr. Dreiser: "So why is it important? Why is Magellan's softness in the head when he came upon the islands important to this country?"

Uncle Gianni stood and walked up and down the room, pacing back and forth.

Uncle Emmanuel sat back, all scrubbed like a schoolboy and looking just as insolent, impassively watching Uncle Gianni.

Uncle Fred was late, and both of my parents' colleagues, Uncle Emmanuel and Uncle Gianni, were nervous. Loquacity and silence were the by-products of their agitation.

Mr. Dreiser was smiling, his head gazing up at Uncle Gianni, so I thought his hair might slide over, in a dangerous tilt of reverence. "I have no idea," Mr. Dreiser said.

"Think about it, after his months and nights at sea, after those disgusting and inhuman places, peopled by grunting giants and women who mutilated their vaginas, really, those Patagonians were barbaric creatures, and then, of course, that miraculous affair, Magellan's long, dreamlike crossing over the Pacific—he came to this. And what were these islands? Just think. Imagine them as lands of memory: an extension of some delirium. Because he thought he'd seen them before, known their women, their words and their music. Pigafetta says as much in the journals. How Magellan on these islands was bedeviled—by a curious tenderness. How suitable for a fanciful man to find memory in alienation, a kind of longing—for that's what familiarity becomes—in a strange place, in this case the Philippine islands. Weirdly, think about it, this man's heart softened in the Philippines. His guard fell. Remember, Magellan was not a kind man. He had butchered sailors, dismembered a mutineer, marooned his king's traitors. He had

watched his men die of fever and suicide. And so the Italian chronicler, Pigafetta, noted a change in Magellan—an emotional conver-
sion in Limasawa. It's in the diary. Check it out. And to mark it, his
heart's strange movement, his epiphanic moment, Magellan took
them, the Philippine islands, the way he hadn't taken those
others—"

"Because they were already owned by Portugal," said Mr.
Fermi.

Uncle Gianni took no notice. "He took them in the name of the
Spanish crown, certainly, but in his heart, when he placed the cross
by those sands and gave the Filipino queen the statue of the little
Jesus, he did it for himself, for his own heart's stirred blood, for the
power of memory coursing through it. Passion tricked him, the
kind some of us may feel when we find a strange place so terribly
plausible, so happily joined with our own longing. And so it was
that a country was founded on delusion: on Magellan's misrecogni-
tion. Because, as you say, sir: he had never been to these islands. He
had been in Indonesia."

Mr. Fermi said, his mouth curled: "A charming romance. Fancy
dress-up for the evils that occurred in the colonizer's name. And it
is not even true. Surely there was more to the beginning of empire
than heartfelt moments of miscast memory. The Spanish conquest
of the Philippines was cruel, rapacious, and ignorant."

"Malignant, systematic, forethought." Uncle Gianni waved his
hands, as if sorrowing over history's adjectives. "All of the above.
That's the sadness of the Philippines. It was raped by plan. Of
course, the Spanish already had a blueprint of governance in Mexico. So the rapacity was lockstep, well-developed, despicable. In this

case, then, novelty might have been less barbarous than Magellan's cruel, misplaced familiarity."

"Well said, but—" Mr. Fermi, a man careful with words, tried to interrupt.

"The pity is that the Philippines was not colonized by Italy," Uncle Gianni continued.

Now Uncle Gianni was on a hobbyhorse, a tired spiel. He had a requited romance with Italy, his adopted country—the way orphans who threw off their parents' memory greedily attached to chosen savants. The great thing about Italy, Uncle Gianni always said, was that no matter how much your passion squeezed it dry, there was always something—an obscure pregnant Madonna in the unlikeliest town, Monterchi, or the way a pedestrian wore a startling yellow rose while shopping for clams on the street—that somehow returned your soul back to you, fairly unharmed.

But I knew at that point when he got to his Italian theme, he was taking old funds out of his war chest of curmudgeonly sayings. "Think of it—the cuisine, the arts, the exile of sugar from their diet! Sugar in pasta sauce! For this barbarity alone, Spaniards should have been tortured before the Inquisition."

"So, you think, like the Filipinos do, that the Philippines got all of its bad habits from Spain?" asked Mr. Dreiser.

"No, only its bad tastes."

"Oh, come on," said Uncle Emmanuel, chuckling and leaning forward. "Your own country, America, had its share in the matter, Gianni. They ruled this country for fifty years—and more."

"Ah," Uncle Gianni said, "but my grandfather, the brute from Abruzzo, only settled in Boston out of—well—I think he had some *agita* disorder, like many other immigrants. He couldn't stay in one place, but he always longed to be back home. My theory about America? Hah. It has been settled by people with short attention spans."

"You're right," said Mr. Dreiser, fingering his embroidered vest. "It should have been colonized by Italy. Filipino fibers and Italian style—good match."

"Or colonized not at all," Mr. Fermi said into his drink.

"Yes—Italy or not at all," said Uncle Gianni laughing, pretending not to understand.

"I didn't mean—I mean that the colonizing of the islands—it's not the most savory chapter in history. It shouldn't have happened at all, if the fates had been kind in any way."

"Should, would, did, had: be my guest. They're all the same to the conquered," said Uncle Gianni.

"A crude way of putting it," said Mr. Fermi.

"We live in the world," Uncle Emmanuel pointed out, "not in the classroom."

Mr. Fermi turned dark red.

Uncle Gianni shook his head at Uncle Emmanuel and moved to bend toward my teacher, saying in a low voice, turning his back on his friend: "I didn't mean it crudely. Please don't misunderstand. I meant it in all the severity of the phrase: it *is* all the same to the conquered. Our 'shoulds' are just fretful and useless: do we, foreigners here, have a right to comment on this country's history? We can't redeem ourselves, we can't repent, we can't even look the people in the eye."

His domestic way, the way he held onto you with maternal interest, contrasting with the silken splendor of his parts, confused you when you confronted Uncle Gianni.

Mr. Fermi looked up at him warily, holding onto his beer.

"So what is there to do?" asked Uncle Gianni, gripping the scientist in the knee with a fiery gaze. A cranial nerve throbbed at his gaunt temple grown red from drink.

And he concluded, slapping Mr. Fermi on the thigh, so that my teacher almost spilled his drink: "Why, rob them blind, of course."

And he laughed. I shook my head at Uncle Gianni. He laughed out loud, his face growing so red I thought maybe I was right— Uncle Gianni was ill. Maybe he had a travel bug.

"Ha-ha. Rob them blind," Mr. Dreiser chuckled. "If you can't look them in the eye, rob them blind."

Mr. Fermi, still in my uncle's grasp, did not laugh.

Uncle Emmanuel took an urbane sip, the red nub of his chin oily with sweat.

Uncle Gianni sobered up. "I'm sorry," he said. He straightened up and looked at no one. "Words have a way of taking away feeling. What I really mean"—and he released the stiff scientist and turned toward us, as if we could supply him with dull alternatives—"is that, as foreigners in the Philippines, we get deluded by our reasons for coming. The land is so welcoming, so generous. We lie to ourselves and imagine we are not only businessmen but also redeemers. The bullshit with which we cover our asses. Unlike Magellan, or McKinley, or MacArthur for that matter, I wouldn't have bothered with a grand scheme, benevolent assimilation, whatnot. Hogwash. Bullshit. Stick to business, I would have said to Magellan. I'd have checked the place out for the best goods, then I'd have moved on, to receive my prize in Sevilla for my goddamned expert circumnavigation. I mean, for a genius who figured out how to circumnavigate the globe, he was dumb. See what happened to Magellan—murdered with his own petard."

"Hoist with it," murmured Mr. Dreiser, a rasp of a giggle rising from his diseased lungs. "Damned petard."

"Hoist, hung, and poison-darted!" laughed Uncle Gianni. "Smart men, those damned petards of Mactan. The cunning Filipino killers of Magellan!"

I waited for the signal for dinner and stood by the stairs, so that I could see the quick shaking of Mr. Fermi's head, the taut torso of Uncle Emmanuel, his stiff pose of polite scorn, and the little dramas in gestures and limbs. I stepped in, not waiting for Mr. Fermi to speak: "But Uncle Gianni, didn't Italy become a country only a few decades before the Philippines started its revolution?"

"Ah, Sol—my precocious historian. Come over and interrupt us."

"Your soupy historical plots," I said, snuggling into his shoulder and kissing him on the cheek.

My teachers were silent, staring at their drinks.

They, too, had not expected this meeting.

I could see my father in his study, on the phone. As for my mother, it was her job to reel in this conversation; but she was in the kitchen, bossing the maids.

Uncle Gianni rambled on: "Both countries have come into the insight of their union too late to reach a lasting stability. This is why Italy is run by gangsters and the Philippines by goons. The notion of nationhood in each is too modern." At this point, he seemed saddened by his dumb generalizations, or maybe just tired from entertaining unexpected strangers. But then, more brightly he added: "But that's why both are more interesting than, say, the Swiss."

"Cuckoo clocks," said Mr. Dreiser, conspiratorially.

"Certainly some other things contribute to the lasting power of—goons, as you call them," Mr. Fermi said.

"What do you mean?" Uncle Gianni smiled, raising his glass to his lips now, with only his index and thumb.

"Nothing," said Mr. Fermi.

Mr. Dreiser interrupted: "Would you say, in your travels around the Philippines, with all these separate islands, is this a coherent country, with its different languages and fiefdoms—does it not seem a mere patchwork of incidental cultures, like Italy before Garibaldi?"

"No," said Uncle Gianni abruptly. "Hollywood unites the world." He walked over to the bar to get more wine.

He was his most reductive when waiting for a deal to close.

Mr. Fermi turned to Uncle Emmanuel, erect and silent to his left.

"So you are a business associate of Soledad's parents?" said Mr. Fermi.

Uncle Emmanuel nodded, barely looking up. He seemed to be examining his hairy hands. He'd flown in from some desert to this meeting, and these civilian interlopers were not welcome. That's what his silent face said.

"And what is your business?" Mr. Fermi continued.

Uncle Emmanuel shifted in his seat, his mouth moving into an uncomfortable smile. He raised his eyes swiftly up then down, with wryness. "Oh, all kinds of deadly business."

Uncle Gianni over at the bar laughed.

My teacher raised his eyebrows but kept quiet.

Then he said: "So which of you sells the F-15s, the Phantom jets?"

Uncle Emmanuel was very quick to say: "Oh, no, no. You go to the U.S. government for those. That's not *our* line." *Idiot*, he seemed to be saying, sliding back into his seat, shaking his head.

"And to which—as your partner calls them—goons do you sell the products of, as you call it, your line?" Mr. Fermi held his drink casually.

Uncle Emmanuel turned red. That is, his pores did. "I don't see that it's any of your business," he said.

"Now, Emmanuel, what's the problem?" Uncle Gianni was laughing. He came back and reached over to clink his glass against Mr. Fermi's beer. "Don't mind him, sir. He's jetlagged. We don't want Sol here to fail in molecular biology just because this dumbass, pardon me, Emman, couldn't sleep in business class."

"Environmental science," Mr. Fermi said. "That's what I teach."

"So, where are you from, Mr. Fermi? That's an appropriate name for a science teacher. You know I met him once?"

"Enrico Fermi?"

"No less. In Cambridge at a lecture. My father brought me to see him. My father was a chemist. I grew up outside Boston, in Lexington. I understand you went to school in that area?"

"I went to Harvard, yes," said Mr. Fermi.

"Ah, yes. The best place to learn to teach middle school ecology."

Pa came in. "Look who's here," Pa announced.

It was Uncle Fred in an all-white suit, in matching fedora and shoes.

"Dinner's served," my mother said, peering out from the dining room screens.

"I did it," Uncle Fred declared, almost skipping. "I have the contract—signed by the Secretary himself!"

"Good job, Fred—we were wondering what happened." Uncle Emmanuel jumped to his feet. "We've been here hours—we've had to sit through whole centuries of Philippine history just waiting for you to get back!"

Uncle Fred was patting my father, hugging his shoulders. Pa was beaming. He had his right thumb up, for victory.

"And it couldn't have been done without help from Frankie," said Uncle Fred, grinning at my father. "The Secretary sends you his regards, Frankie. Golfing trip to Hawaii coming up, right? Now what would we do without Frankie? A toast, a toast."

"Ssh, Fred, let's talk business later. Now let's eat." And my mother winked at us, to show how informal and delightful this mixed assembly was, and we stood up to go to the table.

MY TEACHERS SAT together, opposite me. Uncle Gianni took the seat beside them, next to my father at the head of the table. I have run this dinner through my mind many times, some images in isolation, some in flashes. I suspect, at this point, every single detail I remember is untrue. Maybe Uncle Fred was in blue and not in the color coordinates of the powers that be, or Mr. Dreiser taught science and Mr. Fermi humanities, not vice versa, or that I misremember their names, culled conveniently from an encyclopedia. Maybe I imagined the conversation, and in truth all the boring company came up with was the usual exposition on expatriate vacations in the exfoliated Philippine isles.

But I remember the dinner as if it were yesterday.

I sat on the side, next to my mother at the head of the table. She served my teachers first, her fluttering gestures mitigated by an ironic pout, her signature expression of amiable condescension. There was that give-and-take of mutual hypocrisy—exemplified by the powerful bouffant of my mother's hair and matched by the stiff, splayed tendrils of Mr. Dreiser's fibers—and this careful artifice among people who have no other occasion to be with each other but at a dinner party, mumbling platitudes about New Zealand beef, settled over us while I cut the red meat.

I was seated before Mr. Fermi, whose face even in class would have this absence residing in it; he'd look out the window, with a gaze of melancholy or stupor, you couldn't tell which, as we did our lab reports and took our tests. At dinner, he contemplated his bloody steak, then looked at the other guests with this same vacancy, as if taken by reverie. There were girls who had an ongoing argument on whether he was or was not handsome; the verdict was that, though his eyes were nicely green and his long, wavy black hair had its merits, the bridge of his nose was too high for glamour. Anyway, he often looked preoccupied, as if figuring out a puzzle too complicated for our measly brains. Or as if imagining a long-dead, corny love. That fascinated my vacuous peers.

I don't know why I still dwell on these men, Mr. Dreiser and Mr. Fermi, and what they thought and saw at the dinner table, what they whispered between themselves at dessert when my mother left to check out the crème de menthe. They were nothing to me then and are nothing now. They've gone off to their farms in Iowa and postings in Hanoi, to their irritable wanderlust and homesick enterprise.

Disgusting.

That was Mr. Fermi's word. I dawdled behind them, not on purpose. I was greedy. Mint gelato, streaked with stracciatella, was my favorite dessert. My father had taken his colleagues into his study for a brief chat: so sorry, business, you know. My mother had left us in a rage. The maids had brought out the wrong things, wineglasses instead of liqueur flutes, or something like that, and I stayed behind with the whispering pair.

By the dividing screen, my teachers politely waited for the other guests. They spoke in low tones.

"Absolutely disgusting," Mr. Fermi repeated.

They were facing the Ming vase in the foyer, beside the giant good-luck Buddha.

I was picking at my last bits of mint, a fresh mist melting in my mouth, and I overheard, and I nodded, looking at the ugly Buddha. I, too, had never liked Mr. Kow Lung's feng shui choices—his muddled ethnographic messages needed editing, I had always thought.

"Well, you know, it's not the child's fault," Mr. Dreiser said, almost sighing, his whisper like a bumpy skid of stones from his larynx. "It's her parents' business, not hers."

"I wonder what the kid knows. If you knew that your parents sold arms that prop up your country's military dictatorship, what would you do?"

"I'd keep eating my mint gelato," Mr. Dreiser whispered with a suppressed snort, laughing.

"Yes, it's an interesting ethical question. To have blood on your hands, without having done a single thing."

"Oh, come on now, Dick: that's too much."

"No, it isn't," said Mr. Fermi decidedly, crossing his hands tightly across his chest, as if trying to use up as little space in the house as possible.

"It's a business," Mr. Dreiser intoned, the sigh from his larynx gasping for air. He respired with difficulty, as if with some regret. "Although—it's low on a good trader's list of products. He-he-he. Uh. Uh. Even the worst won't touch two things: drugs and guns. That's what traders say. And guns are at the bottom even of that. But can you believe the way they live? I mean—Louis Quatorze, meet *The King and I*. Chintz! Honestly, I wouldn't care about their money if they did not waste it on such crap."

Mr. Fermi shook his head. "Oh, Harry. You know that's the least of it."

I RETREATED FROM THE dining room the other way, through the hall of Chinese prints and Italian vellum books and my father's lacquered faux-ancient Singaporean opium den.

I locked myself upstairs in the bathroom.

Blood was in my underwear, bright, a strawberry stain. The sight surprised me. At first, I tried to figure out where it had come from. I stood up and realized what had happened. I was surprised by the color: I thought it would be more like batik dye, dark and dripping. Instead it looked like something in store-bought pie, only thinner.

As I stood still, the blood ran down my thigh with haphazard goal, the temper of gravity.

The rest of my thoughts you know.

Hang yourself, you will regret it; do not hang yourself, you will also regret that.

I stood still to see if there might be any pain. There wasn't. My body was as good as new. What a strange thing to change and not be transformed. To be exactly as I was and yet not so.

WHO KNOWS, MAYBE it did happen a week later, on a quiet night before I went to bed, in the bathroom after a sleepy dinner—my faulty memory merely a menarcheal disorder, as my doctors deemed my subsequent malaise. I remember Mr. Fermi's articulated disgust through a whispering screen, like a dart, a punctuated clarity; and I caressed the spot where it clung, something ingrown, an infected thing.

It happened when I was twelve. After this followed a series of distressing incidents, depressions without reason during luxury vacations, collapses in oases of summer instruction. My teachers standing there by the dark screen, whispering, like a sparse Greek chorus.

Disgusting.

Later that evening, Uncle Gianni became more reckless with wine.

He spoke loudly to my teachers after dinner: "Academics, intellectuals, Harvard men! You cannot stand expat business, repulsed by its costs. You men think you have no filth. Where do you live, for whom do you work? Grubbers like the rest of them—you do not escape history's brush. You think you don't mess with the real, the destructive world. Whereas we—we stink in it, you think. We wallow in it like pigs."

"Oh no," said Mr. Dreiser, a kind man and unhappy with this distinction. "No, no. We don't think that."

Uncle Gianni sank into the sofa with his Tuscan bitter, playing air piano on his thigh.

"What's this?" said Uncle Fred. He settled with a cup of tea; ever since he had had his first heart attack, he had stopped drinking. He was a gun dealer with healthy habits. In my hands, I held the twelfth soccer ball he gave me—a red and blue affair, made in Indonesia.

"Ah—" said Uncle Emmanuel, waving his hand away impatiently, "it's nothing. Gianni's going to talk about that Frenchman next."

"Yes: my favorite compatriot. An expatriate like all of us. The first great businessman in America—a great trader. We are, of course, nowhere in his league. Far from it. He was an intellectual like you, Mr. Fermi; in fact, if I remember right, he was a good friend of the great French scientist. Labbatoir."

"Lavoisier," said Mr. Fermi. "Lavoisier was a chemist."

"Yes. Thank you, Mr. Fermi. As you well know, science is necessary for certain endeavors. The marvels of the Renaissance, the discoveries of Billy Bacon."

"Francis—" began Mr. Fermi. "Oh, never mind."

"—And the history of sulphuric acid and nitroglyceride—all of a piece. Who was it who said that? In a movie? A book—Sol here loves books. She's my soul mate. Sol-mate. What was that book, Sol? No matter. This is what tickles me about my Frenchman: the moral side to him, the great radical philosopher. A leading light in the French Revolution. Man of principle. He was a progressive, a freethinker. Good friend of one of the Thomases—Thomas Jefferson, Thomas Paine. Think of it: a French revolutionary, an Enlightenment intellectual, Mr. du Pont, built the first great business in America. *Égalité*, *liberté*, and *munition*."

Uncle Gianni said the last in his French accent, drunken and white-faced by this time, paper-white: his red flush ran out after reaching a peak, leaving him with his death mask.

Mr. Fermi shrugged: "I'm not surprised. Live free or die, as they say in my home state."

"Who was this? Was it General Lafayette?" asked Mr. Dreiser.

"It is Mr. Éleuthère Irénee du Pont," exclaimed Uncle Emmanuel. "Of DuPont chemicals. He started his business manufacturing gunpowder."

"His name doesn't matter," Uncle Gianni said. "This is the thing. It was said that in his factories he kept escaped French revolutionists on staff; they were his forgers, smiths, smelters. Enlightened thinkers of the revolution. Men of adventure. Anarchists and radicals. A commune of freethinkers worked for DuPont's labs. I like that, you know. He took *fraternité* to heart."

"There's humanity in your story," said Mr. Fermi. "Is that what you're getting at?"

"There's humanity, barbarity, comedy, love, irony, happiness, mild manners, stupidity, cupidity, passion—"

"Death," said Mr. Fermi.

"Death: all the demands of opera, in fact. We didn't invent these things."

"Yep," said Uncle Fred placidly. "We only supply the goods."

"We didn't invent human beings," said Uncle Gianni, slumped now in his chair. "We didn't invent war, bloodshed, pettiness, rivalry, nationalism, tribes, dictatorship—"

"You only supply it."

"We're middlemen," Uncle Fred nodded. "And Gianni here, he has the best goods: he doesn't even deal in secondhand anymore. He's one of the best."

"We're internationalists," said Uncle Gianni. "Like you." And he started humming a song, brazenly. He said again, repeating himself like a drunken man: "We supply everyone. But we did not invent human beings."

3

I KNEW SOON ENOUGH they would find me—the nurses in starched uniforms, Victoria Eremita with the evening's experimental souf-flés. They will always find me. A stampede of feet, hullaballoo in the hallway. I felt it—the lump on my wrists. Keloids are not cathar-tic: but they have this comforting familiarity, a pound of flesh that will never go away.

If I were not careful, I'd feel that falling sickness, the drop to the floor and the heaving furniture, pulsating creatures flattening me to bone, to powder.

All around me was danger anyhow: in an opened box, a souve-nir photo from a trip, myself at twelve, ungainly like the scaffolding before the tower of Pisa, my father with his ivory holder, smoking a nonexistent cigarette, and Uncle Gianni in my favorite shoes, two-toned, with the double monk strap, the color of a croissant. In another, I sit in a vaporetto with my lozenge lorgnette, looking like a Peggy Guggenheim, but the brown one, or some other demented heiress in Venice. A recuperative trip, that summer I lost control. Menarcheal hysteria, my doctors said. A hormonal imbalance. And though it seemed to me at times, while we moved from one stuccoed villa to another, that it was not so much that my body was a mess— it was a message—still the trip we took that summer, with Uncle Gianni taking charge as usual, a busybody with the concierges, the museum guides, the maître d's—the trip that summer, though not completely soothing, *was* a salve. Between fits and train stops, fevers at wine festivals, I trembled in rented rooms, but I believe I emerged from the haze intact. I remember at a mountain town—was it Ventimiglia, some sleepy sliver parallel to France—a bear accosted me in a heated revel: a summer pageant not meant for tourists, though by then, after touring all those traps, it was hard for us not to imagine that every pleasure we came to was invented only for us. The animal twirled me around on its tippy toes, until I fell on its scratchy lap. It felt me up my belly. The cold plastic finger on my open midriff down to my crotch was a shock. It was Uncle Gianni who had been watching, watching me in my ruffled Provençal outfit spin and spin and laugh. What he did with the bear was magnificent: he punched it in its empty gut. It was as if it were a display—a spectacle created for my edification. It was so sudden—the way the bear sprawled on the ground, his costume distended, his face unmasked, so that for a moment he seemed to be licking his cheap medieval-circus fur. A girl, a tricolored peasant in a costume, screamed. A man in silver tights stumbled. And Uncle Gianni pulled me from the crowd's confusion, toward my innocent parents checking out ceramic chickens in the town square.

That moment restored me. The wrath of Uncle Gianni, as he harangued the hairy creature in Italian—his funny mix of vulgar speech with perfect pitch—returned me back to myself. It turned out the bear himself was a passing tourist, an idiot in disguise. The

Italians of Ventimiglia, serious men in tights, marched him to us to apologize.

"Sorry, man," the bear implored, in the unmistakable vowels of a drunken American. "Please. Don't let these bastards hurt me."

I have no idea what Uncle Gianni said to the Italians, who took the bear away, still half-dressed as a beast. I never saw the man again. Throughout that trip, my organs, my body, my mind had this obscene soreness, and something in me was infected, a dart, an ingrown thing; but in the end, I had the comfort of my parents' arms, loaded with glazed poultry, and the magnificence of Uncle Gianni, ready to catch me if he could.

I got well.

4

SOLIDARIDAD SOLEDAD WAS the eldest of three sisters. Each girl in her family was expected to be a boy, first Soli, then Noli, then Fili. An oddly literate triumvirate, true, but not so uncommon if you note that my mother, for instance, was named after the Byzantine king Constantine's mom, complete with royal title. Reina Elena, i.e., historic Helen of diluvian tales. I knew my grandmother only from a portrait on the piano, a serious child in a white dress, blue sash and sausage curls. Lola Felma Kierulf, rose-seller and devout believer. In rural Philippines, as my mom explained, the figure of Reina Elena is the star of the yearly flower parades, the regal muse at the head of the summer Santacruzan processions simulating the medieval search for the True Cross. Growing up, Reina Elena, the rose-seller's daughter, Americanized herself to Queenie, suitably following history—but still, the name was a cross to bear.

Soli's life, on the other hand, remains a mystery to me. I caught bits of its outline in snatches. She was not one to elaborate, though a few of the facts were enlightening. Soli's father, a civil engineer from

Leyte, was obsessed not with holy reginas but with a doomed revolution, the fateful tragedy of the Filipino rebels of 1896. Throughout his life he wrote op-ed letters with the rambling sincerity of the autodidact, polishing his wistful theme—the loss of the bells of Balangiga, formerly of a church in Samar, now at a G.I. fort at Cheyenne ("Why Oh Why, Wyoming?" was the title of one of his plaintive screeds). Sadly, in the end he bequeathed only one lasting footnote to his precious war, the naming of his kids. He died young, of literary thrombosis—strike that, a congested heart.

Thus merely by her baptism Soli had earned a pedigree of angst. As a kid, she lapped up the hagiographical picture books of Filipino heroes, scarlet tales of scurrilous pimpernels during the French Revolution, painful rhymes in galloping tetrameter of the midnight antics of Paul Revere. For a time growing up, she told me, she believed she was Jewish, so profound was her longing for Zion, adapted from an education in the novels of Leon Uris that she had found on her late father's shelves. The diary of Anne Frank was a killer, so deep was her identification. And in the seventies, she fasted for the hunger-strikers of Belfast and held her own protest, a backyard bonfire, for Biafra. When Soli was awarded a scholarship to Philippine Science High, she wasted no time being tutored in underground Maoist poetics. And so she pledged allegiance to the Kalashnikov flag by the age of fourteen.

She came across, let me put it this way, like an ember. I have always wondered if it were my own need to burn that made her seem, at this remove, incandescent. As I said, her caramel skin had an illusory sheen, as if something fired her from within. Perhaps her father's unrequited pathos, mournful Quixote of a lost cause, kindled the bonfires of her young compassion. Her conviction was contagious, her views explicit and extreme. I understood how Jed could not withstand her, because in her presence I felt exactly the same.

She was the first, and perhaps only, person I have envied, and maybe because of this I remember her in a skewed dimension, a haze of idolatry more lasting, and just as mistaken, as the impression of those I've loved.

It turned out we were block mates—she and Edwin and I—in that lockstep schedule that kept freshmen in line; but even in June she was already circling in another orbit. She'd come to class to take exams, and it got my goat that while I ground out my heart in calculus, she'd just sail in and ace the tests. She had the gift of clarity. Edwin called her cleverness a passionate reductiveness—but for me, her lucidity was startling. As I said, it's possible I aggrandize her in recall for my own paltry reasons. At the dorm, she was everywhere. A tribe of malcontents, a motley study group of sorts, followed her about. There'd be question-and-answer, history lessons, stupid debates in the dining hall about the labor theory of value, whether it was evident in our culinary choices (was the union chef's surplus value relevant in *both* delicate leche flan *and* cheap powdered nonegg omelets?), and did a change in consciousness in the Chinese peasantry after Mao count as a material condition or sheer unprovable casuistry?—all before everyone else left to play basketball. I met Vita, a lean girl who liked to spit on the floor. Francis "Kiko" Not-Coppola, a kid obsessed with *Apocalypse Now*. Buddyboy Something-something, Beatlemaniac and gun enthusiast. And Sally Vega (yes it was she—not quite unrecognizable from the person she is now)—who always gave money but never marched. None of them liked me. Only Soli kept asking me to join the marches or cornered me in the lobby to give me a book. Some coverless leaflet on political economy. A heavily annotated manifesto. Mao's *Little Red Book*, a cliché cloaked in another, the love poems of Neruda. It was only when I came to the lobby one day, hauling out this beautiful volume, a facsimile manuscript of *El Filibusterismo* in Jose Rizal's hand, after a self-righteous discussion of the hero's failures, that I somehow became part of the group.

My godfather had found it in Kalamazoo, I said. They began giving me lists, eclectic and opportunistic. "Theses on Feuerbach," a slim essay (found). The Bolivian diaries of Che Guevara (nonexistent). *The Art of War* by Mao Tse-Tung (available anyhow at Popular Books). Teenage rebels were just shameless freeloading bookworms. Did I think it odd that I asked Uncle Gianni, on his stopovers from visiting military republics, to get Marx's *Theory of Revolution: State and Bureaucracy*? I think he thought it was funny, an intellectual diversion before I went on with my life. Oh, a dissertation of *demonyo*, my dad said. My dad began to say that he couldn't wait until the term was over and I got better, and I was shuttled off to college in Boston or New York—with all that *demonyo* just crawling around the university, like swamp monsters. And my mom would present me the gift books without much comment, or maybe clue. But Uncle Gianni, I think, was having a laugh.

Anyway, mine was not the kind of family that questioned what children did—my job was to be petted and indulged, as long as I followed in everything else. And so Uncle Gianni unearthed the complete twenty-book edition of *The Philippine Islands, 1493–1898*, by Blair and Robertson, identical to the set in the stacks at the Library of Congress; the letters of Rizal to Blumentritt, two volumes in mediocre binding; *Memorias de un estudiante de Manila, autobiografía escolar inédita*, 1861–1881, a frail impression by an impressionable youth; and for good measure, a bunch of rare French travelogues from the 1870s: Guillaume le Gentil's opus on the Indian Ocean, the findings of a Parisian naturalist in Palawan, and the Duc d'Alençon's terse and romantic *Luzon and Mindanao*. I showed Jed his erstwhile ancestor's chronicle, Antonio de Morga's *Sucesos de las islas filipinas*, not the Hakluyt edition in English, but the Spanish one with Jose Rizal's notes. Jed was the only one among us who spoke Spanish. He returned it to me without comment. He borrowed the *Fili* instead.

That year I read in earnest the history I had not been taught as a child. I remember my anger at the outlandish racism of one Brit journalist, Francis St. Clair, a clericofascist, as Soli called him, reporting on the rebels of 1896 in a joke of a book called, without disclaimer, *The Katipunan*. And as I said, I carried about for months the instructive chronicle of the strategic massacre in 1901 of American soldiers in Balangiga, the town for whom the bells do not toll, in *The Ordeal of Samar,* a Pyrrhic battle narrated, as always, through the enemy's lens.

I discovered that our books of history were invariably in the voice of the colonist, the one who misrecognized us. We were inscrutable apes engaging in implausible insurrections against gun-wielding epic heroes who disdained our culture but wanted our land. The simplicity and rapacity of *their* reductions were consistent, and as counterpoint to Soli's version of the past, these books provided, as I admitted to Soli, the ballast for my tardy revolt.

Soli reproved me. Why do history books persuade you but not the world around you? You live in a puppet totalitarian regime, propped up by guns from America, so that we are no sovereign country but a mere outpost of foreign interests in the Far East. She said this with such conviction, I could barely reply. But, I countered, the military-industrial complex, as you call it, does it not suggest not only an economic order but also a psychiatric *dis*order? It occurred to me that it was a system of oppression that spurred both of our delusions—hers (to save the nation) and mine (to save myself).

Soli nodded, disarmed at the thought, but in the end she disagreed. Obscurantism, she said, does not serve change. The therapeutic couch may be necessary—at least for some, she said pointedly. But it is not the place for action. Next time you drive home to Makati, she said, look around: all you need is to look out your limousine's window to know that it is a problem to be living the good life in such bad times.

Jed held the banner over Soli's curls, like a matrimonial veil, and I walked behind them, not quite understanding the slogans, much less myself. Why had I tagged along that day? Soli had mentioned it to me in passing, and I had come. My first march, a June demonstration at the start of class. Activists never held rallies during school vacation—otherwise no one would come. She was surprised to see me among the crowd, I could tell. She looked at my dumb shoes, a patent pump with a pilgrim buckle (vintage Vivier, but I'd stripped off the label). I told you to wear lace-ups, she said, already mourning the loss of my pretty shoes—you might need to run. But she hugged me to her and whispered: I'm glad you came.

It was a farmers' rally, men in slippers and ragtag groups marching past me in the heat. I didn't see the shields and truncheons until the crowd stood at a halt, an impasse in the shouting—then the bullies ranged before us, in a kind of lockstep rage. I was certain I heard gunfire—it was not just my heart. It all happened so fast, I still do not know how I managed to run, losing sight of Jed and Soli. I was caught in a crush of bodies, shrieks and shouts and groaning: and I remember that rush in my head, like a crazed revelation: this is it, I will die, and what will Helen of Constantinople say? In the end, all I did was lose a buckle: the left pilgrim, of course. And like many subsequent actions, it was anticlimactic—students ducked into alleys, peasants atomized toward their havens: cul-de-sacs, storefronts, friendly roadside restaurants.

It was Jed who came back for me, bright-eyed in his red bandanna, a look of exhilaration as if drunk. The way danger turned him on. I was shuffling down some wretched street, my Vivier pumps a vintage wreck, when I saw him—towering above the mixed crowd, shoppers shielding the dispersing peasants. Bedraggled, in my useless *Belle de Jour* shoes, I saw him turn the corner— I'd recognize him anywhere—and I felt relief and a strange gratitude. Like a found princess. And I understood it to be so right that he would come out of nowhere, just to look for me.

I wobbled toward him, waving.

"Soli," he yelled at me, "over here!"

"Sol," I corrected, speaking to the merging masses. "My name's Sol."

SOL AND SOLI. Soli and Sol. In the dorm, we were twinned in people's eyes. Solidaridad Soledad. Soledad Soliman. Our chiasmic names were some cosmic joke, or perhaps a sloppy choice in a careless novel. People could not get us right. I guess I exploited it, imagining myself less freaky than I was, since now I had a twin with an

identity that seemed better than mine. On the other hand, I was just
the girl with the imported books, asking stupid questions. It made
me uncomfortable to be called Soli, the one, I thought, who had all
the answers.

After the fiasco of the farmer's rally, Soli took me to Monumento, at Caloocan.

The hero Andres Bonifacio's tragic monument was now a
hawker's squall, merchants spilling the guts of the economy on the
highway itself—plastic chairs, pots and pans, bundles of cheap
cotton clothes in baskets. I watched the progress of the city from
the jeep, and a melancholy wash, a stab of something beyond my
witness, something wordless, came over me. A slight man carried
on his scrawny back large metallic basins, one heaped over another,
while on his shoulders were also laden a bunch of spatulas strung
like vegetables and sheaves of underwear stacked like books. Sights
like this crowded the open highway near Monumento—this was
the harvest of the cry of Balintawak. Aluminum spoils on a spit-
grimed street. The undelivered hopes of mundane lives. It was
easy to see how this had once been a swamp, in which the revolutionaries of the nineteenth century had lain in wait for signals and
gunshots; but I found it hard to see the revolution. Instead, I
thought about worms. Walking around in my brand-new, open-
toed leather sandals, I thought you could get all kinds of poxes
instantly on your feet, germs invading the skin, lacerating your
cuticles.

Soli was right: I always wore the wrong shoes.

The funeral home was bare—it had a mottled floor and gray,
undeveloped walls: by one coffin, a steel pediment peeked from the
cement, like a rusty snake.

Five young farmers and one child had died at the rally.

There had been gunshots: I was correct. I was incorrect to think it was normal. It was one of many planned marches, with permits, and peaceful, organized exits guided by megaphones. But it was a march pierced by the mandate of a new militia, Soli said, and the city was in shock. Instant outcry in the papers, revulsion among the middle classes. All this was news to me. I preferred, you know, to read the *Literary Review,* or the (London) *Times Literary Supplement.* Urban military acts in broad daylight were not normal even in revolutionary times (extrajudicial deaths, I was told, of course happened out of sight).

I passed one coffin after another and felt this pain in my ears and the odd sensation of falling apart, though I was walking about looking whole.

Death was a bazaar, multiplied like the merchandise around Monumento.

I felt that stifling in my chest, a familiar horror not quite guilt, not quite sorrow: a numb, hollow, blanketing despair. A falling sickness, the world pulsating, out of whack.

It was easy to distinguish the mourners from the kibitzers. The people who looked out of place, underdressed, wearing sneakers without socks, or plain rubber slippers, were closest in relation to the dead. The mothers and fathers and wives and children of the slain. While the kibitzers were more alert and canny and dressed accordingly, in Sperry Top-Siders and button-down shirts. In one corner, already littered by the props of the living—a coffee thermos on a stool, a comb and hand mirror on the floor—a foreigner was recording his conversation with a woman, while the rest of the family sat in a passive row. An expressionless wizened old man in slippers and a straw hat looked away from the proceedings. A little boy, dressed in underwear, watched the Australian with curious intensity, as if watching television; and a lady, maybe an aunt, kept interrupting the taped conversation, weeping after each of her revelations. The journalist himself looked uncomfortable. He kept wiping with a bare hand his sweating collarbone. And only the grieving woman, it seemed, was in command of the situation. She was a gray-colored lady with a tough pachydermal hide. She had a kerchief tucked into the back of her dress, a gesture of forethought against Manila's heat, and she kept tugging at the piece of cloth, keeping it in place to staunch her sweat: and her brief agitation of the kerchief was the only thing about her, it seemed, that gave away expression. She spoke in a monotone, while a girl in blue eye makeup translated.

An excursion. With friends. She, the mother, didn't know it meant this (vague sweep of fingers across the room, glance toward the coffin).

The military should pay, she said quietly, laying her hand back into her lap.

The girl with caked, blue eyelids dutifully translated, unconsciously imitating even the poise of the woman's hand.

And at a question from the foreigner, the woman answered, promptly understanding him: "*Kinse. Kinse anyos*—" And she said something I did not get amid the Spanish I unearthed in my lost tongue.

The mother looked straight at the girl in blue eye shadow, as if the mother, too, needed a translation for the information she had just relayed.

That her child was only fifteen years old.

The translator shook her head, shifting out of character and waving her white hands: "Those goons. Who says martial law will be lifted? They're sending the militia now into the cities—the CAFGU goons—the counterinsurgency forces have no place in Manila!"

And the aunt on the sideline began weeping again. When she saw Soli, she wept even louder. Soli walked to her and took her in her arms, holding her shaking shoulders. Then Soli picked up the comb on the floor and smiled at the other woman, the gray-eyed mother, who was looking intently at Soli, her poise unmoved.

And Soli started combing wisps of hair on the still mother's brow.

At this point, the multiple coffins began to multiply even more, growing dizzy in my sight. I could not understand what people said—speaking in multiple, accusing tongues—the languages I had overheard all throughout childhood, and which I understood the way I understood the weather: a code beyond my need to comprehend, a sensory mist separate from me, a knowledge of myself I have never grasped.

I stood up, feeling the world spin. It seemed to me that the coffins were heaving against the walls, like bands of trees growing sideways, bloating into horizontal, varnished baobabs, contracting space as they expanded. I felt faint in the windowless room, and the coffins began moving toward me, constricting my breathing. I thought wildly for a moment: All of these dead want me dead.

I passed the door that looked onto the inarticulate mass of the monument in Caloocan—Andres Bonifacio and the heroes of the revolution: farmers, petty merchants, smelters, printing press laborers, government clerks—their bodies in stone and bronze defaced by the city's more tenacious dirt. I looked back at the crowd in the funeral hall. Among them, the mourners and the kibitzers, Soli walked about, her back straight, her stance always correct. She made mundane gestures of solace, completely comfortable among the living. Whereas I could not see my place at all, terrified by the dead.

5

BY AUGUST, I was attending lectures with this stringy-haired guy, Ka Noli, who looked like no Italian cookie. He'd appear in rubber slippers, with dirty hands and unshaved face, at sessions in the provinces, or amid the monsoon damp of nearby suburbs. Ka Noli was a political guide who intoned the doctrines of the *PSR,* a shortcut term for an analytic manual of people's war. I still have no idea what those initials meant. Sometimes, I thought, I imagined I was there for comradeship. An escape from solitude. At others, I thought I was a slut, watching Jed with Soli, noting details of estrangement, irritation. My heart would leap when Jed looked at me. But Jed himself betrayed no obvious concern about his double life, one with Soli and one with me.

My actual attention for the business at hand—the struggle against forces I could barely conceive—was, clearly, incoherent.

I don't think I ever got my priorities straight.

Ka Noli asked us to give ourselves different names, the entire affair a festival of duplicity, as if we were spies or Mafia killers. I called myself Victor. Victor Eremita: Kierkegaard's pseudonym in one of his books—fear and trembling, the sickness unto death.

Even incognito, I was a literary snob.

Hang yourself, you will regret it; do not hang yourself, you will also regret that.

I was a two-faced vermin, worse than a rat.

Jed called himself Simoun—from the book he had borrowed from me, the *Fili,* which he never gave me back.

Soli, our P.O., as she was called, has no name that I can offer. It doesn't matter anyhow: my wit's diseased.

For those after-school teach-ins, we'd take jeeps and buses in dirt darkness to get to homes where people used staircases as book-shelves and floor mats as beds. They hung nets around their straw beds to hide from mosquitoes. The sweet homeowners, someone's schoolteacher father or innocent uncle in the civil service, helped us spray Baygon pesticide over everything, even the sweating plastic of their sofas—but nothing we did could keep away the roaches and the rats. It was as if, as the island of Luzon kept keeling into the Philippine Sea, all the vermin of its vegetation also kept rising from the wreckage to survive. Thus, Manila is this precarious ecology of pests and people merely treading water before extinction. I was always getting a bug in my ear or a dead spider in my espadrilles, and I was ashamed that these disturbances kept me from concentrating on revolution. No one else seemed to be concerned.

Once, they requested a meeting in my house, and I obliged. It was not a good idea. We were polite and well behaved, as prescribed in Mao's *Little Red Book,* and they even took off their slippers at the front door, to my consternation, so that Manang Maring, my half-blind yaya, seeing them *in medias res* (but in *medyas,* no) began shouting in alarm at the ragged barefoot tribe I had brought home with me. But the questions they kept asking me that evening, about what my parents did, where I had been in this picture or that, made me uncomfortable, and though I answered, lame lies, I knew I could never invite the group back. They questioned the portraits in my rooms' hallway (Lola Felma, the scared child with the sausage curls; the headless poet Emily Dickinson's floating white kerchief dress). They oohed and aahed at the vellum in the vestibule and the statues by the stairs. Briefly, they met Reina Elena, on her way out to a dinner party (she and Soli exchanged pleasantries about the hometown they shared). I was annoyed more than distressed by her chatty fascination, my mom with Soli; and Soli, who examined everything with her usual clinical amusement, did not say much on the way back to the dorm but looked at me, I thought, in understanding. The group never met in the house again.

WATERLOGGED TILES IN typhoon homes. A citrine moth tangled in Jed's slip-ons and then alighting in camouflage on his lit-up hair. I was relieved, when finally, after those months of secrecy and delirium—finally, we held a dirge that first week of December, an uncannily wilting time of the year.

Jed and I were finally denounced, for S.A., or D.O., or some other abbreviation for, what the hell, you goddamned fuck.

At the meeting, I learned the name for my sin. Sexual opportunism. S.O. was the plebeian term. So. So. It was out in the open. I guess we were betrayed through some astrologer's gaze. It was odd to hear the clean-cut verdict, the moral purity of the group's outrage.

I agreed with them absolutely, but I sobbed without control.

I was relieved but not absolved.

It was an orderly affair, blame squarely placed, love easily denounced. Jed, admitting all, apologized. In their patriarchal way—the movement had this chauvinist streak, just like the Church—Jed had recourse to a higher court, some assembly of dark lords with goblin wings.

Whereas I had nothing but their denunciation.

I was surprised to be told by the group that they regretted having *me* in their midst.

Looking at their mournful glances, wide-eyed fixtures of reproach, I was mortified by my tardy recognition. I saw in their eyes the person they saw: an obsequious tool, a confused sympathizer with a nice library, carrying an ignorant rattling can of coins. Fucking the boyfriend of Saint Catherine of Siena.

What about my jobs, I said, my paint cans and the copper centavos? Who will do my jobs?

It was an absurd exclamation. Someone laughed. I wailed.

It was odd how it was Soli who comforted me, smoothing hair from my damp face, propping up my shaking frame.

When I should have lain myself at her feet, anointing her with pathetic oils.

"It's all for the best, Victor," she soothed, patting my mouth, my cheek, tenderly, absentminded. That was her gesture: absentmindedness. "You can't even tell us what your parents do, Victor. Do you understand? If you cannot see yourself clearly, it's hard to see the revolution with clear eyes. It is better for you to go to America."

I stared at her: "I already told you what my parents do: my parents are traders."

"Traitors?" one girl asked, as if uncertain about what I said.

"Traders!" I wailed.

"In what goods?" Soli asked.

"Cuckoo clocks," I said. "They sell cuckoo clocks."

Soli stared at me. She shook her head.

"It's all just—weird, Sol—there's something dishonest—just like—." And she blushed, staring away from me and Jed.

Jed did not look at me, and I had nothing to add.

Why was I so hurt when even to me it was no surprise?

Jilted by the proletariat.

There I was thinking it was I who was going to quit the group, but it turned out no one had ever wanted my allegiance. Or something like that. I was told I was no comrade anyhow until I handed in the *T.B.*, the *talambuhay*: my reckoning of my life.

Which I would never do.

Spitting out the lukewarm. Just like that.

If I ever told him (of course I never did), Uncle Gianni would have laughed.

You have not written your *talambuhay*. You have not done your class analysis. You cannot express your class relation to the masses. You cannot envision society as a creature with genuine warmth or pumping heart. We do not believe you can tell us truthfully who you are. You are a coward. A moral void lies in you, large as a copper coin—but a hole nonetheless. You do not have the imagination to possess affection. You have a cadaverous soul. You have not yet read the *PSR*. Comrade: one day, we'll meet again. Change is possible— after all, it is what we believe. We hope one day you will be a part.

Ka Noli, the lecturer, did not say things quite like that: I got their drift. I was dishonorably discharged, so to speak, and in this way my time in Manila was done.

6

O N THE STEPS, the last of the kids who had been waiting for their rides home, smoking a cigarette before their parents came, were already gone. Soli, too, had gone home for Christmas. She left in a rented jeepney stuffed with pillows, buri bags, cookie cans and colored baskets. Soli did not even have suitcases. A crowd of nephews waved at me from the jeepney—we had held a teach-in once at her uncle's home in Marikina, and her uncle's two preschool boys, precocious perverts, had peeked in on me in the bathroom, and I had shrieked. Now I saw one of the talented voyeurs, a cheeky kid with big ears, waving at me happily and calling out my name. *Solosolosolosol.* Disconcerted, I waved back.

Before she left, Soli kissed me goodbye on the cheek, a polite holiday hug.

"Be good in America," she said.

"See you," I said, though I knew I would not.

My semester was over. By the end of the country's Christmas season, after Epiphany, in fact, a month from the day, I would be going off to college in New York or New England—someplace new.

The university was a dreary place without people—just a mess of trees and fading buildings. I stood alone for a while, waiting for Manong Babe. I carried a large shoulder bag, which rattled when I moved. Throughout the last weeks, I had been packing my life in a frenzy, and only a few goods were left behind. I did not know what to do with the rattling can. Then for some reason I decided to keep it, the rectangular tin of Fox's Glacier candy holding the coins and the pamphlets and the notes and the drafts of my *talambuhay*, the life Ka Noli had asked me to write. The copper coins kept rattling as I moved.

I KEPT COLLECTING THE coins during those last days before Christmas break, out of habit, though the group itself I avoided in the dining hall, in the lobby. I was unable to look Soli in the eye. But whenever I found a five-centavo coin, I kept it.

People were kind to me in the meeting's aftermath. Maybe it was the fact of imminent departure, the way some people think better of you when you are leaving, as if departing were the same thing as being dead. Even Vita, the gastric girl with the abundant phlegm, who had seemed to hate me the most at first, asked me how I was doing; but maybe she had ulterior motives because she still had my copy of the selected works of P. G. Wodehouse. For some reason, she liked Jeeves. I let her keep it. And then in a confused confounding of the season's depressions, John Lennon died. We heard the news in the lobby, and shock united all of us freshmen in unspeakable despair. We could not keep straight our anti-imperialist agitation from our profound horror, and Buddyboy the Beatlemaniac, clutching at his red bandanna, howled, literally, like a mutilated calf. In the last couple of days, in the spirit of peace, he kept asking me to listen once again to *Revolver*, his favorite album, if I liked. I declined. I said I hated Paul's voice even more now that John was gone, and Buddyboy nodded and solemnly shook my hand—comrades once again. Francis "Kiko" Not-Coppola, a shy kid, traded a bootleg copy of his favorite movie, *Apocalypse Now*, for a copy of Conrad's "Secret Sharer" (he had many bootleg Betamaxes of the film in his bedroom anyhow).

"When you are homesick," Kiko told me helpfully, giving me his gift, "you can watch *Apocalypse Now*. It's the best movie about our country."

"I will," I said. "When I'm homesick for Manila, I'll watch *Apocalypse Now*."

But I kept to myself that last day—packing with a sense of finality, as if leaving a hospital and wondering what to do with all of my clothes that did not fit.

Above all, I did not wish to see Jed.

"YOU'VE BEEN AVOIDING me."

He was staring down from an amused height.

"No," I said.

"Let's talk. Why won't you talk to me?"

He lowered himself. He sat on his haunches at my feet. The heels of his sandals were raised from the ground: they were worn out now, the heels ground up.

How long had it been—six months?

June to December.

I had lived an entire life in an interim universe, and it was odd to see it whittled down like this, easily measured by the stumps on his shoes.

"Talk to me," he said.

I looked away, at the door, at the burnt, bored guard, then I stared at him.

"Remember," I said, "that night. When the police officer came and you took out your wallet and showed him your name. Remember?"

He took out a cigarette and started twiddling with it.

"We got lucky," he said.

I shook my head.

"That's when I knew."

"What?"

"That I could not be a part."

"Of what?"

"That I was playing a game. That I was not honest. I don't mean about us. About my part in this country. That I could never be like Soli. I could never really join."

"What are you talking about?"

"He saluted you, Jed. Don't you see? We live outside of the country's rules. We can do whatever we want. We can commit crimes. We can even play at revolution. We could kill people, for all we knew. And then in the end we will always get away. We're cockroaches. It's we who are the problem, Jed. Don't you see?"

"Speak for yourself. I'm no cockroach: I'm going to be part of the solution."

"No, you're not. Your fucking family has fucked this country up. You and your family and your goddamned hold on the countryside. I mean, you guys own goddamned Bukidnon or something. You will never be a part. You will always be the problem."

He crushed the empty packet, and he took out the matches for his cigarette. His hands were absolutely sure of their gestures—he stroked, burned, lit. He spoke amid the smoke.

"Does it matter anyhow where we come from if we end up on the right side, Sol?"

"Sol for solipsism. That's what Edwin says."

At that, Jed smiled; he touched my cheek, blowing his smoke the other way.

I shook my head away from him.

"No, Sol," he said. "Don't you see. Sol for solution. Don't you see the role we can play? I *know* it will always be easy for us. The policeman couldn't even arrest us. But he was an idiot. Don't you think I don't think about it every fucking day? That we could have been caught and it would be my fault? What is our country's history, what has happened again and again: what was the failure of Simoun?"

He was fierce in the daylight, face quivering in the haze, though maybe that was only a trick of the smoke about his face. "The hero of *El Filibusterismo*. A diabolical creature, just like us! Addle-brained member of the upper class. But Sol: even *he* was on the side of the good. He failed, but he tried. We *do* have a role to play. We simply have to make a choice. We must choose to be a part."

"No," I said. "We'll always have our wealth, we will always have our names. There is something suspicious, dishonest, in playacting revolt. We're cockroaches. We'll outlast even our crimes."

"We can give them up," he said. "Our wealth, our names."

"Will you? Will you give up your family? Your mother? Your home?"

"Well, no need to be absolutist. Give yourself a break, Sol. You know the world's evils are not your fault."

At that, I laughed.

He took my face in his hands.

"I was scared that night, when the policeman came."

"You did not look it."

"I was scared. For you."

"Chauvinist bullshit," I said.

He did not laugh.

"I was scared. I always knew it would happen. I knew I would do it."

"Do what?"

"That one day I would get you into trouble, and you would do whatever I wanted."

"No," I said. "No, I won't."

I shook myself out of his hands.

I started moving away.

"Yes, you will, Sol. Sol for solution. I'll see you during break."

I turned away. I saw Sally—Sally Vega—coming out of the dorm.

"Sally!" I yelled. "Wait for me."

"I'll see you, Sol," he said.

I grabbed my bags and sped out to the street.

Sally Vega, Sally Vega. I believe that was her name. Mystery woman of the dorm. She looked like Gertrude Stein in that picture of the artist looking like a Roman emperor. Claudius or Caligula. Sally Vega compounded her alienation from the world with neglect—her jowly flab and amphibious flesh, a desert patch of rosaceae roosting on her chin—she looked unhealthy, unhygienic.

"Why do you do what you do, Sally?" I ran to her. "Sally Vega. Sally Vega. Why do you donate money regularly to Soli's group but do not join?"

Sally's flaky cheeks seemed to extend in folds to her neck, as if her self-pity had turned her into a blob of desiccated blubber. I watched her cheek folds move as she talked.

"I hope my parents come," she said. "I'd like you to meet them."

I waited politely for more information, but as usual her walrus chin did not elaborate.

Once again, her mystery parents didn't arrive—instead, a chauffeur in a black car picked her up. She looked disappointed.

"I knew he wouldn't come," she said. "My dad's always busy."

She sat in the back and did not look at me when the car drove off.

Jed, too, had disappeared. He didn't linger when he saw me with Sally Vega, as I pumped her with questions I knew she wouldn't answer, just as long as I had the excuse to turn away from Jed's certainty, that yes, I would succumb.

7

M Y PARENTS ARRIVED in the white limousine. It looked more ridiculous than usual beside the withered banana leaves of the driveway; but my heart leapt when I saw it. Now even the flame trees looked alien—their leaves turned dull in December, like scabs in the sky's kneecap.

Frankie and Reina Elena came out of the car together, holding hands, their faces shining. I was surprised at my emotion when I saw them: I was happy to be going back home.

Ma wore a flared pantsuit in silk chartreuse, with rainbow geometrics at her neck, like some wafting optical illusion. She was a walking patch of green powered entirely by Emilio Pucci. A jeepney braked, and passengers stared at her plumage. She wore wide dark glasses, like her idol, Gina Lollobrigida, a celebrated tourist in Manila.

The first thing I noticed about Pa were the white shoes with the woven pattern; the white safari suit, the straw Stetson, his figure all white, in his white suit and white patent loafers, white hat and white shirt. I always thought it must annoy the dictator, to see himself slavishly duplicated among his minions, as if his own figure were not excessive enough.

But I was a spoiled brat, a split soul.

I was happy to see them, even though watching them stride toward me, I had to admit I wished I were also not their child.

"Inday!" Gina Lollobrigida exclaimed, stretching out her hands. Even the burnt bored guard turned.

I ran to my mother and was swept into her perfumed arms.

She took my head in her hands and kissed me over and over, so extravagantly you could mistake her exuberance for acting.

"Oh, inday, we've missed you so much."

"How could you," I said, "you've barely been home."

"Oh, yes—we've been busy. But we have such great news!"

Pa folded me into his arms.

"Guess who's here, Sol, guess."

"I can't guess," I said. "I know."

He was grinning, his arms open wide.

"Uncle Gianni!"

"Just in time, too," Pa said, flicking invisible ash off his suit, his pinky delicately lifted. He had stopped smoking at my command, when I had learned of the evils of tobacco in Mr. Dreiser's middle school wellness class.

My dad always followed all my wishes—how could I complain?

"Where are you all off to?" I asked, holding on to Uncle Gianni.

"He came in honor of you," said my mother, kissing me again.

"No, he didn't," I said, wriggling away. "You all look dressed to kill."

"We're going to have lunch," said Pa. "To celebrate your return home from this—place. I told Queenie—it was a mistake to send you, even if Don Mariano's son is here, too. It's full of *demonyo*. But I'm so glad you're coming home."

And he hugged me, a smokeless caress.

"Oh, shush, Frankie. You went to this university yourself, what are you talking about? And everything's just fine, now she's going to college in America! Inday, Uncle Gianni came just for your home-coming," beamed Ma. "He will take you to New York himself in January."

"I came to organize the soccer games," Uncle Gianni reminded me. "Don't forget. You have to help me, Sol."

"But that's weeks from now," I said. "I thought you were coming for my birthday."

"That goes without saying, *carina*. But will you come help me with the games?"

"Okay," I said. "Same dates?"

"December 28, yes, Holy Innocents' Day! To slide us into New Year's cheer!"

Even Manong Babe, standing by with my bag, kept nodding at me as if at some prospect of a reversal, a happy turn in a plot.

"I thought you were abroad," I said as we got in.

"I was," said Uncle Gianni. "I came straight from Germany."

"Is America dismantling bases?" I said.

"What do you know about that, inday?" said my mom, laughing. "You will stick to your studies in America, become a historical scholar, and leave us to our business. She thinks she's so smart, Gianni. It's all your fault."

"How is your social studies group?" Uncle Gianni said. "Any new titles on the horizon?"

"All done," I answered brightly. "Course completed. Moving on!"

I saluted the air.

"Too bad," he said. "I bought you the best book."

And he presented a volume I had never heard of before, Antonio Gramsci's abridged prison notebooks, a beautiful book of analysis in leather binding, and he leaned out from the front seat to be kissed.

"*Ciao, bellezza*," he whispered, in his extravagant way, as I kissed him on his scrofulous neck.

Manong babe took us down Katipunan, along the highway and down the back roads of leafy streets into New Manila. After Diliman, this was the greenest part of the capital, shadowed by old acacias, splashed with bougainvillea. The road was still dirt in parts, and the dust in the noon heat caught the rays, so that it looked as if the light sizzled, then blinded.

"We're going first on a quick detour, inday, before we get home," Ma said. "We could not get out of the meeting. He wouldn't change the date. I mixed up the calendar. I forgot it was your Christmas break."

"Meaning—you put business first, Ma, and you forgot me again. That's all right."

"And oh, inday—you've met him. Colonel Grier. Remember him? At the concert?"

"The man with the coin collection," I said. "The scholar of the Philippine revolution."

"He said, Gianni, he could only give us thirty minutes," said Pa.

"The nerve." But Pa all in white, holding up his empty luminous holder in the backseat, looked like a Cuban tango dancer, absolutely unconcerned.

"Hah. Let's see who's got the nerve. He doesn't know what he's dealing with," laughed Uncle Gianni.

"He's so new to the country," Ma sighed. "He doesn't know a thing."

8

I REMEMBER THAT AVENUE in sheer light—the haze of dust motes rankling the air. In recall it is purely sensual, a number of distinct elements—dry, friable leaves, with a kind of muffled crackle, a static spark as they decomposed; the simmer of gardener's hose, the way water fell on earth so hot it vaporized when it touched ground, so that there was a curious smell of boiling on the block. Strangely, dimly, I recall the hiss of firecrackers. A sulphurous smoke, the skittish demeanor of light—even the street seemed nervous in spirit, its san francisco leaves quivering, smelling of flame. Our progress had telltale smoke in its wake, the omen of New Year's cheer.

VICTORIA EREMITA WAS taking away the snacks, the pictures on the table. She made such a commotion I almost fell from my rest in the rocking chair.

She began straightening up the boxes and the crates.

"No!" I shouted.

Startled, she stopped in her tracks, bent over some neat stacks—
cartons tied up in strings.

"Ma'am Sol, I am just trying to clean—"

"No," I said quietly. "Do not touch."

I knew it must be there somewhere—the rattling can of
memory.

THE STREET OF entry was full of gardeners, caretakers, drivers—
underdressed, pacific men. Who were the witnesses? A Metro aide
with her scudding broom. A startled, somnolent houseboy? Some
anonymous gaze.

On the street, someone was always watering a garden, and the
suppressed sense of heat, that raised muggy moistness, overlays my
vision, like the vague blue rinse of a blank canvas. At the corner
before you reached the street was the empty gas station with its festering weeds. Grass and dirt still clung against its cement base,
growing through its cracks. A cement wall near the gas pump was
overgrown with trash—like a place unsettled, though this business
must have moldered there for years. The earth, it seemed, was only
a few years removed from jungle, from swamp. Transient attempts
at trade, a corrugated shingle here or there, had the forlorn trace of
foiled ambition. Everywhere there dwelt that smell of hydration,
even on the pavement. Frying vapor. When you reached the store
with the lame man at a door and a fervid monkey by the window,
you turned to the right on Third Street. Those musky gardens of
the British Council met you.

"My favorite library," I pointed out when we passed it.

"Nice mansion," said Uncle Gianni.

We drove straight on and turned another corner. In front of a long, tall gate, Manong Babe stopped the car.

A guard came up, and Manong Babe gave him his license.

The guard, unsmiling, took it, then looked at us.

Ma waved at him, but the guard was unmoved.

A second man came over and gazed at the papers, at Manong Babe's face, then he peered at us inside.

He went to the guardhouse and buzzed the gate open.

As we drove in, the guard saluted, an abbreviated gesture.

"Unfriendly guy," I said.

"Don't blame them," said my dad. "People picket them every week, it's disgusting."

My mother looked at me inquisitively, caressing my fingers on her lap; she frowned at my dad. "Honey, why bring that up at all?"

A uniformed servant with a walkie-talkie came to meet us at the house's entrance.

It was a meandering bungalow with garden chairs set out on the patio that faced us.

The lawn was carpeted in deep green: you noticed that instantly. Grass from Kentucky. But the splotched leaves of common san francisco, stained lime and purple and tooth-yellow, lined the garden's edges, just as they did in those dirt yards I'd seen in the provinces at those teach-ins with the group. Various Filipino common flowers, gumamelas and yellow bells, were dispersed among a profusion of roses. Arching toward the eaves, brilliant bougainvilleas hung like thick, clustered bracelets on the bungalow's low limbs.

"We've been here before," I said.

"It's the headquarters of LOTUS," my father said.

"Didn't someone celebrate a birthday here?" I asked.

"Maybe," Pa said.

Ma went up to meet the uniformed men. My dad and uncle hung back.

"Remember the parties we used to have here? Bourbon all over the place, people acting like baboons. That was fun," Uncle Gianni said.

"No more of that," said Pa, speaking low. "This new guy's different."

"He must be unpopular," said Uncle Gianni. "I mean, this place was Animal House."

"I've been told he scares the shit out of everyone. He has more war experience than all of them put together, even the general. But I'm sure you'll find the opening, Gianni. You'll crack the shell."

Uncle Gianni grinned, his lips disappearing as if he relished the battle.

"We'll see," he said.

Ma came up.

"He's waiting for us."

It was a cool, shadowy place, a maze of halls paneled in hardwood, with walnut-like dark cuts in the wood, their centers like eyes. The uniformed man, his walkie-talkie buzzing all the while, led us across the hall, then down a staircase and into a cool basement-like area, with a view of a garden—a redesigned old bunker.

Some white men in plainclothes ate at a few tables, their expatriate presence transforming the tropical décor. These scenes of foreigners in vague military drag—wrinkled dress whites unbuttoned, camouflage khaki shorts hiked up—these random soldiers lounging amid the palms always looked like historical black and white pictures of the forties, during the time of the Commonwealth, as if the country had not moved beyond the past and were still ruled by American commandos, men in battle fatigues planning for war.

I almost didn't recognize the man I had met at the concert. He'd become eerily tanned—a beet-red conflagration all about his body, as if he had an allergy to the tropics. His own men seemed to shy away from him, though he was talking with one of them, ignoring us. He sat by himself, while his men at other tables listened in desultory groups. He sat near the bar, one of those wooden, accordion-paneled affairs. A monotonous mahogany sheen cloaked the entire place.

Unlike the others, Colonel Arthur Grier was dressed in old-style gym clothes—a tight, faded pink tank and extremely brief nylon shorts. An old muscled Marine: he knew his body looked good, and he did not care if his nakedness was obscene or his clothes ridiculous. His pink, pumped flesh ripped out of his clothes' seams. It's true, he looked disgusting, but compelling—like some reptile that engendered this evolutionary response: my alert revulsion. In the months since I'd first met him, his face had turned tropical-leathery and tanned, and it was hard to tell if he were older than I thought or deceptively younger. His rank vigor overwhelmed judgment. He looked up, barely apprehending our arrival.

Clothes always mean something. The Colonel's were an understatement, surely an insult. My parents were overdressed, a supplicant pair. Uncle Gianni, in his sheer dark *La Dolce Vita* suit, so fine it swayed when he moved, was unconcerned as always about his troubling effect, as if he were starring in his own production. He looked like an Italian cinematographer from *Apocalypse Now,* about to accept an Oscar.

The Colonel moved slightly when Uncle Gianni offered his

hand, making a gesture as if he were about to stand up, except he didn't. He motioned us to sit down, across from him at the mahogany bar. He didn't speak.

"I had to pick up my daughter, Colonel, she's just back for Christmas break—do you mind if she's with us?" said my mother. Her voice, a shrill pitch, carried in the wood-lined room.

"No, not at all," he said. I remembered those carved-out spaces in his speech. Connecticut or Colorado, something like that. "I remember you," he said to me. "Defender of the *insurrectos*." He didn't smile.

"Whadja like to drink?"

All the grown-ups made their choices quickly. I ordered San Miguel beer.

My mother looked at me: "Soledad? Excuse me? She's having wine. She's joking," she said. "She's never had San Miguel in her life."

"A beer drinker?" the Colonel said with approval. "That's all I drink now, you know. It's good for the heart."

"Pretty soon, doctors will be recommending death to get rid of goiters," Uncle Gianni said.

"Well, then you can have a beer," said my mom. "Just one."

"Are you making fun of me?" Colonel Grier said to my uncle, not looking offended.

"No, man," said Uncle Gianni instantly. "I wouldn't dream of it," he said smoothly. "I wish the longest life for you."

The Colonel laughed. Uncle Gianni saluted.

One to one, I thought. Each had scored a point.

In that way the lunch went; if you looked for openings and parries, there was a lot to watch out for. But it was all just silt and garbage—trash talk. Just lunch, after all. I looked at the keloids, the scars on the Colonel's arms, and tried to imagine how they got there. I tried to imagine Colonel Grier as a victim in Vietnam. It was hard: he had the broad, wall-like body of a carabao; his muscles were alarming. He terrified me, frankly. I thought that easily his large hands could break my neck in two. I tried to focus on his story. To train soldiers in counterinsurgency, he said, he made them practice by beheading chickens with their bare hands; it was easy, he said, but messy. He got this idea from reading history books—the history books about the native peoples.

"*The Ordeal of Samar*?" I asked. "Have you read that?"

He shrugged.

"Perhaps."

"So why has the U.S. Army not returned the bells of Balangiga? I mean, why oh why, Wyoming?"

Everyone stared at me as if I were insane.

I almost giggled.

Colonel Grier turned his leathery back to me.

In the tropics, he told my uncle, what you need to do is terrify your enemies.

"Somehow that works," he said. "You know what the Filipino rebels would do to American soldiers in the 1899 war?"

"What?" asked my dad, all eagerly polite.

"Filipinos liked to pour sugar concoctions, syrups and jams, on the wounded men's heads, tie them to a pole in the sun, and let the ants eat them up."

"Sweet," said Uncle Gianni.

The Colonel snorted. "Saccharine's more like it."

"Sucrose torture," laughed Uncle Gianni.

"Ant cure," said the Colonel.

"But how horrible," said Ma.

The Colonel nodded. "Got to admire them for that—they used all the weapons they had. All the pests in their arsenal. It's good to learn from the natives. That's how you win. Kill the cockroaches with their own demons."

"Hoist them with their own petard! Damned petards!"

You could tell Uncle Gianni was in his element. He had met his match, and he could not stop grinning.

"Well, young scholar," Colonel Grier suddenly turned to me. "Would you like to see my coins? Not the Byzantine ones—they're in a safe," he explained. "But the American pieces. I like to take them out—it's like holding history in your hands. Lincoln cents and Latin doubloons. I'll show them to you, if you wish. Including my Philippine hoard. A minor branch of my Americana."

And you know—honestly, I could not tell if the Colonel was laughing at me or dead serious: it's hard to tell with guys like him. Their ambiguity is their weapon.

IN THE END, my parents looked vanquished. As far as I could tell, they never took the offensive. Their agenda was unsaid. The only concession they could get was that Colonel Grier promised to see them again, at their Christmas party or the soccer tournament hosted for expatriates on Holy Innocents' Day, December 28, by Uncle Gianni, to usher out the old year and launch the new. Into New Year's cheer! The meeting ended with frilly piña coladas in our hands. I held the piña colada and kept sloshing the ice in it, stirring with the cheap little umbrella, holding on and not looking up.

My mother's laugh, as talk subsided, rang about the murmuring room, rising toward the whirring fans.

Colonel Grier stood up. At his move, we rose, too.

"Time for the gym," he said. "Three o'clock sharp."

"You're a regular?" said Uncle Gianni.

"As regular as anyone can get. My wife tells me I'm obsessed. I go everyday at three o'clock, rain or shine. It's a habit you get from captivity, I think. You hang on to routine. That is my experience."

"You're a regular guy," said Uncle Gianni.

"What do you mean?"

"You're a very orderly person. I like orderly people."

The Colonel walked ahead, not bothering to acknowledge my uncle.

Nothing resolved. Going down the stairs, I couldn't help noticing the Colonel's thighs, like blocks, the iron grip he had on his body. He looked invincible, though dressed in a pink tank top. A car was waiting by the curb. The Colonel strode up to it. The guard saluted the sockless man in his running shoes, his underwear apparent under his tight shorts. We watched, waiting for our own car, as the Colonel bent down to pat one of his front hubcaps. In this way, politely we stared at his wedgie, contemplating his oblivious ass. Then he straightened and walked to the other side of his car, staring at the wheels.

The uniformed man remained silent beside the car. We watched, not quite sure what to make of it, then Colonel Grier looked at us. "They're all there," he said.

"Anything wrong, Colonel?" Uncle Gianni asked.

"Some crazy native tried to steal my hubcaps: right in the compound. From that wall over there," he pointed to a gauze of bougainvillea in the corner, "they climbed in through that gap. Arrogant son of a bitch. Right in the heart of the bunker. Fuckers. They'd die for hubcaps."

"Did they die?" I said, horrified.

"Probably just neighborhood boys," said Pa. "Easy enough to fix."

"You're right," the Colonel said, waving his hand in contempt, "the motherfuckers. Since then we raised the wall, of course; and we have more guards. But I check anyway. Over my dead body if I let some fucking Charlie get away with that kind of shit."

My dad nodded in agreement.

"Did you shoot them?" I asked again.

"Of course not," the Colonel said. "That's not my job."

The Filipino guard standing beside the car was grinning.

I looked at them, the Colonel and his guard. I imagined it was the piña colada rushing up my guts, this sudden, bittersweet nausea.

"I thought for a minute you were looking for a bomb," said Uncle Gianni.

The Colonel looked scornful.

"Who would dare?" he spat. "They'd be sorry if they tried."

As we got into the white limousine, I said to Uncle Gianni:

"Seems as if he got you. He won."

"What do you mean?"

"He wouldn't let any of you get a word in. About whatever new deal you want him to approve."

"What deal, Sol? You know nothing about it," my mother said.

"Oh that? I don't know," Uncle Gianni said thoughtfully. "Remember, Sol, the first trick of reconnaissance."

"What?"

"You watch. That's it: you just watch. You learn a lot from just looking."

"What did you learn here?"

"Should I spell it out for you? Give me something you've learned, Sol, from this lunch. Come on. There were many, many things."

"Such as?"

"Well, what does he do at three o'clock, rain or shine?"

I thought about that.

"He's a very orderly guy," said Uncle Gianni thoughtfully, "though he should vary his itinerary. I bet he's never late for work."

9

"Nonsense," my mother was saying. She was standing in my doorway. "Of course you're attending the Christmas party. You have to be there—it's a celebration of your birthday!"

"My birthday is next week."

"Well, in celebration of your birthday, we're exhibiting the portrait."

I had forgotten about that—after the triumph of Madame Vera's gallery retrospective, Ma was finally going to install *Reina Elena, with Child,* on the mezzanine.

"But we had to do it a week early, inday—Madame Vera, you know, she's superstitious. She thinks the solstice is bad karma."

"So good luck to me," I said, "Sol for solstice."

I'd rather die, I thought, than celebrate my seventeenth birthday with Madame Vera.

"Come on, darling. Get dressed. Of course you're going. You're the star of the show!"

I lay amid a spill of books. My head ached from lying down too much; I felt moisture in my arms, despite the central air. I was in a

marooned waste of being, a sensual muck, the usual worthless surplus of Manila's endless Christmas season—we were always let off
earlier than everyone else in the world, even at the American School,
which wasn't Catholic. It seemed to me the whole world got off its
carousel at Christmas, standing still to be harassed by carolers until
Epiphany, January 6, the day of revelations that always marked the
end of eternity for me.

Ma urged: "You know, the Colonel will be there. He asked
about you when I called to remind him."

"Which means," I said, "he had to acknowledge remembering
me when he didn't have anything to say to you. So what's happening
to your deal with the Colonel?"

"Oh, inday, it has nothing to do with you. Our business has
nothing to do with you. Just become a scholar of histrionics and go
to Harvard School of Law. It is all I ask. But, inday, didn't you talk
about the coins? He invited you to see them. Why don't you go and
see his special coins?"

"What do you want with him?"

"Inday, he's an educated man! You can learn from him. He'll
make general one day. That's what they say. Especially with General Tom so ill. Although I do like our own General Tom better:
Tom's so much more *simpatico*."

"But what do you want from him, the other one, the
antipatico?"

"Oh, can you imagine, Colonel Grier wants us to make a bid?
If he agrees to the plan, he wants a public bidding for the new
equipment."

"What new equipment?"

"Oh, you know, the plan. For national security. When the presi-

dent lifts martial law, the country will need a new blueprint for its
defense. But oh, it is none of your business, inday. He's so new to the
country, that colonel." My mother laughed. "Uncle Gianni will fix
him, don't worry. Don't worry your smart head about that. Well,
you must come out of your room. Your vacation will soon be over,
you're going to leave us for America, oh, inday—and you still haven't
done a thing! You have not had one adventure! You can invite a
friend to your birthday. Someone from school."

"They're all home in the provinces."

"I don't mean that school. I mean the American School. How
about Don Mariano's son? That melancholiac boy, Jared."

"Jed."

"Jed, Jared, Jiminy, Jack. Ha-ha. Why don't you invite that boy
Jared, Jack? Don Mariano should take him along, what do you
think?"

I shrugged. "Do what you want."

THE CHRISTMAS BALL was a signature event, for which the house
was turned upside down in preparation for a costumed hell.

My mother always imported the chef, a monumental German
who had once dominated the country's foremost hotel. He was
rumored to have served General MacArthur himself (a slander he
failed to correct—as he said to me once: I'd have poisoned the man
if I'd lain eyes on him, *Deutschland über alles;* during the war, he
confided, I was only thirteen and breeding Hitler's mustache—it
was the fashion). The chef was now retired and owned an island off
Zamboanga; but occasionally, with totally superb disdain, he would
leave his fiefdom to enact favors for valued old friends. The sight of

this man (name withheld, a policy I reserve only for him, a magnifi-
cently nasty character) threw the maids into fits and completely
silenced Manang Lita, my mother's chief cook, who treated him
without rancor as a god. Manang Maring, my old blind yaya now
retired from her duties, didn't dare emerge from her domestic cave
while the German was in residence.

Guests were already arriving at the house in droves. Fancy
women came with their housemaids and powerful men with
their mistresses. Everyone arrived with guards. I kept watching
out for Don Mariano, just in case. I remember the discomfort
and hollowness of it, waiting to see if Jed would arrive. In my
high heels, I felt groggy and listless from lying in bed, from the
vertigo of so much sleep. I tottered about my mother's party with
boredom and a dim verge of tears. It was bad enough that the
people at the party, expatriates, ambassadors and businessmen,
had nothing in common with my inertia. People were in kinetic
Christmas cheer, fueled by drink and other excellent traders'
goods. A Frenchman fell into the pool, bringing his lovely trans-
vestite companion with him. If he weren't a consul, my mother
would have thrown him out of the house when she saw him arrive
with two tarts, one chocolate, the other Cambodian, a gorgeous
boy in velvet and feathers. The two men floated in the warm
water, like large fowls dipped for plucking. I watched their beautiful sequined clothes rise like bedraggled wings; their slender
calves acted like ballast before they went under. When they
emerged, heads up, they had their tongues in each other's mouths,
a well-rehearsed act, and people clapped. Another couple took
pictures of themselves atop the Gothic gargoyles sculpted on the
marble fountain. A man and a lady took turns chuting through

the grassy slough from the pool to the garden, yodeling Christmas songs all the way down.

Everyone came. Bumbum Esdrújula and the Secretary, dressed as Antony and Cleopatra, with the midget and her towels trailing along, bearing the suicide asp (plastic) for theatrical effect. Zubiri de Zoroastre, the gossip columnist, with his cohort of lensmen, muscle boys with bare chests and Kodak cameras. The Colonel and his mammary wife, dressed as Dorothy of Oz: "Actually, I really *am* from Kansas!" she kept explaining to sundry transvestites, who couldn't care less. General Tom arrived as Frankenstein: a nice pun on his twitchy face; for a man whose doctors had been saying for months he was going to die, he had a sense of humor. A slew of bodyguards enclosed him, not so out of place in the masked mix. Movie stars met sugar tycoons, and gigolos and justices waited their turn at karaoke.

Before dinner, my mother emerged on the mezzanine, a marble balcony above the banquet, to gather people for the big event. People cheered, and Madame Vera, dressed this time in a matador's costume, an affair in black and gold rickrack epaulets, swept up a dusty cape and took her bow, sending revelers around her into asthmatic fits.

I was standing near the door, as far from the upstairs crowd as I could get, when a woman entered the lobby. I froze, my heart stopped.

"Prima!" someone called out from the living room, where the more orderly and catty had taken up space, watching the gate-crashers.

"Is that Prima De Rivera?" someone behind me whispered. "*Qué pasó?*"

The lady advanced through the mirrored foyer. I was the only one close enough to see. The curls, wide-spaced cheeks and pale brow looked anomalously like Jed's. It was a precarious resemblance, disconcerting—Jed's cheekbones and Jed's light hair in reflection, simulated in perfect glass in the mirrors about the hall. It was clear from the hollow-eyed Prima how Jed's looks were the fine result of a manic sowing of proper seed, for which foreign brides were imported for their coloring and chosen for their cheekbones. The Morgas through the centuries had long-established mating habits, like hummingbirds or iguanas. All the male Morgas went to Spain to find a wife. Don Mariano was the first Morga to marry a Filipino—the beauty queen and toothpaste model Prima de Rivera, Miss Caltex. Or Miss Shellane Propane. Anyway, some diesel diva. And although she was part Italian, part Spaniard, she was also somehow Ilocano, a sad mongrel. Sure, she was a mongrel of the type certain circles of Manila spawn and prize, like Argentine cattle or Alpine dogs, but Prima had unfortunately grown up in Makati, not Madrid, an ignominious start to their union.

Her still-lovely face, marred by confusion, a nightmared look, questioned her fractured sight in the Versailles mirrors. Eyes like smoke and ash, green-veined hands—she gazed at the shards of her reflection and smiled, an eerie multiplication. A torso pocked with scabs: punctured, cut open.

She was practically naked.

I tried not to stare at the purple blotches and drugged decay all across her arms.

Another door opened, and I looked. But it was only a maid, running after the runaway.

Prima De Rivera Morga stood in the gauntlet of the evening's guests in her nightgown—a wrinkled silk *camisa china*. Her ghostly

ankles were bare, and for a moment there, I thought she would tot-
ter into the giant Ming vase and shatter the house's feng shui, splin-
tering her bones along with the vase. But her scrupulous maid
caught her skinny arm—the gentle maid put her shawl across her
shoulders and steadied her backward, toward the door.

Standing sidewise across from her, near the screen door, I saw
the slight tremble as Prima moved forward, her hands wavering
as she held her Spanish shawl. I witnessed her son's height and
languor—a simulacrum that exposed the vigor she had lost. I felt
a deep flush suffuse me as she stared back at me before she turned
to move away. But I was mistaken: she was staring right through
me, her vacant gaze spent. Her absent eyes, so empty in the glare
they looked almost white, blind, gave one an awkward pain: a pang
of guilt, from having witnessed this—this human dissolution.
Wobbling, she looked at the vase in the hallway, then she kissed it,
tonguing the ancient porcelain.

The room was silent. Musicians held their breaths and the wait-
ers stopped in their tracks. People upstairs turned their eyes from
the unveiling of the society portrait to watch its inverse version, a
naked truth in the room below.

My mother was descending the staircase. At that moment it
seemed hers were the only actions in Manila, click, clack, click,
clack. Her high heels crushing a cracked bone, a breaking thing.

Finally she reached the woman. My mother tiptoed to reach up
to kiss Prima de Rivera Morga on the cheeks, *beso-beso*. Everyone
noted how admirably Queenie kept her composure. Prima bent a
little, smiling shyly, as if trying to remember who my mother was.
As Ma took her by the hand, Prima allowed herself to be led, towering over my mother; then Prima De Rivera Morga spoke into my

mother's ear, bending as she did so, her tall gaunt body, like a high arched C, a harpy or a harp, looming over Reina Elena.

"*Hija de puta*," she whispered audibly to Reina Elena before the rest of Manila. "*Joderse, que se joda*."

And giggling, she watched my mother's stupefied face.

The shawl slipped inattentively, so that now everyone in the room could see her sad scars: splotches of gray all along her flesh, until they reached a gnarled entry at her wrists, the roots of her twig-like veins branched toward her apoplexed fingers. The kind of hand Madame Vera would render smooth as a rose petal, a fresh garland of dewy flesh.

Then a servant closed the door on Prima De Rivera Morga, who was shaking like a lunatic in her Spanish shawl.

Dinner was announced soon after.

And now, as if broken from enchantment, everyone charged into speech.

He had driven her to drugs. Or was it drink? Anyhow, her husband had a kind of disease, someone added. *Satyriasis*. It was social philanthropy, someone tittered: he did it only with the masses. Giggles, snorting and guffaws. Another provided an explanation: "She's haunted by the spirits of the graves she's robbed." The accusing mystic held up her scapular for good measure. People smirked at the nutty peanut in the gallery. "It's true: she has robbed ancient graves for their vases, for their porcelain!" You should see her house, someone digressed: she has the best collection of ancient Chinese pottery in the country. She used to have a sharp eye, the person said. Grave-robber, said the woman with the scapular. That's not the point, another person countered: you can be rich and own foolish things, like, you know. Someone laughed. And Prima's collection of Spanish-era documents, they're invaluable: I've seen them, a historian said. Rivals those of Secretary Esdrújula—and that's saying something. Is it she who owns the only manuscript extant of *Noli Me Tangere?* Nitwit. *Gaga tonta.* The National Library owns that. But someone stole it! It was returned, you retarded bookworm, two decades ago! When she used to host dinners, someone said, it was better than dining at Malacañang Palace.

Prima de Rivera Morga lived a charmed life, another agreed, if it weren't for the fact that marrying Don Mariano had turned her into a nervous wreck.

And so it was that poor Prima, by word of mouth and speculation, was transformed from ghoul to gastronome, klepto to connoisseur, in the short span between hors d'oeuvres and the first meats.

THE HEIGHT OF the evening? Of course, on such an occasion, she came. It was no surprise. The tension in the kitchen weeks before the event foretold her coming. The lordly German's sweating carcass permeated the kitchen for a week, brutish portent of the guest to come.

She arrived with her retinue, a cascade of ladies in blue. Her hair in its upsweep, her laugh in its glory, the Lady kissed my mother in the way of old friendship—a fiction they each achieved with grace. I understood my mother's reasons for her idolatry, but on her side, the Lady's motivations for attending, I have no clue. However, the kiss's effect on the party was electric—it was as if, finally, everyone was ready to dance. Scream and murder. Her arrival was the beginning of a beautiful evening. Power has that effect. No wonder the transvestites had a ball.

10

COMMODUS, THE SON of Marcus Aurelius, did not turn out well. He liked to club cripples with a lion's pelt, pretending he was killing giants, and fought butt-naked in gladiatorial combats. Of course, he always won, since he was emperor. His tendency to believe he was Hercules, going about beating up dumb animals, annoyed the Romans so much they assassinated him. His dead father, the bookish emperor and stoic philosopher, meditating on his heir Commodus mauling to death an awkward giraffe, perhaps said in his grave, No comment.

Caligula, on the other hand, had a clever successor, his uncle Claudius, the famous *I* of legend. Though Claudius, too, liked to slay dumb animals, for example killing a whale in a public spectacle, he was a man of learning, the last king who spoke Etruscan and a writer of histories, including eight volumes on the lost history of Carthage, as well as a statistician of dice. Claudius had cerebral palsy or Tourette's, which explains his reputation as an idiot; however, history was not fooled.

Thus a man of learning begat a beast while the monster Caligula ushered forth a scholar.

I had a lot of time to myself that Christmas. I understood that I did not have to be tied down to my fate as a daughter. I could cast my own light, maybe, I hoped, scratching out a few possible lives—pondering instructive examples of the reversal of genetics and diverted destinies. There was no reason that I could not spend the rest of my days living productively, annotating annals of late Roman ironies or perusing the voids of contemporary lives. I was leaving for an education abroad—yes, to live in comparative luxury, but that did not mean I could not contemplate with care the patterns of the past. As my mother said, I should become a scholar of histrionics and spend my life researching ancient history with a focus on understanding family ties. I could leave the Philippines and never come back: to eke out volumes from its tragedies through my craft or sullen art. As for Jed, who knew what he was going to do?

I was startled when I heard his voice; I had been mulling over the party, thinking about his mother.

"Are you there?" he said again on the phone.

"Yes. Where are you?"

"We'd like to see you, Sol."

"I'm not interested."

"But it's important. You'll see. Come see us. We would like you to see us. I saw your picture in the papers. You're looking great, Sol. I want to see you."

"With whom?"

"Just me. I've missed you."

The last is perhaps my addition, wishful thinking.

I KNEW WHERE I'D find him anyhow.

It didn't seem to matter, by then, that I didn't trust him. Anyway, he'd wear you down with his charm, which lay precisely in the fact that he didn't use it—it hung in reserve, like a beautiful cloak, worn regretfully, knowing its power.

I asked Manong Babe to drop me off at a shopping center.

"Are you sure?" he asked. "Where are you going? Are you walking?"

He sounded horrified at the thought.

"You sound like Ma," I laughed.

He grinned at me, his right eye disappearing under his mole. "I can pick you up," he said. "Just tell me the time and place."

"No, Manong Babe. I'll get home by myself."

I looked back before I went a few more paces. Cars were honking at Manong Babe.

I walked back toward him.

Manong Babe rolled down the window.

"Don't you dare follow me," I commanded. "Go on now. Those jeepney drivers will kill you if you don't move. Go!"

At that, he moved with the wave of traffic, which was driven into frenzy by the crackling signal from the holiday traffic announcer, a woman in a neon police outfit carrying a violent megaphone.

WHAT WOULD I have done without Manong Babe? Once, when an unexpected squall marooned us in Marikina, and the jeeps and the tricycles could not get to the canals of Soli's uncle's home, I told the group I would call Manong Babe and ask him to pick us up. Soli said, sure, but Jed dissented. He always thought ahead. He said: It's too conspicuous—think of all your uncle's neighbors wondering about the white limousine. It would be so easy to trace that car, he said, and figure out who had been where. And so we waited for the rain to stop in her uncle's crowded home.

And when Manong Babe once drove us all in the car—the day that we had a session at my house in Makati—Jed, too, had his misgivings. But it was a lark, a great adventure, and everyone wanted to see my home. Finally even Jed gave in.

Manong Babe was in his element that day, asking all the kids their names and where they were from: Taguig, Ozamiz, Tagbilaran. We were all from so many different parts, myself the lone kid from Makati (Jed was absent). Manong Babe and Soli shared a bond—they were both from Leyte, my mother's province.

"Tacloban? Really? What's your family name?"

"Soledad," Soli said. "My father was a professor. Of engineering. At the university there."

"Ah. My father was a fisherman—at the other university there! Ha-ha. Soledad, ha? From Housing—on Mountainside?"

"Yes," exclaimed Soli. "We lived in Housing when my father was alive—on Mountainside, by the children's playground."

"I used to drive a jeepney there—*binulan*."

Soli was delighted: "Who knows? I could have ridden your jeep when I was little—and look—here we are!"

"It's a good car, huh?"

"You take good care of it," said Soli.

He beamed with pride.

"We call it the other Babe," I said. "Manong Babe's baby!"

He laughed, the gray hairs on his mole trembling.

"And I know your family, the Kierulfs," Soli added.

"What?"

"I know all about them," Soli told me. "Queenie Kierulf, who married a rich man and went off to Manila. Everyone knows about Queenie Kierulf, daughter of the flower-sellers. We used to buy our Maytime roses from your grandmother's gardens, in Cabalawan, where they built the bridge."

"Who else lived on Mountainside?" said Manong Babe, "I used to drive the children of the Cubilla Delgados—on your side. Are they still there?"

I WAS NOT SURE Manong Babe would leave me alone—so I walked in the opposite direction. Jed had ingrained these little precautions—the apartment was our secret, he said, and no one needed to know. Our pestilent Eden. *Nuestro peste Eden.*

When I arrived at the place, opening it with my own key, he was reading. He did not stir as I approached. I watched him. For a moment, I gazed at his missing figure, a long athlete's body in messy clothes.

Jed looked up in the dark from what he was reading but stared straight, his hands on his chin, with that melancholy profile, looking offhand, briefly, like his mother.

He hadn't noticed me, or pretended not to.

His vaguely neurasthenic, glassy look of solitude. Papers fell from his fingers. I imagined he had not been expecting me, but I doubt it. And for a moment, that still image rips through a raw core: his ripe mouth and blue absent eyes. His ears looked funny, with his hair cut short, his curls shorn from his temples.

He wore a military cut, an ugly buzz.

"Your hair!" I exclaimed.

"Sol!"

He looked sheepish, rubbing his naked neck.

"You don't like it?"

I shrugged my shoulders.

"It's none of my business."

He grinned, shaking his head.

"Sol for solitude," he laughed. "I *vant* to be alone."

Newspaper articles were strewn on the bedside table, and paper fluttered to the floor as he rose from the bed. He had already had coffee; when he got up and walked over to kiss me, I smelled it on his breath. Without thinking, I kissed him, cheek against cheek, the way I did with my mother's friends.

He made a face.

"I'm not such an old Makati *matrona*, you know."

I sat down on a chair across from the bedside table.

"I didn't think you'd come," he said.

"I shouldn't have."

"I kept hoping you would."

I looked at the paper in his hand. It was a page of scenes from my mother's party.

"What's that?" I asked.

"That's you," Jed pointed. "Nice dress."

I took the paper and looked at myself, a dark, gawky figure.

"That's Prima," I noted: "That's your mother."

He nodded, staring at her. "Yes, it is," he said.

"Your dad was supposed to come."

He nodded. "They had a fight."

"I'm sorry," I said.

"About what? That my family's a mess?"

"But your mother—"

"Married my father knowing who he was," Jed said. "He's always been that way. He is who he is. She knew he would never change. I guess no one can believe he's been a good father to me. He is. But he has absolutely no scruples as a man."

"I'm sorry. She looks so sad."

"She's sick. But she won't get help. But it's not my problem now. I cannot be her keeper."

But in spite of himself, Jed looked sad, looking at his mother.

I noted a newspaper face, circled in blue ink.

"That's Colonel Grier," I exclaimed. "That's him—the Colonel I told you about, the one I met at the concert."

"Who cares?" Jed reached across the picture-strewn table and took my hand. "I've missed you, Sol. How've you been?"

"I'm well," I answered. I withdrew my hand but then placed both again in front of me, clasped, so that they were beside his long fingers, his palm half-open, and he leaned forward. His thumb was downcast, near my wrist, large beside my small bones.

"Do you want some coffee?" he asked.

I shook my head.

"That's right." He smiled. "You only take it in the mornings."

"Well, what was it you wanted to tell me?" I asked.

I watched his thumb on the table, the way absently it moved against his index finger, along the length of his carpal hollow. "What is it, Jed?"

"Would you like to go out for a while, watch a movie?"

"No," I said, "not that."

I SUPPOSE I WORRY Jed's figure in my mind, almost afraid that it might stir. I was a sorry person. Do I remember any terrible discipline in his mental habits, do I recall with fondness what he liked to read, did I debate whether his purposes were good or evil? There was something—muddy, I must admit, a kind of murky tenor, a sump of silt in my love. When something sinks in me, stupidly like an ache, what my recall poorly finds in the depths is not some noble emotion, a fine substance—but murk. The mess of the body. Soggy things. It distresses me. The last things that surface, in this distinctly unhealthy reverie, are gross farm animals and such, perhaps appropriate in this view of the Hudson Valley, the oleographic grime of the farms in this distance, beyond the river. My thoughts revert to muddy matters, cows, animals stupidly savoring cud, and nearby maybe is some pig, snorting in a hovel.

"WHAT'S THIS?" I looked down at what we had cast off to the floor, with our pants and shirts and shoes. The apartment was musty but clean—it had a visual sense of decay, but an actual surface tidiness. On the floor, I found these aberrant bits of newspaper, gray, almost incoherent pictures on the clean, vacuumed rug.

Photos of diplomats in drunken poses.

I moved off the bed to look at one picture. I put on my shirt to get the photograph. Jed laughed at me. He, on the other hand, like a dumb colossus, lay around naked, a sweaty beast atop unironed sheets.

"That's Uncle Gianni." I picked up the article. "What are you collecting, a society album?"

Jed held a cigarette, ashes trembling against the wheezing, hyperventilating fan.

"You know, the others would like to see you," he said, his face screwed up as he spat out smoke. He coughed.

I stood up to open a window.

A snaking light fell on him, a gold, uneven thread.

"Don't," Jed said. "Pull the curtain down."

"Why are you guys all chain-smokers?" I asked. "Does the revolution require emphysema?" I did what he told me. Looking at the sooty cloth, I saw faded coconut trees stamped on the curtain, with serial leaves arranged between each printed tree, like patterns in a math lesson.

I can still see, with eyes closed, everything about that room.

Sometimes, I think, I still walk in it—I am locked in that parallel, inescapable place. I have disoriented moments. Snatches of furniture distend—palm-printed lamps attaining the heft of Greek pillars, creepy creeping fixtures. Bamboo and baobab visions. Strange dislocation: objects shifting while I stay, stunted, in place.

"Didn't you think it was funny," I said, looking surreptitiously out the window, clutching the curtain, then staring back at Jed, "those cloak-and dagger-confessions at our meetings with the group, the false names?"

"No," Jed said, shaking his head. "Not at all. In fact, I wish you'd come back—come back to the university. Don't leave for America yet."

"How's Soli?" I asked.

"She's fine. She's leaving school for good after Christmas. You know she dropped out of school?"

"I'm not surprised."

"She made the decision to work full-time in the movement."

"Have you seen her since?"

"No," he said. "They say she's happy. She'll be organizing factory workers in the city. It's what she wants to do."

"She's throwing her life away."

"No, she's giving it."

"Her form of soul-searching, I guess," I said.

"Not everyone is in an existential crisis, Sol." His body turned upon the bed. "Some people choose clear-eyed what they want to do."

He stared at me. When a male body is unaware like that, and it seems to lose its consequence, its old terrible hold, one wonders how on earth this absurd bastard, hoary ball of hair and limp bedraggled lump, ever held one's attention at all.

I started giggling at his look of gravity while his penis drooped.

"Stop it," he said.

"Your prick looks funny."

"I know. It always looks better on you."

He adjusted himself and blew smoke across the fan, which, in the afterthought of its wheeze, blew smoke back to him. He coughed again.

"Well, Jed, you should have come to that party, if you were so interested in it. I look hideous in these pictures, my God."

Jed came to stand beside me. He looked at the news pictures in my hand.

"Who's that?" he asked. His flat, pink nail pointed to a face in a group.

I peered closely. "I think that's the general. Tom. He's been in Manila for quite a while."

"With the LOTUS military group," Jed said.

"Yeah," I said, "LOTUS. That American operation. You know what? Their headquarters are just around the corner from here. You can walk to it. Beyond the British library."

"I know. And him?"

"That's the Colonel. The one I told you about. An educated man. He says he did a master's thesis on the Philippine-American War."

"Really? And what was his thesis?" Jed held his cigarette unaccompanied on his mouth, idly moving his hands.

His cigarette clamped to his mouth like that, he looked like a boy playing a game, his eyes narrowed.

"You look funny," I said.

"So what was his thesis?"

"I told you. He studied the tactics of the Samar rebels, you know, in the last years of the Philippine-American War, and explained how the American containment, their methods of war—"

"The retaliations in Balangiga, after the rebel massacre," Jed said. "The American atrocities during the war."

"Yes, the Samar massacres—the howling wilderness. His thesis was that, in many of its details, the war with the Philippines foreshadowed Vietnam. But he saw it only through a military lens. He claims he's apolitical. Who knows? The idea wasn't so original, he says. Anyway, Francis Ford Coppola had thought the same thing."

"You mean Joseph Conrad," Jed said.

"Hah! The Colonel wrote it in the early years before he was drafted into Vietnam, he said. His point was that knowledge of indigenous tactics would be useful in a modern war, in similar terrain. But his focus was on Filipino methods, on the ruses of tropical guerrillas during the Phil-Am War. He's interesting. He was introduced to me as a scholar. He's a smart man who looks like a redneck. He invited me to see a collection of his: he collects coins."

"Why don't you?" said Jed.

"See his coins?"

"You should," said Jed.

"That's funny. Ma says the same thing. You know, he kept using those old colonial terms—the language of old history books about the Philippines. It was like being in a time warp, especially after the lectures with the group: going back to the days of 1899, the Spanish-American War chronicles, stuff like that—the racist speech of ancient times."

"Not so ancient," Jed said, "if it's still walking about. Wasn't that strange, talking to that man after the lectures with Ka Noli?"

"How do you know that?"

"You just said," he said.

"Yes. It was strange."

"You know what your parents are doing with that colonel, don't you?"

"Yes."

"So you know what your parents are doing with Colonel Grier?"

"They're trying to get him to approve a shipment, a big contract of military equipment. Expensive brand-new arms. It's a multimillion-dollar deal. Really. Big bucks. You have no idea. They need his word, his go-ahead."

"And why is that?" Jed said.

"You know, the Philippine-U.S. military pact. The Philippine government buys matériel for its army at the discretion of the Amer-

icans. One of the colonial conditions for independence was the sign-
ing of the 1947 pact that created the Joint U.S. Military Assistance
Group. With LOTUS as its administrative arm, the pact remains in
effect. It won't go until the U.S. bases go. Which means never. The
hand of God couldn't make them go, who knows. It sets—I mean it
advises on—Philippine military supplies, army training, and so on.
President Manuel Roxas signed it, but what choice did the guy have?
Anyone could see that it is a good way to remain in power: keep on
the good side of the Americans, whose businesses in turn rake in
millons from the arms trade with anticommunist states. The cleverness of the colonizer was that it gave us independence, but it kept its
hold by controlling the material fact that keeps a government in
power—its military."

"Very good," said Jed. "Are you sure you haven't read the *PSR*?"

"Ha-ha. You don't need the *PSR* to know—just watch my parents. They are upset with the Colonel. They've always had their way
with the old guy, General Tom, but Tom is sick. It seems the Colonel's a stickler. He wants public biddings, transparency, et cetera."

"He just wants his own people to have a slice of the pie.
That's all."

"No. I don't know if he's interested," I said. "As I said, he doesn't
seem political."

"Everyone's political, Sol."

"I mean, he just doesn't seem interested in my parents' concern.
The Philippine army uses secondhand arms, old stuff. We don't
really bother with new guns. We cannot afford them. That's what
my Uncle Gianni says. The new deal my parents want is a new
era—a big military boondoggle. They swear the insurgents are
moving from the countryside into the city, and new arms are needed,

a new policy. They want, I think, an exclusive contract. I don't know if the Colonel is even interested in dealing with that issue, buying new matériel or not; but my parents want him to okay their deal."

"Very good," Jed said again, smiling approvingly. "Good girl. But I don't care about your parents' deal," said Jed. "That's their business. You know what Colonel Grier's real specialty is, don't you?"

I shook my head.

"Counterinsurgency."

"I guess."

"He came specifically to Manila to train militia groups. The rest is not my concern." He moved away to stub out his cigarette on a tin ashtray, shaped like a volcano. Dust motes floated in the cracks of light, mute indivisible creatures. The room itself, I now remember, was organized rather unconvincingly around that theme: a dreary tropical motif.

Brown-dotted seashells, like turtles' backs, were scattered about, embossed with faded ink—beach souvenirs on the brink of some revelation. The green sofa had sketchy palm drawings on its arms. The curtains had coconuts. The lamp stand was a bamboo monstrosity, with watercolor bamboo shoots grimed into its sides, more like mold than paint. The lampshade, a ghastly, now-unanimous version of puke, was meant to portray bright parrots amid jungle cover, but the fabric had worn out and all you saw were vague traces of the birds' casques and the watery smudge of parrots' plumes.

"He's a specialist in jungle warfare," Jed was saying, walking to the window. "He's a Vietnam veteran. A decorated POW. His is an interesting story—if you're on his side. He spent forty-nine months in captivity in North Vietnam. One of very few—only around thirty or so—to escape his captors. He's a celebrated guy. Now he's an expert in guerrilla tactics; he teaches men how to encircle villages, how to kill specific targets. Specialist killings, torture. He's a specialist in methods of counterinsurgency: infiltrating cadres, extracting confessions, inspiring surrender. He comes from teaching at Fort Bragg."

"The School of the Assassins."

"Yes. The government is beefing up its military forces. It's setting up CAFGU: you know what that is."

"The paramilitary groups. They are turning private armies into special forces."

"The government is using private armies for its own purposes. How do they think that won't rise up to bite them? The new militias—it's all in the papers now."

"Of course. I've read about it. I'm not dumb, even though I quit your movement. It looks like a positive sign, for the communist rebels. The government is taking them seriously."

"Sol. You're nuts. Is that how your father explains his deals?" he asked.

"So the U.S. and the Philippine military are assembling forces against the communists, the New People's Army," I said. "It's just one murderer going after another."

He shook his head at me, almost sadly.

"It's even bigger than that, who knows," he said slowly. "The communist rebels are small fry. They're inconsequential."

"What do you mean?"

"These men—your father and his friends—they are always thinking ahead. For them, there's bigger game than ragged revolutionaries. Do you think they care about us, I mean, really? They see the big picture. Everyone knows the rebel army has no teeth, no guns. I mean, the rebels collect goddamned copper five-centavo coins for bullets. The rebels will not make a move even if a million peasants are killed in Manila. But these men—they just need a good reason for a deal. Commies in the countryside are just fodder. Small fry."

I looked at the clippings.

"This was a party to clinch it," Jed pointed to the pictures.

"I don't think so. No. My parents are not certain they have a deal."

"Or maybe the deal is on the way."

"Here he is," I said. "That's a better picture of the general, without his mask. General Tom. He came as Frankenstein, you know. Oddly enough. He's a sick man. He has an iron lung. Or a metallic heart. Or something. Our Tom, as my mom calls him. He's an old friend. They like him." I looked at another picture of Tom singing a ballad with Uncle Gianni. Their features were almost unrecognizable, blurred by their straining gestures as much as by the paper's cheap pulp. The old American general's shadowy figure, singing into the mike, was circled in blue ink.

"Why is he circled?" I asked. "The colonel's circled, too."

"They're important guys," Jed said.

11

THERE WAS, IN fact, a peaceful prelude. A day or so. Before the feverish fortnight of activity, we took these long walks, avoiding the holiday crowds if we could. We talked about books, about random, neutral sights. (I pointed out the street, Elcano, the oddly placed name in cramped Binondo of the false circumnavigator, the one who took the spoils of the dead Magellan—"what funny bits of knowledge you have," he said, kissing me on the brow. He knew of a beggar, a wispy child on U.N. Avenue, who looked like a replica of our erstwhile comrade, Buddyboy Wong, the Beatlemaniac, and he always passed by to give the look-alike kid some coins). Sometimes, it's true, Manong Babe drove us; but most of the time we traveled by ourselves.

That lone, magically quiet Sunday in Ermita, when the sidewalks were empty except for trash, cats, and the liquid dreaminess of morning light, we kept walking. There were makeshift homes of sleeping families parked on the sidewalks, the first time I had come across them close enough to look. Jed stopped at one dwelling, an open cart, peering through the structure at the barely constructed furniture, the mundane details of disrepair, while the family, a mother, father, and sons, slept softly, their dreams offered to us. Jed's face was serious, without pity, his brow, shorn of his curls, looking oddly bereft; I stopped to wait for him, and he turned back to me, again saying nothing.

Maybe Jed's subsequent actions had in them the same humanitarian resolve as his pitiless expression; I would like to make excuses. My head aches, recalling those weeks, so knotted and tangled have they become.

I remember that walk down spaghetti streets and closed restaurants, through an eerie, sleeping city. So spookily beautiful was Manila's rare silence, but inconvenient and disappointing, too; we couldn't get into the bookstore we looked for. It was closed.

And in the climax of the morning, we were stopped for a traffic violation.

Jed's sheepish face as he looked at me, his ears red as the policeman approached, was amusing. He was flustered. I'd never seen him lose his calm, and he ended up overpaying the bribe, I noticed, handing over one hundred pesos in his confusion. He looked at me, his embarrassed, half-turned gaze bright, and all I could do was laugh.

I remember that, walking the streets, my hand in his, I felt luminous, inwardly, in his presence; maybe it was because of his own glowering, glowing figure—the heat of his pale cheeks and burnish of his hair. In that day's limbo, he went with me everywhere I wished. The warmth it generated in me (a silly, respondent giddiness that surprised me, always) when I glanced at him, at Jed's pettish, distant gaze, walking quietly beside me, was a constant thrum. Disappeared now, lost, traces legally unknown. Gone. The word itself seems abandoned, a stripped, unfinished syllable. But at the time, he was by my side, a man hunched by thought, with squinting eyes gazing wistfully at the pavement. I sometimes felt awkward, too ready with speech, beside him.

Our wandering had enough language for shared recall: "Remember that night we painted a sign by what turned out to be a guava tree?"

"The fruit was raw and bitter; we threw it away with our paint."

"I didn't," I said, "I kept it and ate it. I love guavas."

"Remember how, as children, we could just sit in the gazebo and hide from everyone and make our plans for justice and democracy, with G.I. Joes and fighter planes? I did that."

"I didn't," I said, "we were never children in gazebos together, Jed. Though that's a pleasant thought."

"I thought my mother was the most beautiful woman in the world and I didn't know what I would do without her, when I was a boy; I used to have dreams about losing my mother to cannibals and outlaws."

"I have dreams about finding things. Hairpins. A book."

A̋ND WHEN JED asked me to go and meet them, finally I did. Walking to the shop with Jed, I felt a woozy creep, I must admit—the onslaught of my recidivating sickness, a glut gathered in my gut. There was also the way being a pedestrian full-tilt in the city's mob still dazed me. All my life, I'd been taught never to cross a street. To get to a shop up ahead on the other side, my mother would call up Manong Babe from his dungeon in the hotel parking lot and wait for him to stop at the curb, and so, if she could help it, I never walked through traffic.

But in those days, we walked and walked; an endless parade of our anonymous selves, mingling with the city. I felt that slow slush in my loins, my legs hurt. Beside Jed, his footsteps longer than mine, I skipped along and then stopped keeping up. By the shop, he waited for me, then he came over, shaking his head.

"You keep walking behind me," he said. "Is that a habit or an accusation?"

He took me by the hand.

We stepped up to the shop and looked around.

"There he is," Jed muttered. "Come on."

Together, we moved toward the man in the corner, indistinguishable in the crowd of shopworkers, salesmen, idlers and commuters, people who seemed to come from nowhere and make up the city. In the city's daily maelstrom, everywhere this bustle of everyday acts, eating, walking, shopping, spitting, staring at women, crossing a street—all of this did make Manila seem wonderfully alive, maybe even significant, but at the same time improbable and illusory to me. The multiplication of so many mundane gestures in so many lives compelled thought to shut down. And walking like that, I'd feel that Jed and I, hands clasped, were the only warm, living creatures in this swamp of humanity. Or maybe it was the other way around: they were alive, and we were the city's ghosts.

In his corner, Ka Noli in rubber slippers, with dry, uncut hair, face oily and growing a mustache, sparse like slivers of rice in early season, looked pretty much like the men around him, drinking coffee and reading *People's Tonight*.

He looked up and acknowledged us by offering a cigarette. I took a seat in a cramped space between the counter and another occupied table. Jed, his legs too long for the chairs, looked out of

place at first. How would a guy like Jed ever disappear in the countryside, looking like that? But when he lit up the cigarette, hunched
in a denim jacket like the others, bending low to the table, pale-
faced and dumbly smoking, he looked like anyone else, a tired
pedestrian in a pastry shop.

We sat for a moment, exchanging greetings; they ordered coffee. Ka Noli was high-spirited. It was the first time I had seen him
outside, in broad daylight. I always saw him at the teach-ins hidden
in a corner, lost in shadows and obsessive about doors; he liked to sit
facing doors. He still had that doomed cough, so that his chronic
clamor punctuated, in my mind, the progress of the country's
history.

He spoke in a dexterous mix of Tagalog and English, street
talk, and on his tongue it seemed more vigorous than either language; he made stray comments, mostly jokes, in the way, among
Filipinos, an easy familiarity arises among people who see someone
again to whom they are related, though they barely know them.

Ka Noli's lightness made me feel at ease.

"Did you get the pictures?" asked Jed.

"Cool *ka lang*," Ka Noli said, waving a hand at him. "Cool it,
makulit." He chided Jed. "Let's have coffee first. *Relaks*." He slumped
even more in his chair, turning to me: "Can he save the world by hur-
rying? Like White Rabbit, you know. Hello, Alice. In Wonderland.
Be careful of this guy: *tarantado yan*. Coffee here's *da* best." And he
took a sip. The place was called Da King Donuts, a miserable pun.
We watched the shoppers coming in with their bags and carrying out
boxes of cakes by the dozen, a steady flow of unsteady pastry.

"You know what I want for Christmas?" Ka Noli said. He
spoke in clear English.

"What?" I asked.

"A skateboard. I wonder where the kids at Luneta get them? They sniff rugby, then they skateboard. *Galing. Yan ang* trip!"

"Imported from Saudi," I said.

Ka Noli made a whistling sound. We turned our heads to see what he was looking at.

"Hah," I said, "look, it's Edwin."

Edwin Cardozo was walking toward us, looking like a painter down on his luck, wearing a ponytail and trench coat, without his umbrella. The two men nodded when he reached us. Standing before us, he took one hand from his pocket and waved at me. When he smiled, I saw that he looked changed, but I couldn't quite place why.

I laughed: "Fancy seeing you here. Have a seat, Ed. I thought you'd be home in Samar."

"Christmas makes more sense in the city. You need a nice, vulgar commercial setting for Christmas," Edwin said, smiling broadly.

That's it, I thought: Edwin had finally gotten rid of his braces.

Edwin sat down, taking the chair nearest the counter, all white-toothed. He was even smooth-shaven, as if newborn.

"So, what's up?" I asked. "Small world, huh?"

"Sorry I'm late."

Ka Noli nodded: "That's okay. Jed just got here."

"You know him?" I asked Ka Noli. I looked at Jed.

Edwin was very amused. "Not at all, Sol. What do you think?" he asked.

"You know Ka Noli," I stated in confusion. "But you were never at his lectures."

"The world *is* small, Sol," Jed said, patting my hand. "They're actually long-lost brothers."

"We're twins," said Ka Noli. "He's the ugly one, I'm the good-looking one. Separated at birth. We just found each other."

Edwin was beginning to giggle.

"What's so funny?" I asked.

"I thought you knew I was with the group," Edwin said. "I thought you were just pretending not to know. Give me five, man."

Jed stood up and slapped his hand.

"I had my suspicions," I said. "Don't get bigheaded. It was pretty obvious: you protested too much."

"It was a good disguise, don't you think? Coca-Cola philosopher. He's good at pretending to be the exact opposite of who he is," Jed said, settling into his chair, still chuckling.

"I thought you hated rallies," I said.

"I do," Edwin said. "That's not my business."

"You pretended to be a book-lover at the British Council," I said.

"No," said Edwin. "I was not pretending." He grinned, his newly liberated mouth gleaming. "I like books."

"You were stalking me all over Diliman."

"Not really. I was just following orders."

"But why? How long have you been part of the group?" I asked.

"Since high school," Edwin said. He was serious now. "Since I was at Science High. I recruited him."

Jed nodded. "He recruited me. In the dorm. At chess."

"I thought Soli recruited you."

"I introduced Jed to Soli."

"So you pretended to be a jerk, you pretended you only wanted to play chess."

"We really did play chess," Jed revised. "It's just Edwin was very bad at it."

"Ed's one of our best," Ka Noli said. "At least, in your area. One of the best recruiters."

"I'm very disappointed," I shook my head. Ed began grinning again. I reached across the table and started punching him in the shoulders.

"Stop," he said, moving closer to the counter. "Stop!"

"That's what you get," I said. "Commie."

"Sssh!" Ka Noli said.

Edwin's chair toppled to the floor, and he fell with it. I bent to the floor to get at him.

"Let's leave," Ka Noli announced, looking around at the shoppers. "*Hoy, tama na yan!*" He strode off.

Jed picked Edwin up from the floor, then put the chairs and table in order, and, running to the door, we followed the smoke of Ka Noli's figure.

"No," I said. "Don't even think of it. Don't you dare ask me again."

Jed sat on the bed. He shrugged his shoulders, looking at Ka Noli.

Ka Noli was by the window, the one that looked out onto another dark, unpainted concrete slab, framed by the rotting curtains.

Edwin orbited the bed, his raincoat still on, hands in his pockets.

"It's just a thought," said Ka Noli.

"Is that why I was recruited in the first place?" I asked.

"No. This has nothing to do with that," said Edwin. "That was a different—sector."

"This is very different work," said Ka Noli.

"I would say it is. How do you know you can trust me? You're crazy." I looked at them. "You think you can get away with a plan like that? There would be goons with guns on you in a minute. You'd be swimming in the Pasig with dead dogs, no questions asked."

"Changes in the political arena require tactical reconsiderations."

"We've planned it all out, we have ideas."

"We've been on the lookout," added Edwin. "We know what can be done."

I shook my head.

"It is just a request," said Ka Noli. "An exploration. We shouldn't have bothered with you."

"Don't mention it," I said.

Jed looked with warning at Ka Noli. He sat closer to me on his bed.

"Forget it, Sol," Jed said. Ka Noli moved impatiently at his gesture. "Forget we mentioned it. I just thought—"

"You don't," I said. I put my hands on my face. "I can't believe—"

"How about this?" Edwin asked.

"No," Jed said. "Look, guys, she said no. I thought she would."

"Then why did you bring us here?" asked Ka Noli.

"I hoped otherwise," Jed said. "I'm sorry."

"Look, maybe if I show her what I have," Edwin interrupted. "Maybe she'd like to see these."

Edwin stopped wandering, and I looked up. He stood before me, by the coffee table. He lifted something from his coat, what he had been hiding, and from beneath his shirt, clumsily, he took out a large Manila envelope, the cheap kind used by messengers, with that fuzzy surface, a crumpled embrace in his palms.

Carefully, he shook something into his hand. Slowly, it eased out of the envelope. On the table, he placed an eight-by-eleven sheet in front of me. The wayward gust from the fan ruffled it. He placed one of the spotty seashells on the picture's edge.

I looked at it and shook my head; I covered my eyes with my hands and sat still. No one moved or talked.

Then Edwin said: "There are others. I have many more like it. All different, all the same. These—" and I heard paper settling in front of me, a thick, soft flutter, "these are all from one village. There are others. And if you like, you can visit the place itself."

Set like that, arrayed like posters in a shop, the group of pictures looked like a jumble of grays and blacks, and you wished it to remain so. You wished it to remain an optical mystery. That textured abscess, the dark abyss, for instance, could be the heart of a banana flower, or maybe a close-up recording of a narra's gnarls. And the little roils of white and gray, raised and bracketed amid a blood-seeming dark flood, looked somewhat like a mother's pregnant, triumphant skin, undulant flesh, which you discovered in slow motion. But then these volumes of gray moved and fluttered, like a riverbed losing its water as you watch, and the spatial matter of mud becomes more of a tint than a crevice, shadow rather than soil. Then it suggested a sea, a garbage facility, a severed hand.

A dark, terrifying head.

It was the severed head of a child. The darknesses (you began to note them with some calm) were maybe her eyes and mouth, grimed and bloody, one with the earth. The larger, bleeding blacks, you saw, were palm leaves or banana trunks—a domestic jungle. Coconuts and rocks and a hut loomed beyond the disordered limbs, the fantastic rot on her arms, her repose, separate, on the ground. A Nike shoe on her foot. Separate from her was a body with legs upended, like a woman in labor. Her skirt a clump above her waist. A private army aimed at her parts. I moaned. But I looked.

I could tell the other was a child because of the adults around her—full-bodied creatures lying silently aground, in the last gestures of their dying. One woman, all covered in dried mud, cradled the child's still body, the way the sleeping woman in the cart in Ermita had held her son; except that in the black and white picture, the woman held one whose eyes were lost, indecipherable—her head had rolled away in the mud, toward me: foreground in the picture, the black heart of the abyss. It hovered in my vision, the missing head of a headless ghost.

I rushed up to leave. I rushed to the bathroom and stood above the sink, willing myself to retch.

A dry, heartless cough came out.

In the rusting mirror, I saw the child's head, its wavering blacknesses, as if it gleamed in my dark eyes.

"Are you okay?" Jed asked when I came out.

I sat down.

"What are those?" I asked, barely able to ask. "Where did you get them?"

The three men were still, and except for Ka Noli's coughing and the flap of Edwin's coat, and the gasps of the fan that kept lifting the edges of a picture, disturbing it, like air in a helicopter's wake, we made no sound or movement.

"That corner there, Sol. See that line, that shadow?" Edwin said.

I nodded, looking.

"That's a gun: an automatic. Your parents sold it to the government, through the auspices of Don Mariano Morga, friend of the Secretary, who in turn fronts for the big fish—a long chain of trade, just buying and selling, that's all. And that's the trade's trajectory: perfectly angled, toward that child."

"There's a drive to speed up arrangements for these new forces, the civilian militias. Every so often they visit a village they suspect protects the rebels. That's the official gist. This is one of those operations. The government, of course, has its own reasons; your parents have theirs; the Secretary has his own. We have ours," Edwin explained, like a teacher.

"They can be stopped," Ka Noli said.

"We can at least send a message," Ed said.

"This man," Jed said. He plucked a piece of paper from his snare, the old newspaper photo of the general singing at Christmas, "this man is at the center of plans for the counterinsurgency. And this," he pointed to the American colonel standing almost primly in a velvet jacket in the circled photograph, "this man executes the plans. He came to Manila specifically for this. To run training in the countryside."

"Look at this, look at how neatly displayed they all are, the enemies of the people." Edwin spoke in his deadpan way, taking Jed's society pictures. He pointed to each figure as he archly labeled them, a facetious pose: "*Feudalista. Burukrata-kapitalista. Imperi-*

alista. Look at that: all neatly gathered under one roof. It's almost too neat, Sol."

"From your point of view," I said.

"We don't blame you."

"You're part of the solution."

"You can help us."

"You don't have to do it if you don't wish," Jed said, as if he were being kind.

"What do you want from me then?" I asked.

"Just some guns," said Edwin. "They're already in your parents' warehouses."

"We need the special kind, the brand-new ones."

"Which warehouse?"

"You know," said Jed. "And if you don't, we'll show you."

"That's it?" I asked. "That's all?"

"You don't have to if you don't wish," Jed said.

"But I could do so much more," I said.

12

THE COLONEL'S HOUSE was a choice location on Roxas Boulevard. Another trim, sweet lawn: the moist mulch of gardens. The smell of earth lingered with the waft of seawater in the marina beyond, a brief balm, and momentarily you forgot the diesel-plumed city. I was ushered into a wide, dark-floored living room in the colonial style: high-ceilinged, capacious, good enough for a minor ball. I heard a cry—a baby—as I passed a room. Then muted music in the background. Down a little corridor was the den. I entered a cubicle dominated by low glass counters set in velvet. There I found Colonel Arthur Grier, relaxed, politely dressed, already looking expansive. He was holding a glass of beer. He was expecting me.

I marked this day for him—the solstice. My birthday gift.

He looked older, softer in his home: as if at rest, he stopped holding in his tired age, that strenuous way he clutched his years, wild, unscrupulous birds, within his gut, his diaphragm and stiff shoulders; at home, he let them go, and the birds of his experience settled, soft flitting wings on his face, gaze and body, so that he looked what he was, a scarred fifty-eight-year-old man.

"Over here," he said, getting to the point. "This will interest you."

I moved toward the hoard at which he pointed: a pair of large silver coins, origin Acapulco, provenance Zamboanga, I believe he said. I was looking around the room, testing the layout in my mind, an interloper's stealthy obligations toward furniture, fixtures, and roaming, muffled servants.

"See," he said, "these are called the pillars of Hercules. The dos mundos, they call it. They have a literary history, if you must know."

"Hm?" I said.

"These are the dos mundos, the kind mentioned in *Treasure Island*. Also mentioned in Melville."

"*Moby-Dick*?"

"Yeah. Never read it myself. But that's what they say."

"The giant doubloon," I said, impressed.

I looked again at his catch. The so-called pillars on one large ovate coin were overlaid by what looked like chicken scratches.

"Why are they—?"

"A whole *real*," he continued with satisfaction, tapping on the glass. "I'm lucky I have a pair whole. They were cut into bits, you know, into half-*reales* and all that. Cut-up *reales* were legitimate tender. Literally, they were quartered. Quarters. See over there. Yes, I see what you're pointing at. Even those scratch marks, they tell us something—"

I glanced at a servant entering with a tray. I watched a palm leaf swaying from a window, over the shoulder of the uniformed houseboy: a framed view across from the door. I tried to guess the lengths of spaces. How many footsteps would one need?

"Chinese traders made marks on the coins—like a merchant

ledger—to check the silver. Chop marks. This type here: it was the most widely used legal tender of its time in the world," said the Colonel, shuffling around in his slippers, putting his bottle of beer back on the tray and taking a new one from the boy. "What would you like to drink, child? Beer? Coffee?" With his other hand, he tapped again on the glass: "This was legal tender even in the United States; precursor of the dollar, did you know that?"

I turned to him. I nodded respectfully. I surveyed his plunder.

"What about this?" I asked, pointing to a coin with a ribbon attached to it.

"That's an interesting one." As he drank some more, I heard his heavy, slow breaths; he smacked his tongue against his lips, licking away foam. "It's no coin. That's a medal of merit," he said. "You can see for which campaign."

"The war of 1899."

"The Philippine Insurrection. See? It's a beauty. I got it in pristine shape. It was minted for the American soldiers of 1899. The Philippine campaign. Here, hold it." He put down his beer, took a key from his shirt and lifted the glass. Gently, almost lovingly, with shaking fingers, he took the medallion from its velvet-laden case.

"I got this years ago, oh, in the late fifties. It was one of many designed just for that campaign. I was doing my thesis at the time, on leave from the army. My father gave this to me when I received my diploma. It's not too expensive. I keep it for sentimental reasons." He looked at me with a smile, as if I of all people, a student of history, should understand his pride. "We come from a long line of soldiers. My great-grandfather was in the Civil War. Do you know"—and he said this with narrowed, meditative eyes—"he was called on to join that Philippine campaign; he could have ended up in Samar, who knows: he could have been an actor in my thesis. Many veterans of the Civil War fought in the Philippines—Union and Confederate battled together bravely. They had a common enemy. But my great-grandfather Lieutenant Major Waller Augustus Grier died on the boat coming over to the Philippines. Isn't that strange? This medallion—it was one of my father's last gifts to me."

I held it in my hands. It was heavy, with that curiously lush patina of rust, a green-flecked wine color that settles on old metals, as much part of the beauty of collecting as the coin itself—the witness of time. And it was, at the same time, heavy in my hand, a barbaric weight, and my fingers trembled. I had to tighten my hold on it to look at it closely. And I felt it, a rude gush in me, a weeping rumble in my womb, at the sight of this souvenir so precious to Colonel Arthur Grier.

It had a raised, absurd palm tree, with unnatural coconuts hanging below its crown of leaves like scrota, and on the medallion's sinister half, its heraldic left, was a set of scales—"for justice and democracy," said Colonel Grier—and beside the scales was a lamp, for freedom. A wreath of letters garlanded the coin: "Philippine Insurrection 1899."

I felt my legs trembling, in that weakness that seemed to have nothing to do with the world around me but seemed allied to it nevertheless, these physical flashes before a dark, harmful swirl. I felt in me the bend of a river, a brooding, phosphorescent stream. I clutched the medal in my palm; my fingers could barely fold over its broad sides.

"Yes," I said, "I'd like some coffee."

The servant glided over and handed me a cup. He smiled a

broad, childish grin when I thanked him. I watched the boy as he left, his soft, shuffling footsteps sliding away in the hall.

"Careful," said Colonel Grier, "it's very hot. Sugar?"

"Yes," I said. I looked for a chair. I sat on a desk, still holding the medal, its stiff ribbon hanging down the curve of my thumb. I sat down, agitated. I put the coffee on the desk. My other hand tugged at the ribbon.

As the Colonel leaned over and gave me the sugar, I hefted the medallion again, testing its width. I took the sugar from Colonel Grier, poured some in my coffee and stirred. Then I dipped the medallion into my burning cup. Carefully, slowly. Vaguely, I remembered something from my traps of reading, how certain chemical mutations occur on rusted metal, especially on aging coins, especially in steaming water. I stirred the coffee with Colonel Grier's medallion, stirring and stirring the dull stream. I watched with curiosity the dark liquid's slow, thick swirl, its calm vortex of memory, of long, old years and weeping children, men and women, from both sides of the ocean, then and now, this almost dilatory reverie as I spooned more sugar into the coffee, stirring with the Colonel's precious, loudly clinking medallion.

"What the fuck—what are you doing—That coffee's acidic, goddamn—you're destroying my medallion! Motherfuck—Give me that, you bitch!"

I see my figure scampering, like a cat. Or was that a calculated stammer, my swift departure from the room. I walked out of Colonel Grier's mansion as fast as I could. I startled the houseboy, who met me in the hallway with a kind of happy, unspeaking look of camaraderie, of kinship, maybe because he was a kid like me, and I ran past the bedrooms, sprinting as if I had a ball at my feet. I'm a winger after all, and I raced. I almost bumped into a lady, a loose-haired, humming blonde, from Kansas, and I raced past the lazy windows of swaying palms, through the lawn to the limousine, where Manong Babe was waiting for me, as always. Always ready for me, whenever I happened to need his help.

THAT WHITE HOUSE on Roxas. The bougainvillea headquarters in New Manila. His gym. Golfing jaunts at Mandaluyong. Even the soccer tournament before New Year's. Possibilities were perused, responsibilities declared. Amid ugly cigarette smoke, the hoary clank of the beastly fan, within the decaying walls of the apartment, we argued, and it seemed to me, as I said, that even the objects in the room attained a nervous refinement. Their outlines trembled in my eye, as if the room itself had gained this hypersensitive awareness of life, a troubled vitality.

Our quarters—the single bed, our corny props (the jungle metaphors of the furniture), the lusty vibrations of the fan—have this dreadful clarity, like those surreally factual Dutch paintings, in which even light is nailed down and shadows are carved in place, just so. It seemed that places and objects, physical matters, gained a strident existence; while my own motives and purposes, the soul, as it were, of the matter, have this lank, depressed substance, an unfleshed state.

I was aware that Manila had shapes, sounds and pigments that had not occurred to me before, my senses tuned to its excitable parade, its pendulous rains, the mint, bellyish look of its sky, rash, wounded people walking at a tilt, and the different cries of grass— the clamorous insects I never noticed in the cracks on the streets.

The Christmas season gave all this a nightmarish velocity as our hushed speeches and the loud spirit of the times seemed to swell a Manila envelope of tragedy.

I remember listening to Edwin, that limp, owlish boy, and how I forgot to marvel at the things he said, his tense abstraction (I discovered it was his salient numbing vice) inserted in our heated conversations. It was as if, stripped of his dilettante disguise, he'd turned into the vitriolic essence of the ideologue.

"Foreign monopoly capitalism and the comprador bourgeoisie hinder the growth of industry: they must be opposed by the people's democratic revolution."

Saliva still rained through his unbraced mouth, oddly enough.

"The foreign policy of the bourgeois Philippine government is dictated by U.S. imperialism and internal reactionary classes: they must be opposed by the national democratic state."

"Just kill the fuckers," Jed said from the bed, lazily.

IT WOULD BE too much if I could recall our exact phrases. I know I could crib mendaciously from the group's published Bylaws and Programmes and still be true to the spirit of Edwin's spit, his ponderous bile. And Jed's laconic venom might have, as you suspect, this improvisational, slapdash aspect, just to keep the plot along: a significant dash would do just as well, a violent aposiopesis on the page. It was Jed who was the calming figure, a center of repose and introspection but with an adamant intensity, that smoked concentration. And should I talk about Ed and Ka Noli's gradual disappearance, how they fairly vanished as the days progressed, so that by the end Jed and I were mostly on our own, and I am left to imagine their furtive, paranoiac presence at our few encounters, the way it seemed each was suspicious even of the dust holes in the walls.

I wonder now if I have made their presence up.

As for me—I can barely tolerate the memory of it, my pathetic figure. I don't mean the act, the plot itself. Newspapers, pundits, sociologists and even psychics have already made hay of its stink.

No: I mean my inexplicable bloom.

I felt that the world suddenly seemed clarified; and in this incandescent room, I, too, began to glow. My role in it all was a gradual unfolding—I had always longed to be a part. It was as if, oddly, I had finally discovered myself. I had found my voice and my value and my purpose. In making plans for the day, the time, the victim, I acquired, if I recall right, an almost offensive insight, a scary, concise reasoning, and confidence. It's true. Plotting a murder built self-esteem.

In hindsight, our self-importance was predictable—but depressing. We had this increasing notion of ourselves, as if this seedy, pat vengeance gave us dignity. I do not even talk of glamour, something shallow, tabloidy. No, I talk of self-respect, honor. An inflated notion of virtue infected our brains. Or maybe it kept us going like the target object (a nail, a mold on the wall) that you need to stare at in prayer in order to keep from losing concentration and feeling like a fraud.

I suppose it's true of anyone whipped into the eye of a busy, seething project (let's call it), no matter how it was one got there. You feel your confidence level is up—then that superman, Nietzschean, egomongering stuff comes later. Especially if there's any slightly (okay, let's say frankly) diabolical aspect to it—a hellish, Raskolnikov factor.

The fact is, if I may state so, I am demoralized, remorseful now (tepid, tepid word, but we'll let it pass), as I find language, roaming images for my recall. My own heart lurches—as in a slim, shaky step, the airy, uncomprehending slip before the avalanche—when I think of it—this abyss, this fall from the travertine ledge—into which I have launched.

But I can't help it, I am also amused. In this sick way, like a secret laugh beneath a hand. I'm amused by our approximal, jejune dialogue (that is what we were), our morbid, fanatical lines, the loud, ludicrous intensity of my mind's movie, even as I note, with the background crescendo of a disheartening bass in my chest, the amoral progress of those off-kilter, off-putting scenes.

13

JED POINTED THE building out to me as we drove to Uncle Gianni's soccer tournament: Holy Innocents' Day—December 28—into a new year's cheer!

"The Colonel's residence, up ahead," he muttered, driving on.

"Roxas is too busy," I said, shaking my head.

"We're not targeting him."

"What?"

"I want the General."

"But I thought—"

"I want the General. He's the big, public fish. We want him."

"But he's dying anyway," I said. "Let his heart kill him. Whereas the Colonel—"

"We want the big man."

I was silent as we passed the white house, with its neat lawn. I saw a lumbering figure move on the far side of the garden. I turned away. I did not glance back at the Colonel's house.

"By all means," I said. "Bomb Tom away."

"It was that bad," Jed asked, though it was a statement. He was concentrating on the road and not looking at me. "You know what I think," he said. He turned to me.

"What?"

"You really just don't like that colonel."

I didn't speak.

He turned away, staring at the road, holding back a grin: "You know it's not personal, Sol. You do know that's not the point of the exercise."

MY FATHER'S WAREHOUSE was close to the decayed parts of the harbor, which rambled on into the slums built by smugglers and sailors. Gnawed, Spanish-era residences, eminently decaying, were strewn along our path.

Once, from these homes, old traders smelled without cease the coming and going of their fortunes. They brought European brocade and fancy lingerie for Manila's lost generations, the blight of emigrants after Magellan. It wasn't just a Spanish scene: close to the water, Chinese settlers confirmed the rumor of their kinship with the globe whenever they sniffed the salt breeze. The heavy air brought junks—wind-driven receptacles of silks, lacquerware, sandalwood cabinets, chickens, which were exchanged regularly for far-flung goods. Silver from Acapulco. Mindoro's birds' nests. Butuan's trinkets. Sulu's pearls. Transubstantiation was the harbor's theme: desire into doubloons. In this way, Manila, ancient stopping place, port of exchange, was a restless place for those who were only passing through. This might explain its wildly cosmopolitan hunger, even in the early seventeenth century, when Siamese chiefs and Muslim pirates were already part of age-old trade.

My family's business, deep into the twentieth, continued the city's old preoccupations.

Jed drove through side streets following the shoreline obscured by tenements and commercial buildings. Soon we reached solid cement blocks, streets that seemed to consist of garages or walls. The shipping companies' trucks were regular patrons of ghost-town streets, and pedestrians walked at their own risk; still, some homes thrived, displaying clotheslines and potted plants in the windows, and junkyards reached up to the roads, where kids played among old tires and rotting tricycle skeletons.

Down a long dirt road we turned into a sunken compass of green; the well-kept area could be turned into a double-decker soccer field overnight. On each side during the right season you'd find a pair of fluttering goals. Two games could be played simultaneously; not the full-length eleven-a-side, but maybe up to seven players each. It was a scheme I had had in high school, a century ago, to embellish my résumé for the schools I had planned to attend. Soccer for Scholars. To notch up points for the Ivy League, I rounded up a bunch of kids from different charities in Makati and hosted soccer clinics for a month, with a finale for the children and their families, a tournament, a spectacle, including medals, most valuable athletes, and a lot of hot dogs. It was a whimsical activity, of pure Uncle Gianni design. The Philippines, after all, is a basketball country, and soccer was an expatriate, anachronistic sport, in the past played locally mainly by the Spaniards, called *coños* without irony.

That was how the Mini-World Cup National Tournament came about.

Uncle Gianni had thought out all the trappings of my original event. My father had paid for everything, including the nets and uniforms, the construction of stands, state-of-the-art toilets. It was worth it, he thought. Uncle Gianni ended up using the field afterward for his own games. That, in full, was how he came to sponsor this holiday bash for his colleagues, friends and hangers-on. The day was a prologue to the smoke and debris of New Year's, coming before the participants' deep, well-deserved hangovers, a long weekend of revelry and stupor.

I had tried to warn Jed about it, but nothing could really prepare one for Uncle Gianni's event deep in Manila's bowels, a conceptual spectacle in the tropical heat.

The show had already begun, balloons were up, and far off in the grassy open-air plot a loudspeaker blared dance music, which we heard from as far away as the gravel parking lot. A few drivers loitered in the dust, but most were out on the fields: it seemed to me the drivers were the most avid fans of the games. From this distance, I could already make out Uncle Gianni's voice—whether it was my radar imagining the tenor of past events or, in fact, his hoarse, actual presence, excited and conspicuous, publicly exhorting his friends. This muffled, mounting microphone bleat reached us up on the gravel.

Stopping on a height before we descended into the compound, I pointed him out to Jed; and as I said, nothing could prepare one for the sight in Manila of Uncle Gianni in casual array, with a wireless mic in hand, emceeing the event, this time, for a change, in complete Texan costume, knives glinting on his boots, a distinct, I hope ironic, ten-gallon hat, and, I could barely tell and yet I knew, a daintily folded kerchief on his sunburned neck.

They were all there, athletes and alcoholics, dressed in their sweats or in what passed for sportsman gear, these ghosts of the galleon trade. Milanese leather-goods makers, French attachés, German restaurateurs, English salesmen, American pharmaceutical agents, Spanish opportunists, African oilmen, Dutch beach bums, Canadian do-gooders, Japanese engineers, all the Filipino oligarchs who fed from their hands, and, at this event, a lost, blue-eyed Mormon, a sweaty gate-crasher whom we bumped into as we marched to the main fields.

People were arriving and strolling about. Many were seminaked: obese men in transparent shorts, fine-boned women in backless shirts; but this lone, scared-looking youth wore the white shirt, dark suit, and tight tie of his trade, his raw, scratched face sautéing in the sun.

"This is Mr. Fortunato's party, isn't it?" said the Mormon, who was a bit older than us, it seemed, but the onslaught of manhood had not treated him well. He had pustular pimples on his cheek. Repetitive welts also adorned his outsized Adam's apple, phallic and repulsive.

We were hopping over the rope fence, and Jed strode ahead.

"He's over there," I said to the Mormon, trying to move away from him but not succeeding: he blocked my way past the gate. "There," I said, "the man in the cowboy hat."

"I see," the boy said, looking a bit skeptical. "My friends told me he could introduce me to people."

"I doubt it," I said. "I don't think anyone came up here looking for redemption. Excuse me."

"Oh, I'm sorry," he muttered, and he moved away and walked beside me, like a puppy terrified of being stranded.

"Well, then, maybe you can help me," he said shyly. "May I ask what is your vision of the apocalypse?" He swallowed hopefully, and I stared at him.

Just ahead of us, I saw a seventy-year-old Belgian, practically

naked, with his arm around a pubescent Filipino girl. Nearby, a
bunch of drunken Englishmen were singing what they called the
Irish national anthem, God Save the Queen, one of their favorite
jokes. We walked past so-called, self-labeled *coños*, pink-skinned
Spanish mestizos talking about their Jet Skis.

"Take your pick," I said, waving my hand. "Here's your latter-
day set of apocalypse now."

I regretted the statement when I spoke it. I did not want him to
remember me. And the frenzy of these games, after all, exhilarated
me. I loved the purity of soccer—passion deliberately tuned and precisely, patiently enacted. But I was impatient, looking for Jed. I thought
I saw his bag, an outsized sportsman's Adidas; I thought I saw it on his
shoulders, like a bulwark by the stands, behind Uncle Gianni.

"Thanks for sharing," the Mormon said, mumbling. I watched
the kid scamper away, his lanky, woolen legs fending off brambles
and loose earth, up onto the curved, sliding grass, the main fields of
the tournament.

"Joaqui!" someone squealed as I noted Jed talking to a blondish
boy near the stands. His name was pronounced like that, "Wacky."

A girl in shorts ran up and hugged Jed.

I recognized her. She had been a cotillion girl and cheerleader
at our high school.

"Wacky! Where have you been, *maldito*!"

"Ramona," Jed said. "Mong. How are you?"

And they kissed each other on the cheek, a bit exuberantly on
Jed's part, I thought.

"Bad, bad boy. Do you know I had my debut and you did not
go? And you were in Manila *pala ha*. You did not answer the
invitation."

"You did? You turned old so early."

She bumped her hip against his.

"You, ha. I had to settle for Pochie *na lang* for the first dance because you were not around. *Maldito*. Where are you hiding? Is it true you're going out with—"

"Wacky," I mimicked. "How've you been?"

Jed turned, still smiling as I approached.

The girl stared at me.

"Who's she?" Mong asked, even though she knew.

"Victor, say hi. Remember Mong?"

"But that's not your name. Aren't you Soltera Soliman?"

"Nuh-uh," I said. "I'm a Danish scoliotic with a ruined brain. Pleased to meet you again, Mong. Ramona."

She didn't hold out her hand.

She turned to Jed.

"Well, see us again sometime, ha? We all miss you, Wacky. You haven't been to a single Christmas party—*ninguna*. How bad you are. I've just flown back from New York, but everyone talks about you, you're so *snabero daw*. Where are you hiding, ha? You didn't even ask me—I have so much *cuento* about New York."

"See you, Mong," Jed said.

"Are you playing, Wack?" the vaguely foreign-looking boy called Pochie asked, looking at the bag in Jed's hands. The boy had been doing stretches on the ground, one hand rolling on his hairless tummy and the other seeming to oil his calf, though both gestures were aimless, likely like his brain.

Jed shook his head. "I'll watch you," he said, as he tried to walk away. "Good luck. Ciao!"

"Ciao," said the boy.

"Ciao, Wacky! Remember, Tuesday at Carmela's, Wacky! Pochie's going, too, aren't you, Poch? Wacky! We called your mom. She knows. *Sorpresa!* Carmela's having a baby shower! Can you believe? Before she even got to college! You should come—the shower's going to be bigger than her debut!"

"Ciao, Mong," Jed said, waving goodbye, but she was already bugging the boy Pochie about something.

"Where were you?" Jed asked.

"Yes, Wacky? What, Wacky?"

"Oh shut up. C'mon. Let's go."

ON THE EDGE of the sports barracks was one of my dad's warehouses. A low-roofed set of adjoining buildings and the compound's oldest tenement. To reach it, on normal days you had to go through the barred, tall gate by the road, usually guarded by a pair called Mundo and Al. They had been in our employ forever, like many of my parents' faithful. On the day of the tournament, they kept these gates open. Mundo and Al stood sentry, a rather distracted one, I knew, at the covered path during the games, in the utilitarian area where the new toilets had been installed. Beyond that outpost, jutting more boldly onto the main grounds, there was an afterthought bar, which seemed the demarcation line between revelers and domestic staff, except for a few white-dressed nannies near the playing fields, obediently following tottering kids.

Rifles in hand, toothpicking and making serious bets, Mundo and Al were judging the nationalities of Team Malta, composed of a crew of Europeans, all non-Maltese—"O, Dutchman," Al would say knowledgeably. "Look at bald head." They commented on the fitness of their favored *coños*, who usually won, because they could claim players from a wider selection than any of the Belgians or Brits or even Japanese could. Al and Mundo were happily absorbed in this way, like a pair of boys engaged in ant bouts, heads to the ground inspecting their contenders, watching the thrashing, minute legs of their chosen beasts, their bets depending on optimistic intuition as the black and red ants raced to gobble each other up; they did not take their eyes away from the skirmish until the pushed, tangled bodies revealed the winner: in an ant bout, it was easy to tell which side won. The winners gobbled up the vanquished.

I knew Al and Mundo would be absorbed in this way, watching the soccer tournament without pause: there'd be no need to worry about them.

"Hello, Mang Al, Mang Munding."

"Ma'am Sol," Al said. "This year, Philippines will win." Al had a childish face, because of the way his eyes seemed always smiling in a round plain. I used to think he was a sorry excuse for a guard, until once I saw him lift his gun to shoot at a sound on the grounds, a long time ago, when the soccer field was still brambles and weed. He shot a rat with one bullet, just like that. Muhammad Al, he was dubbed, flies like a butterfly, kills like a bee.

"Well, what did you bet?" I said.

"Nothing," Mundo retorted, spitting. "Al is putting the money on Spain again."

Every year, both Al and Mundo secretly hoped that the Philippine players would win the tournament, but, like true nationalists, they never bet on them.

"And you?"

"Belgium. This year, they have the two small Italians. Very good with the feet."

I nodded. "Sounds good. Have you seen my dad?"

"He is out of the town, ma'am. Sir Gianni—he is over there."

"That's what I thought," I said. "Well, go ahead with your business. We're just watching the game."

I LED JED TO the windowless building up ahead leaning toward the street. It had large steel doors in the back, near the gates, away from the playing fields; but I walked up to the small side door, near the mess of weeds and dirty ground. A rooster, Al's pet, made a ruffled sound. Its cage was set against the property's natural boundary, a thicket of bamboo. Beyond the bird was the concrete wall surrounding the compound, hard to scale and difficult to compass. The rooster squawked at me. I opened the door on the rooster side. It crowed a warning as we went in, but it was an indifferent bird and made a useless, lackadaisical appeal. Anyway, no one was listening.

Jed followed me in. I had been inside a few times when I ran the soccer clinic. The equipment had been stored here: nets, balls, goal frames. When Uncle Gianni first set up his tournaments, it used to be my job to make sure the equipment was ready for use. But I had never gone into the innards of the buildings or walked about the crates that loomed as each door opened. Down by the first door, I settled my bags, oversized, with strongly seamed nylon compartments, chosen for the event. We went through a long hallway studded with wood, slats of shipment crates, wooden shavings, the pale, smooth paper of crate-stuffing. It smelled of dry packing, the crimped smell of bunched pulp, ticklish to the nose. I sneezed. Jed turned on lights for the next suite of rooms, veering to the right. The rooms interconnected and snaked; large, neat boxes were lined against the wall.

"Here," Jed said, making a turn. "Look at this. He said it would be here."

"Who said?"

"I have my sources."

"Have you been pumping information from Manong Babe?"

Jed didn't answer.

"Don't you dare include him in this plot, Jed."

In the room's dark pulp, he stopped and kissed me: "I wouldn't dare involve Manong Babe," he said. "I love Manong Babe."

"Stop it," I said.

"There's something about guns," he laughed, clutching me from behind.

I giggled.

"Teargasm," I said.

"Let's do it," he said.

"Right here?"

It was a secluded niche; I was ready before he closed the door. We didn't wait to take off our clothes. Come to think of it, I liked sex in stupid places—where novelty matched my body's surprise. It always shocked me, like electric wiring, the scratch of his shirt against my breast, his wet mouth—and the oddness of our placement between plaster wall and wood-shaving pile gave the gross grappling just the right pitch of madness in that creepy cave.

Later we almost missed it: a doorway to a dark, noncommittal space. I switched the light on for Jed. I sat on top of the crate. He began tapping on it. He took his sports bag from his shoulder and unzipped it. He was ready: he had wire pliers, pocketknives with different blades, a heavy-duty pair of scissors. Hammers and nails. All he needed to do was find the loot in one box.

I watched while he went through the first box, feeling the wrapped object.

"They should be locked and sealed in a metal bind," Jed muttered. "This can't be it: they wouldn't be covered in paper."

The fact is, the warehouse also had other goods. A harmless trade. Watches, toys and shirts: cuckoo clocks. We opened up several boxes. I hammered the tops shut when we had the wrong box. You had to look for the right-sized one; the containers were smaller than you expected.

Jed whistled.

"Ssh," I said, walking over.

They were packed unassembled, with cartridge, trigger, and muzzle in separate wrap, like incoherent scraps. An expert, I imagine, could easily conjure wholeness from the loose parts, with that voodoo of knowledge like a snap of vision in a gun-lover's heart. But I had never held a gun. Jed held out a part for me to hold. It was a bunch of metal, inarticulate, not even foreboding, surprisingly greasy, slippery, inert and senseless in my ignorant hands.

Later, I felt that dread, that mild flush of death, when I saw the ammunition, a tidy, bunched pack.

"See this?" said Jed. "When this hits the flesh, it explodes in you, like metal batter. Let's see: it's called—'the Winchester Silver-tip.' This one shatters your bones but lodges inside. This one can go right through you, if you had the right caliber. We don't want them. They're not the right ones; we can take one set, though, just in case. We need the ones for the machine guns, the ones that can shatter bulletproof cars. Look at these brand-new beautiful babies. You know, your uncle Gianni has the best goods among the private dealers. He really does. Did you know that? Excellent stuff. Look. Kiss that baby."

He handled the wrapped metal with an eager gaze, an expression I recognized, that intense look he made as he pressed against my chest, for instance, his face breathing hard and finger pivoting. He caressed a loose muzzle. Watching him, his apparent thrill, was frightening, and I felt my own nipples shyly rising, a rash, favorable fit, the way I always responded to Jed.

A vague convulsion met us outside. We had to shield our eyes when we stepped out of the warehouse. As we walked out to the field, carrying our heavy bags, we heard that low, massed hum in the distance, a crowd in heat. I had to adjust a bit, coming from artificial glare into the bright sunshine of the tournament and the game's loud abandoned noises. A deciding half was in full swing. One could tell from spectators' cheers, vowels rising to follow this ball or that man. Our feet walked to the rhythm of their frenetic calls. The urgent expectation of victory roused the crowds (a flushed, sweetly tanned interracial mix, united by thrill) to that shrill frisson resembling passion: loud shrieks from a woman otherwise sedately dressed while she hissed, wanton moans when a ball grazed the post, and the mortal wounding notes when the enemy made its incursions, delicately balling the mouth of the goal. We stopped, dropping our bags.

Jed stood by and watched, as he had promised his friend; he became absorbed in the game, squinting and biting his lip. His large-bodied friend Pochie, blond hair now in a ponytail, was playing for Team Spain. He hogged the ball with agile greed, and then, by what seemed a trick, causing a groan in the crowd, he hit the ball into the far post—on an error from the Filipino goalie, whose chest spun on the ground, like a chagrined cow. Team Philippines lost, bad luck, the young prostitutes imported from Pasay said, shaking their heads; and the Filipinos had had control of the play for two halves, too bad; all they had needed was one lucky break, said Mang Munding. It was only Sir Pochie's fair share, after all, muttered Al, who had bet on the man though he shook his head in disappointment, and the young women admired Pochie's broad, bullocky thighs.

We stood there watching, Jed and I, our bags on the grass, and after a while I lay down, gauging the progress of the games from the noises of the crowd, while I closed my eyes beside Jed's feet. I smelled the whiff of leather, grass, sweat.

There, that remnant moment, when unruly hopes still mattered and floated in the breeze, the air warm and sweet. The din was like a deep rocking, my head against our bags, wind rustling while I rearranged my shape to fit the bags' awkward, metallic edges. That moment: hold it—a sense of utter expectation, a temporal vacuum, the act yet to be done, and our souls in pendulous sway. Nothing yet scratched on the coin of time.

I felt some febrile, exquisite contact, like a ghostly clitoral shiver: my taut breasts and soft, spread-eagled body tremulous and open to Manila's sky. I imagine that I remember it—that lone, orgastic moment—when the future lay in wait, still innocent, eyes closed and mouth parted, breathing softly in the wind.

Part III

1

I HATE NEW YEAR'S. It's the noise. I hate the noise. And the raucous monster celebration, the fatal sounds of the city—whenever I spent New Year's in the city, it always depressed and enervated me: I locked myself up; I wouldn't go out. It was as if the whole of Manila—this vulnerable, already volcanic, accidental place—were erupting into its revolution, its hoped-for radical transformation. Briefly, my heart thudding to the rage outside, I'd imagine that the grand, passionate bedlam scream, the ugly, stupefying rockets, torpedo-tortures, hand-damaging devices, et cetera, had some more momentous glamour. But, in fact, what is it? A mindless conflagration, a festive, retarded splendor—and each New Year's debris moves Manila even more brazenly into its polluted, stupid demise. Nothing much to crow about.

I spent those days after the tournament almost tranquilly, if you could call that thoughtless, heavy torpor tranquil, in which I rarely ventured from my room and read a lot of books, one paperback after another. One green book I closed with heavy, sweating arms, with sluggish hollowness. I found these penciled words on the book flap, which I turned when I reached the end: a bland vocabulary list. "Jejune, oleograph, grisaille, Duchess of Malfi, scrofulous, milieu"—all carefully scribbled using different pens, in a terse, optimistic row. I didn't recognize my own handwriting. I hadn't realized that I had read the book before. I was taking books from the bookcase, one after another, and reading them with mindless passion. Briefly, looking at the list and recognizing, with a near pang, my academic, childish hand, I stopped. The pious diligence of my younger self looking up those words, "scrofulous," "jejune." I wondered at it, how that time was so distant—I shook my head. I took another book, and I lay there, sunk in the uncommitted rapacity of my reading, my dense soothing indolence.

It was the way it would be if one were trapped on a desert island, hard-pressed to find relief from the minute-by-minute hope of rescue, the daily distress in looking constantly for signs on the water, sounds of arrival above the trees; haunted by expectation, sure to be concluded any minute; if you could know exactly when and how and if; but instead there's the deadly wait, and you take up a book, an object of time in itself, a measure of duration. A book holds the fitful infinity of time miserably passing.

And yet it was soothing. On the other hand. A lulling, desperate state, but comforting, the way the extreme inactivity forced on us by illness has a morbid, feculent pleasure, the drowsy miasma of languor: there's that sensual garb, this state of malaise—a faked proximity to death—but who am I to speak of comparisons?

AT FIRST, JED said my deed was done, my part was finished. Others would take my place.

"Right now I really wish you'd stay away," he said that day of the tournament.

Jed repeated, answering the protest on my face: "Go home with Manong Babe. Stay there. It's best if you don't see us after today. Do you understand? In fact, you should leave the country sooner than you planned. Aren't you supposed to go to school? Go to school in America?"

"No."

"Suit yourself," he said. "But don't go out of your house. Stay home." He sighed. "It's better, really, Sol, if you leave the country."

And then I asked, a small, petulant mistake, my voice scratchy and shrill, to the tune of the crowd's cranky din.

"So where will Soli be in this?" I squeaked. "Will you now be seeing Soli and not me?"

I heard the pitch in my voice and was ashamed at the squawking self-pity.

I had these embarrassing visions. I understood things were coming to a head, and I had begun to have dreams—of phosphorescent snaky couplings, forest writhings. Soli and Jed, Jed and Soli. If he were not going to be with me, where would he be? I had stark, fantastic notions.

I trusted jealousy because it was always there, a sure nagging omniscience, a delicate nerve that ran parallel to the best impulses of love; in a way you could not understand, I longed, too, for my friendship with Soli, the thought of her rigid, straight back as she had left me that last day on her uncle's jeepney still weirdly haunted me, sometimes, when I was with Jed; and at the same time I had these carious, jealous twinges, like a bad tooth I lived with and had begun to caress with pleasure. The thought of Soli, my old rival, my Doppelgänger: the first person I had envied—the thought made me miss her and hate her both.

When I had those recurring dreams of the amphisbaena, of the white two-headed snake in a primeval forest, I knew somehow in a pathetic flash, weakening me as I woke up, that the writhing snake, each head tugging away from the other and the slim, luminous length (passion wrangling at each end) wriggling and slithering horribly in its frenzy amid bamboo and grass, was a potent figure of something abominable and treacherous: and it lay deep within me.

Jed shook his head at me. "Jesus: you think only of yourself, Sol."

"I'm sorry."

"We've already talked about that," he said.

"But I don't remember. Tell me again."

"No," he said harshly. "She has no idea about what we're doing. She's in the provinces on vacation. I told you. She has no knowledge at all. If you want to know, Soli thinks I'm an idiot. A lightweight. But she is wrong. She made clear a while ago that she wants nothing to do with me at all."

"Are we out of bounds, Jed?"

"What do you mean?"

"Who else in the group knows about it? Is it against the rules, what we're doing?"

"So what if it is?" he said. "We're doing our part."

"But for what, Jed?"

"For the country."

As I said, I kept to my rooms, dreading there would be news in the papers, some leak; but for a sinking, bookbound eternity, there was no news. Perhaps, in fact, nothing would happen. I wallowed in my bed; I didn't get up. I kept scanning the papers. Instead, there were reports on New Year's Eve balls; 172 dead in firecracker incidents, with the numbers rising; shopworkers in Cubao threatening to go on strike, but who cared after the Christmas binges?; proclamations of peace in the countryside, a holiday truce, with a rare endnote on a raid somewhere in a far-off village, no names mentioned. The country was in that holiday quietus of restive calm, a citizenry suddenly, almost despondently aimless, the streets still reeking of the cheap sulphur of New Year cheer. Even on my glassed-in patio, the solarium, I could hear the muffled thunder of some tail-end thrills.

I kept reading my books. I put down the volume I was reading, Evelyn James, Henry Waugh. I could barely sleep. I don't think it was quite dawn when my phone rang. It was still dark out. Despite everything I knew, my heart fell: Would they start out so early? I lifted the phone, and I was pleased, an instant, instinctive warmth waylaid me, when I heard her voice.

"Soli? Soli, is it you? How've you been? It's so good to hear from you. It's so—so wonderful to hear from you."

"Good. I've been good."

"Where are you? Where have you been?"

"I just got back from the province. I've been on vacation. But, you know, I've been busy. There's a strike in Cubao—you know. Stuff. But I wanted to call. There's something—Can we see each other, Sol?"

"When? Sure. Today?"

She gave me the time and place.

"Well, actually—." I hesitated. "I might be busy today."

"I have to see you now. Today."

"Then I'll see you. Right now."

Before we hung up, I said: "It's so good to hear from you, Soli."

"It is, Sol. It's good to hear your voice. Well, I'll see you then."

Almost immediately after I hung up, the phone rang again.

MANONG ARMANDO STOPPED me in the garden. In the glimmering day, he was sweeping debris off fragile earthworms in the dirt path.

"No driver today, Ma'am Sol," the gardener said. "Manong Babe still not here."

"That's okay. I thought you were off for the holiday? I'm just going for a jog."

It would take days to clear away the black haze, the collected tar in the acid sky. Even now, this early in the morning, some triangle bombs boomed, like a giant's throat clearing; it seemed to come from the village opposite, or from the tardy, abundant crop of the feeble crackpot right next door. Then a concatenated spark, rat-tat-tat-tat of the firecracker, *Sinturon ni Hudas*, the curt machine-gun fire of a grown-up at play. It followed me as I walked to the village's gates. So did the rancid smell of burning rubber, favored form of ignition for homemade New Year's bombs. New Year's always ended with this deserted, damaged feel of war. I left the gate to descend on the rubble of the village's backside, where a bunch of grimed kids tried to spook me with their leftover *watusi*, a tepid hiss that made me jump just the same. The street kids laughed and ran away when I looked behind me. Beyond the gas station, I jogged to

Ah Me! Kitchenette, a shack near the highway. Lightheaded, tensile and brittle from my lack of movement during the past days, I was still trying to recover from the timorous surprise of that dumb *watusi* as I ran, my long-dormant, static nerves now stirring into exaggerated, jangling action. I breathed in the pungent foulness of the air, a thick clump that tickled my throat, and I coughed; simply by strolling out, one risked ingesting the temper of the city.

2

AH ME! KITCHENETTE was an open-air stall facing the highway that had only a bench before a linoleum table. Ami, the owner, I presume, bustled about plying fried bananas and boiled cakes. Dried mackerel and fish balls. Pungent takeaways I could not stand. Soli sat on the bench in full view. She waved at me, drinking 7-Up from a straw in a transparent, plastic bag.

Ami offered me a 7-Up, pouring another botttle into plastic before I could speak, and I was left there, my arm arrested, holding the murky bag.

We sat with the rumble of the highway gathering its potential on this groggy morning: motorcycles sputtered in the distance. Our feet dangled over the street's neatly swept trash. No one else was around. We seemed the only people awake that morning in sulphurous Makati.

"I don't see him anymore. I don't know where he is," I said. I crossed my fingers behind me, sweat rising, I thought, from her question. I watched the 7-Up slosh in my dangling hand.

"But where does he live? No one seems to be able to tell me."

"You really don't know?" I asked.

Soli shook her head.

I gave her an address. Pasay. Punta. Something like that. Places we never went.

"I'll look for him if you won't," she said. "I can't believe the stories."

"Then they're probably not true," I said.

I felt like a fool, waiting for her revelation.

"I hope so. I hope it's just a rumor. It's so ridiculous, Sol. I couldn't believe the idea. It can't be sanctioned at all. I heard rumors when I got back. It must be just gossip. It's a plain, criminal act. Sheer adventurism."

"What are you talking about? What's the rumor?"

"Nothing is clear. I think Jed is planning something—something stupid. People used to laugh about it—his adventurist streak. I used to worry. The story going around is: He's hanging out with the wrong people. They call them red freaks. The people I know think it's a joke. But you know I've been thinking—my God, he's going after the Secretary, his father's friend."

"The Secretary?"

And I dropped it. I dropped the bag.

I watched with relief as it broke open in a puddle on the street.

Soli knew absolutely nothing.

"Do you know anything about it?" Soli demanded.

"The Secretary? No. I don't know what you're talking about."

"I hope you have no hand in anything Jed's doing."

I didn't speak.

She sighed. "I shouldn't have done it."

"What?"

She looked at me, smiling at me in her old maternal way: "'What?' You're always saying 'what?' I shouldn't have recruited you. That's what."

"It wasn't you," I said. "I went to the meetings on my own. It was my decision. I wanted to be a part."

"At first, it was Edwin's idea," she went on, seeming not to listen, looking at her still-life hands. "When I told him who you were, a gun dealer's daughter, the daughter of Queenie Kierulf Soliman, a famous lady in my hometown, he thought it would be smart to know you. Just in case you could be useful. I saw your name on the roster, next to mine, and I told him who you were. Jed, you know—well, he corroborated my rumor. Anyway, Edwin thought it would be good to get to know you. And so I sought you out. And when I began to know you, I liked you. You listened so seriously to Ka Noli. You asked the right questions at the lectures. You took it all in. And I honestly thought it was worth it for you—the lectures, the study, seeing more of the countryside, thinking about history. It's important that everyone should understand—even people like you. Sorry to be so blunt. That's what I think. I don't agree with the narrow-minded bullshit of the cadres. Everyone should be on our side. We can all join in our own ways. I thought it was good for you: to see other kinds of people, know how they lived. I mean, you didn't even know how to use public transportation! Edwin told me not to recruit you, in the end, but I disagreed. I thought I was right. But I guess I wasn't." She caught how I was staring at her. "It's okay if you hate me," she said.

"Hate you? It's I who should ask forgiveness."

"For seeking you out like that—"

I shook my head.

"I'm sorry," I said suddenly. "I'm really sorry about Jed."

I finally said it. I said it in a burst, an exhalation.

She shook her head. "No. No. No. It's all right. All under the bridge. You know, of course, I didn't feel like this then. Though it's funny: I never blamed you."

"Yeah. I'm too dumb to even think about."

She shook her head. "Don't be silly." She raised her eyes: "If I could just know for sure that it isn't true—that the story I hear is wrong—"

"I wanted to be a part," I said.

"Useful fool." She sighed.

"What?"

"U.F. Useful fool. It's a term they used." Soli shook her head. "I was wrong. I shouldn't have done it. I shouldn't have sought you out."

"Useful fool," I repeated, questioning the phrase. Then I said: "So it was all premeditated. Our friendship?"

"No. Of course not." She reached over briefly to hug me, to smooth my hair as she used to do, absentmindedly. That was Soli's gesture: absentmindedness. She said: "Of course, it wasn't diabolical like that. It was Edwin's idea to talk to you, but then when I got to know you, I hoped you would be with us. I thought you *should* be with us. But then, remember, when I took you to that funeral parlor—in Monumento."

I didn't speak.

"You vomited on the street. I felt helpless when I saw—maybe I was wrong. Edwin told me you'd be the worst kind of recruit—"

"Thanks—"

"But it seemed right at the time that you should join."

"How strange." I stared at Soli.

"You're right to be mad. I'm sorry. I should have thought about it a bit more. I should have thought of the consequences for you—the burden on you."

"The burden?"

"That you would hate yourself," she said.

For a moment there, I hated Soli all over again: I hated the way she pitied me.

But she sat with that repose she had in the right moments—her impressive control. Her dark, long fingers rested on the tabletop, in devotional clasp; her back was straight, leaning slightly toward me. Her eyes seemed to darken with her alertness as she looked at me squarely.

"But it was I," I said, speaking more softly. "I did it all myself. It was not your plan: it was mine. I did wish to be a part. It was I who wished to join your group. I thought—I thought it was the one thing that would make me whole."

"That's what Edwin said."

"I know."

I looked at her. We started to laugh.

Soli reached for my hand and held it.

"Jed was not a part of it, Sol," she said softly. "Jed had no hand in our investigation of you."

"Investigation?"

"We investigated you, of course. S.I. Social investigation. Your background, your friends, your interests."

"Edwin was stalking me."

"Not really."

"I don't care," I said. "I don't care about any of that. What are you going to do now? Don't go looking for them, Soli. It's not worth it."

I felt her grip on my wrist, a moist, tight squeeze. Smell of butterscotch and fish.

"I have to go now anyhow," she said. "Want to go with me to the factory picket line?"

I shook my head. "No," I said. "I have to go—."

"Well then."

I stood up as she did. "Are you really going to look for them?" I asked. I decided. "I'll go with you, Soli, if you want to look for Jed. You can tell him what you think. That he is out of bounds. That he is doing stupid things."

"No, stay." She sighed. "You know, you're right. I shouldn't believe those stories. The idea's stupid—a macho fantasy. It's absurd. For one thing, Ed's a coward. He'd be too scared even to be a lookout, you know. Jed, on the other hand. You're right. It can't be true. I have to go back to the workers. The strike's in Cubao. You don't want to come? Pay the bill anyway." She grinned.

"Right," I said. "Once a useful fool, always a useful fool."

She stooped to hug me. I hugged her back. Fish. She hated mackerel—or I do. I smelled it, the fish balls and the mackerel, a long time after she left: the afterlude of her takeout from Ah Me! Kitchenette. That gesture she made as she smoothed hair on my brow before she walked away, her tall, straight-backed figure, fleeting glimpse of rare mahogany.

I should have run after Soli, but I didn't.

Instead, I gave her the wrong address. My little prevarication: useless lies from a useful fool.

I picked up the tab. I looked absently onto the splattered mess on the street. Ants were already at it, circling the soft-drinks stain, taking in the sulphur of Makati.

3

As I said, in those last days in Jed's apartment, I had gained an aggressive clarity.

Jed shook his head at my insistence.

No, he said, it can't be, he said.

It was I who insisted: I insisted that it be the Colonel.

"It has to be," I said. "He's a regular man. He goes to the gym at exactly three o'clock. He's probably never late for work."

"How do you know?" said Jed.

"The first trick about reconnaissance," I said, "is this: you watch."

"You're right: He's very regular. He has very orderly habits. He would be the best target, certainly. And yes: He's the enemy. He's the brains. The general's just for show. We know that. But, Sol, he's too cautious. The others think he's too cautious, and I agree. He will be hard to get. The Colonel doesn't even ride his car without checking at it on all sides, inspecting the works. The General will be easier to kill."

"He's just caressing his stupid hubcaps," I said.

"What do you mean?"

I looked at Jed. "It's true. He's not inspecting anything. He doesn't think anyone will shoot him. He just wants to know his hubcaps are there."

"What are you talking about?"

"That's what he said at LOTUS, at his headquarters. He checked the tires on both sides that day, and Uncle Gianni noticed."

"Explain the whole thing," Jed said. "Slow down."

"When we all had lunch with him once. Trust me. He's not afraid of bombs. Far from it. He's an arrogant man. That's why he sticks to his schedule. Don't you see? He doesn't even travel with guards. His hubcaps had been stolen once, and now he obsessively checks them out everytime he travels. It must be something about Vietnam, being a prisoner—he hates loss."

"The day you had lunch with him he did this?"

I nodded. "I saw him bending over his car. Just as you said. But he wasn't looking for bombs. He was just looking down at a hubcap, tapping on it, cleaning off a scratch or something. He's arrogant, really. He's pretty sure he won't be killed. He's right, if you think about it. It would be a diplomatic uproar, an all-out hunt for the criminals, and very bad P.R. He's a war hero. A P.O.W. A decorated Vietnam vet. It's the kind of death out of which, I imagine, old-timers would make a howling wilderness."

"He's just checking his hubcaps," Jed mused.

"Yes," I said.

"When did you have lunch with him again?" Jed walked away from me to light a cigarette. The fan whirred his way, and his hand held steady against the flame, blocking it against the hoary air.

"The day we were let out for Christmas. My uncle is still mad at him."

"Yeah, you were telling me," Jed said.

"Did I tell you about that? The Colonel promised to be at my uncle's tournament, the one we're going to."

"He's a funny guy, your uncle," Jed said, politely blowing smoke away from me. He smiled. "Edwin thinks we should kill him instead."

"That's not funny," I said.

You can't just let me stay home." I was so angry with Jed my ears hurt, that sharp tension in the back of my head that signified a migraine, a tantrum.

"There's nothing for you to do. Everything's in place. Stay home, stay put, go away."

"I will not. At least tell me when you're doing it, let me know your plans. I want to be a part."

Jed sat shaking his head.

"No one tells me what to do, Jed. Not even my dad."

"It's not a slumber party, Sol."

"Oh, come on, if she just wants to be near—"

Jed shot angrily at Edwin: "Easy for you to say—shut up, Ed. You're not even going anywhere near the place on the day—you know it's dangerous."

"Where's Ed going?"

"He's going to the provinces to visit a dying aunt."

Ed shrugged, looking sheepish.

"She's sick. I owe her everything—my tuition fees, even my dentist."

"Hah," I said. "Then let *me* be a part, instead of Edwin."

"No. You hear me, Ed. I want her safe in her house, or on a beach in Thailand, or some place. I want you to go on to college in America and research dead Romans. Why don't you leave the country early, go shopping in Hong Kong?"

"You think that's all I'm good for."

Edwin was smirking.

"If that's what you want to think. Just go away. For your own good."

"Bok," Edwin said. "What's the harm? Let them call her. They do need one last errand."

4

IT WAS EARLY in the morning, but the household was already in motion. The gardener greeted Mr. Kow Lung, the feng shui man, who always came around during the holidays. He lived in a smaller village nearby named after an archangel or a beer company; the gardener Manong Armando always greeted him with a bow—he looked so dignified but spoke so little, like a kung fu sage—and he led him from the living room where the Ming vase and the Buddha held sway, like stout philosophers, like those gigantic icons arising from the sandstone of a temple, cross-legged, omnipotent, and expressing the recklessness of everyone else's fate. Mr. Kow Lung inspected the décor, the way the shadows fell on the Buddha; the house was at peace. The furniture had already been dusted; the curtains let in the light. And Mr. Kow Lung went on to the kitchen where he had breakfast, his third meal of the day; in this way, houses in Makati retained their auspicious glamour, and during Christmas Mr. Kow Lung never stepped foot in a grocery store or paid for his meals. It was a good exchange.

In fact, before Mr. Kow Lung's arrival, the help had already started their own party. It was their New Year's Day celebration, an anachronistic moment that lagged behind the country's, perhaps the busiest time in the kitchen. Postmen, cake-deliverers, blind masseurs, linen-vendors, psychics of different specialties, traveling knife-sharpeners, amateur painters of Philippine farm scenes, milkmen on motorbikes, all came by at one point or another on this appointed day. It was a time of community, when all of the deliverers claimed their yearly reward—Peace on Earth, Goodwill Toward Men— and ate Manang Lita's honey ham and rice. The place was so busy no one would have noticed my disappearance, or the absence of other regulars at the table, except that even then, who knows, maybe rumors were already in the wind.

OVER IN NEW Manila, a dark-blood saloon reached its turn near the gasoline station. The Metro Manila cleaning aide in charge of the street was humming, sweating but humming, in the rising heat, her bandanna keeping her trim hair in place, her red and yellow outfit marking in random, zigzag streaks the gray tidiness of the sleeping street, where if one noticed the car coming in the other direction— was it white or green? two men or four?—who would have risen up, lazily on one's elbows, shielding light from one's brow as the sound neared and uttered its soft drone? No one. It was too early in the day for most drunk people in Manila.

I REMEMBER SOLI WRAPPING her takeaway lunch: dried mackerel and warm rice. The whiff of the fish would remain for days. Skin of mahogany. A woman of repose. I hated mackerel—the greasy brown fat and mordant stench. I imagine things in broad details, fish smells, the garish sunlight of Manila's rising day on the long jeep ride she would take to the picket lines, her straightforward destination. The aluminum foil crackled as she put the fish in her bag; I wrinkled my nose. It stank.

It would seem, at first, like a New Year's prank. A tardy firecracking explosion, a hissing Roman candle. Then (too early in the morning) the rat-tat-tat of the guns sounded like a Judas Belt, *Sinturon ni Hudas*, the usual belated medley of holiday cheer. It was the distinct memory of the street-cleaner that she smelled the sulphur first, the wild *watusi* air, before she heard the bullets: but from the beginning of the holiday season, the street itself had smelled daily like a war zone, a debris-filled, cacophonous smoke. The aftermath of New Year's was one of the most hectic times for Metro Manila cleaning aides.

And so he died with his head splashed, like a dull pitcher, against the pierced armored glass. His driver made a blind, swerving dash as the car was hit at the gas-station corner, that empty, festering region that Jed and I had walked so often, counting even our steps. No one was in sight, not even the monkey and his crippled captor by the store on Third Avenue. The street was asleep. The stores were boarded up, blind. It was true that, later on, various witnesses were said to have arisen like crickets from the cracks, trilling their tall tales of license plates and other things; but early morning on that street, we knew, had a mint, unstamped aura to it—a blank reverie. You could walk it like a lover and feel free.

The street-cleaner, yellow kerchief tightly tasseled on her head, was almost swiped by Colonel Grier's car, the maroon Mitsubishi saloon, armored and impregnable (so they say), as his shocked, desperate driver made the futile, unseeing hurtle down the street, carrying his car's riddled right side like a flopping organ, an ear, a lung. The sight of the damaged car was such that the getaway group got away—the street-cleaner gawking. Decent-looking face, sleeveless shirt. Red bandannas. A long barrel—a gleaming weapon—obscured one man's fate. She couldn't see him behind his gun. But then the witness could not be sure if it was one or three, those gunmen, or white or blue, the car. Was it a white limousine, a long white car driven by a spoiled brat?

Later, when she was asked to identify the abandoned vehicle, the so-called getaway car, she hesitated, she wasn't sure. The car had gone toward San Francisco del Monte? Yes, she said: that is true. Anyway, she herself had almost been killed as she sidestepped from the wounded, wobbling saloon. Colonel Arthur Grier's last sight was a bright yellow flap outside as he bent to the left, a fluttering coin, a golden bird wing, a glinting medallion, or was that the sun, as he turned his head, and the street cleaner made a wild dancing leap, blindly hopping away.

5

I DID THE LAST job out of jealousy, out of spite and anger with Jed. I refused to accept that in the end I had been merely a useful fool. But on the way to the apartment, leaving Ah Me! Kitchenette, down the rutted streets, familiar potholes, and landmarks of cloud-shaved trees, through the ruins of Kalentong shops into the ordinary roads of New Manila, I already began to feel the pulse, that quickening in my wrists, that signaled, like a conditioned dog, my stupid lust. The entire route was a map to Jed—stones, houses and stoops. A turn down the alley from a vacant movie palace, a silent church, a streetlight, then the first glimpse of that obsolete gas station—all these played, in scattered overture, prologues to his presence.

The apartment window looked out upon the unpaved road leading to the gas station, from which Jed, daily, had kept his faithful watch on the comings and goings of the street.

Looking up at the window, I imagined his hunched shape, with the throb in my breast that I thought must be the sentiment of cancer, a livid nerve that drove my blood. I thought I saw the mist of Jed's curls, or was that cigarette smoke.

He would be gone, of course. My job was a tail-end adjunct to the event. But I at last would be a part. Jed had chosen the apartment window for its angle. Often we had watched the car make its turn, its careful decision by the corner; daily he knew where it slowed. Even its cunning schedules—never arriving at the street at the same time or route—could be ferreted out, for those who planned ahead.

By the time I arrived, it was over. I saw the commotion at the corner, the street was not yet blocked. I entered the apartment. I watched from the window, noting all the necessary events—police cars, kibitzers, taxis and jeeps clogging the street to make their drive-by assessments. One has those dreams where the sound track is screwy. Sirens and car horns before the ambulances actually arrived. I hear the sound of gunshots, again and again, though Jed was gone, vanished with his cohorts, and the getaway car (I hoped) had long removed itself to the city's suburbs. I see Soli repeatedly, walking down William McKinley Road, hailing a jeep from Ah Me! Kitchenette, to the picket lines in Cubao. The opposite direction. I hear the sound of shots, like triangle bombs, *watusi* rockets— over and over: while dust motes roved through the air in distinct, gross forms in the apartment in New Manila, that glazed, cheap room, oddly, with its windows like iron grisaille, looking like a decrepit set from *Apocalypse Now*—fan whirring like a dying breath in the late morning, light particulating even as it glowed—the fan beating its monotonous, clunky groan.

In truth, it was the only sound I must have heard: the bleared fan's groggy whine. And the staid, steady ornaments in the room— the faded mimesis of a tropical jungle—were the most truthful witnesses of what I knew.

I checked the room completely for any evidence, for any scrap of their crime. That was my job. Everything was in place. As I said, Jed liked danger, but he always planned ahead. On the way out, I took a spotted seashell and put it in my purse—I don't know why, unless it was for memory.

But I omit a detail. This is the thing. I went to look. Not part of the plan. I couldn't help it. I still don't know what came over me; the knot of adventure in us all, the curious malice of ordinary persons. Because I could. I walked off. I see the sun at its height, heat stammering, skewering the light. No one noticed me—or I noticed no one. I shouldered my way in: stupefaction still held sway, the crowd a ruckus of distraction. I saw the body. Bent toward the side window, eyes to heaven. Wide eyes. Indecent eyes: motherfucking—goddamn—blank medallion eyes. To my surprise, he looked alive. Something about the body holds on to life—the turn of his cheek, which had an air of boredom. But then I shifted my view, jostled by the crowd—and that sudden movement—a mere nail-shaving of an inch—revised my deceived glance. His sunburned jaw was a grimace, a cubist pose, frozen between panic and oblivion. Blood on his slack chin attracted flies and dust. There was no doubt about it. I trudged back to the apartment. I made a call, an extra errand, my last words. Colonel Grier—he was dead.

6

WHEN THE NEWS was splashed in the papers, the household saw nothing amiss. I had sat in bed for days reading books and speaking to no one; and I believed that when my mother saw my mood, she announced in her prim, moderating way, her lips pursed: "You know, it's a good thing you are going to America. Maybe you should leave right now, right this minute. That university was never a good place for you."

Or at least that's what I think she said through a drowsy din.

Surreptitious activity had been going on in my rooms. People were still packing me away. As I read one book after another, I knew that, in the background, action was in full swing—stacking, buying, delivering, whispering. They were crating me off at last into the world of my mother's choosing. All the details of my person—my wits, clothing, desires, sports equipment, books—were being arranged and assembled for dispatch abroad, all of the things my mother determined I wished to carry. A new life was on order, a whole catalog of freedoms. I knew there was something amiss in this, I couldn't put my finger to it. I was too preoccupied, impotent and distracted, to find out what it was. Old Manang Maring was out, emerging from the caverns of her retired rooms, hobbling about with her obliterated, white eye for remnants of my closets, knickknacks and accessories, all of which people were trying to sneak out from beneath my glassy gaze—with all the stealth of dump trucks. Ever since Manang Maring had gone in her middle age to Saudi, to try her bad luck abroad, she'd been displaced from her position as my yaya; but on her return, damaged in one eye, her superfluous presence led to these inconvenient attentions, her blind fawning over me.

To compensate for her role in my departure, Manang Maring strictly followed my old daily routine—the routine of my childhood. As if receding into the past would keep my spirits up. In the morning, toast, fruit and orange juice on a breakfast table lay outside my room. Milk. Stuffed animals propped on my bed. Coffee and cookies at eleven. Manang Maring gave my final schedule the exacting touches of a distinct farewell—offering my meals with the silence and respect given to condemned prisoners. Newspapers had been added to the breakfast tray early on in my career as house brat, as well as selected book reviews and magazines. And I read the papers she offered, dismissing the loyal old woman with hardly a wave.

I was riveted, holding on to the news, orange juice in hand and head stiffened toward the portent of what I read; the slightly intolerable acidic aftertaste of the juice nicked at my gorge, and I felt that critical bitterness curl up my gut, a citric burp. I don't think my hands shook, but neither did my brains work, except to exhale solemnly and read. I read the news and can't say I was horrified; although I felt, strangely, a kind of surprise: in the mundane way the completion of a story, no matter how predictable, has in it a gross, goose-bump value. And at the same time I didn't believe it. I couldn't see it: the congruence between what we had planned and the gory surplus of this story. Drinking orange juice, back in my pajamas, I didn't see the chain of these events, what I knew versus what I read, as coherent and clearly following. And then, devouring the papers and looking for word in the evening news, I slowly came to this revelation.

It had nothing to do with me.

In my bustling, unseeing house, against the pillows of my raised, flowered bed, my Roald Dahl wallpaper and velveteen toys, I didn't have any hand in it, I had no signature in this grisly, premeditated evil. Not the smooth down of my sheets, nor the comforting silence of the air conditioner, nor the careful imprint of my initials all across my beautiful walls, nor the pulp of fresh, peeled fruit held any witness or connection to the pocked, shattered glass, the riddled bulletproof saloon, hubcaps spattered but all in place, and the inert body barely visible in the report, next to the square inset photograph of the murdered man in better times, bulb-nosed and younger, fatcheeked, unsmiling, and wearing a Yankees baseball cap.

And so it was that as I discovered more and more about the case—the vicious caliber of the guns, which the Americans themselves knew (so it was reported) could overpower the not-so-dependable panels of their cars (the windows were bulletproof, but the car's body was not, knowledgeable kibitzers said, without providing sources); the unique awful boldness of the enterprise ("the first direct attack against an American official in the Philippines since the Filipino-American war!" yelled a yellow editorial); the atypical character of the arms (brand-new Western-bloc weapons in a country with proliferating second-rate arms); the apparent youthfulness of the suspects; the lack of reliable witnesses (an incoherent Metro sweeping aide; a mute monkey); the arcane, complicated details of the American operation LOTUS that seeped into the arena of public consciousness—("created under the RP-US assistance pact on March 21, 1947, paid for by the Philippine government to advise the armed forces on military matters," the foreign agency, in its turn, had "a reputation for excellent beef, imported cigarettes, wine, chocolates, and bingo where dollars were at stake"—a kind of "Animal House of a diplomatic home," with "real-live dirty dancing")—the more I read, the more I recognized my separation and distance, the improbability of my connivance with the event. I was not a part. I was, as Edwin prophesied, irrelevant; events rumbled on without any hint of my aspect in them, no sign of my acts.

But even beyond that (the no-less-dire footnotes, on the op-ed pages, of blame and suspicion and paranoia), there was that curious mental distraction that I felt: like a vehicle careering mindlessly, without brakes or rear-wheel drive, on a guileless track, dangerously unconnected to the pavement. Instead, I read with an outsider's calm and even with a thrill for ghastly happenings, the Metro Manilan's lust for squalid detail.

Predictably, on television, in a repetitive, irritating refrain, the commander in chief, generals of the armed forces, the minister of defense and other individuals proclaimed the urgent investigation of the horrific case. The Secretary, in a rare national appearance, declared: "The killing has brought a new dimension to the guerrilla war!" People asked, looking at Mr. Esdrújula, "And who's he?"

Most important: vigilante groups with brand-new guns were mobilizing toward the city, in preparation for an urban war. A massive arms movement was beginning, shifting government priorities from peace escapades to wartime plans. Before the Colonel's blood was dry, the president demanded money for counterinsurgent funds; and no doubt lawmakers would rubber-stamp his cry.

The next day, letters to the editor demanded speedy results; parliament made terrifying promises. Of course, out came from their prehistoric lairs squawking pro-America hacks and Christian charlatans who denounced the perfidy of fellow Filipinos, the soullessness of the decade and even of the millennium, and our failure thus to win the honor of becoming the fifty-first American state—an embarrassing chorus of hysteria.

On the other hand, in equally raucous, dyspeptic tones, sibilant voices in a left-leaning daily gloated over this just murder of a murderer, as they called him, tit for tat in the tide of time, a surprising but suitable casualty in the increasingly brutal war against insurgents; and on their part they denounced the military and the dictator for their share in the blood, while editorials and feature articles explored in jubilant detail the ironies in the death of an American warmonger.

Colonel Grier had posthumous fame as a schizophrenic man. On one hand, his general, speaking from the hospital where his mortal frame was wearing him out, his frail, plaster-of-Paris heart, said, his head shaking in grief: "And to think he had come to help the Filipino people in their efforts to defend democracy." The U.S. military attaché spoke in a ceremony: "He was a brave man who served his country well." A wealthy expatriate, a suntanned Italian, offered the reward of a $200,000 watch for information on the crime.

On the other hand, a list of the Colonel's talents was alleged in the press. "Sponsored low-intensity conflicts . . . an instructor at the School of the Assassins in Fort Bragg . . . projects sowing confusion and conflict in rebel-taken areas . . . CAFGU was his brainchild . . .

proposed and trained head-hunting vigilantes . . . Alsa Masa, Bantay Bayan . . . troops that gouged the eyes of children after they were killed . . . littered the countryside with Garands and carbines . . . dead women . . . dead children, their severed heads . . ."

There was a deadlock in opinion. A public relations strategic stalemate, so to speak.

No one was surprised when, two days into the investigation, names of suspects cropped up in the news like so much grain separated from chaff—unpolished, raw grains of facts, for sure, with earth and moldering aphids still fresh on them, so that the actual ripeness of the details was unclear, and maybe, who knows, they had just popped from a rash mill of evidence and incrimination; but the names were published nevertheless. No one was surprised at the swift results. Everyone knew that the police, when they wished, could ferret out any sort of criminal with just the right push and shove; it had long been said that, for the constabulary, Metro Manila was such a tightly knit community that each criminal and civilian barely bore the proverbial six degrees of separation.

However, as I said, the released names seemed more like bait than the result of careful investigation. And in fact, in the news stories, they may as well have been lines of dirt, for all they mattered to the public; there were no figures, no human notations to the names. No one cared much about the details. Shock was all.

Jared Tango, also known as Simon; Ching Byun Co, no alias; Soltera Solidum. In one report, the suspect was said to be Joaquin "Wack Wack" Mongo; in another, all three parts of his name were held out, as if manipulating the alphabet were a police tactic: Jet Migra, alias Riverside; in one, more cheekily, he was Jack de Morgue. They were curious, unsettling, these revelations. In my mind, he seemed to dart from one hiding place to another, an anagrammatic fugitive taking refuge under the finite resources of his name. And it was not clear, now or then, if this scrambling were journalistic error or an ingenious police tactic: if, somewhere in a piss-flavored precinct, the name had, in fact, already been conjured, and it was a curious, problematic puzzle. An actual Morga. Fancy that.

I didn't think about this as much as I wished that the errors were, I hoped, providential—and so the interstitial Jed running through the phonemic gamble would not be caught. I began to look at the changing names and find in them clues to the investigation. I imagined that the early vagrancy of diphthongs was a good sign, "oa" interchangeable with "ue"; and I appreciated, with a lurch in my heart, the introduction of middling, superfluous syllables late in the game; as I read paper after paper, the uncorrected spellings and distracting vowels foolishly made me happy. As his name remained enigmatic and, in fact, receded in the limelight, as revelations and developments occurred, I felt justified in my pale fantasy of his safety, secure as Jed was in his obscurity, as far as I could tell—and, perhaps, we all could be truly absolved because the right morphemes of our names remained unknown.

I saw the fallacy of my belief—the cunning of the naming game. When events were replayed ad nauseam and holy masses were scheduled to be prayed, and I must admit I was not so clear-eyed or pronounced so healthy myself—the precise question that occurred to me was: why was it, of all the names, that these ones in question seemed changed so cleverly—so full of art?

In subsequent reports, the girl was said to be unknown; in others, she was called Sally; in many, she was not mentioned at all. In a torrent of factual fancy, in serpentine moltings of *S*'s, she was Selena,

Semilla, Solidaridad, Sonrisa. And the last name's vagaries had a certain wit. Soli-Man. Sole-Dad. But they never got it right.

However, even then I felt (admittedly under the influence of some medically noted wild glandular disease) that there was logic in the error—somehow, the rampant dysgraphia, the frank misnaming, held in itself a clue: though it was a lead I was better off not following.

As I SAID, even as my thoughts wandered, developments occurred. Details jumbled out within hours. The papers gave a name to a suspected sect of left-wing bandits. Some clunky revolutionary acronym, based on variations of the terms "urban defense elite hit squads" or "miserable red adventurists with fancy, stolen guns," depending on how you looked at it. Urban Sparrow Unit: fancy name for nameless fowls. Raids were made on different groups, including a church headquarters peacefully ensconced near the scene of the crime. A Catholic bishop denounced the police's actions. Police surprised a bunch of students in a movie house. Arrests were made. A student was released; mistaken identity, it was proved; plus, her father turned out to be a congressman, and the student herself, an innocuous economics major with walrus cheeks, was only a dabbler in a campus rag. She'd never even joined a march. The police were clutching at straws.

Should I have laughed when I read the descriptions of the gang in the newspapers? They were "highly trained urban guerrillas, an elite group within the red army." They had "planned the action months in advance," patrolling the headquarters of LOTUS using unsuspicious lookouts such as an old Chinese chauffeur, Ching Byun Co, also known as—

Should I have laughed? When Manang Maring came in to work that day, she was in such hysterics that I thought her Saudi Arabian–induced injury had finally kicked in and shown its last, damaging blows. She was heaving and crying in spastic commotion, her blind white eye emitting tears that looked eerie, because they seemed rootless, pouring from a void. Her vast breasts shook in miserable, self-conscious despair, as she spoke in tongues, a mixture of Waray, Tagalog, English, and the gastric residue of her chorizo-and-garlic-rice breakfast.

"Calm down, Maria, calm down," my mother said impatiently when we entered the kitchen to catch the reason for the excitement.

I had been startled away from my cup of coffee by the early morning noise. All the packing was done and epiphany was at hand: only one more day, and I was set to leave for America. I'll be honest: at that point, I wished to go.

I climbed down to the kitchen—I had yet to finish my newspaper.

"Oh, Madame, Madame," Manang Lita the cook, always the reasonable one, looked at us with her grave, wide eyes, her stare cluing us in on the degree of the tragedy. The more serious the matter, the less emotion registered in Manang Lita's eyes.

Manang Maring was still gibbering, whispering names and sorrows. Servants were huddled around her, a few with charged, red-eyed sentiment, going to and fro, from the medicine cabinet to the refrigerators, fetching and carrying things.

"Lita, what is it?" my mother said sharply. "You tell us. Is Maria having a stroke? Should she see a doctor? Why did she come to work if she needed to see a doctor? I told her not to go to that Saudi, but does anyone listen to me? It has damaged her brains. Not that there was much to destroy. Maring never listened to me. I told her what would happen if she ever worked in Riyadh. What is going on? Lita, you tell me."

All of us, the maids and the houseboys and the gardener and the other driver and I, waited for Lita, who calmly wiped Maring's face, ordering a girl to return a bucket of ice to the cooler as she did so. When Maring was calmer, reverting to sighs and sipping a glass of water, she looked almost satisfied by the attention. Lita spoke to us.

"It's not about her," Lita said finally. "It's not about Maring. It's about Manong Babe."

"About Babe?" my mother said. "They found him then?"

"What's going on?" I asked. "What do you mean?"

My mother continued: "Well, if he's back, then what is she going on about? What's the problem with Maring?"

Maring started sighing again, falling apart on someone's shoulder. She started to wail. One of the kitchen maids giggled. The gardener Armando, on the edge of the crowd, silenced the girl with a rap on her scalp. Another woman started moaning, turning away from the rest.

Lita said: "She was with his family this morning. They finally found him."

My mother was listening, nodding her head.

"So where did he go? Did they find him drunk somewhere?"

"Babe doesn't drink," piped up the gardener.

"Ssh," they all said to him.

"No, Madame," answered Lita.

"So tell us, Lita. Come on. Why is she shaking like that?"

Servants were holding on to Maring, who moaned dramatically at this point in the story. The others stood by watching, some sniffling with a distinct choral fade, and all listening with my intentness and curiosity, ranged before me with the look of my own stupefied face.

"Madame, he is dead."

At this Manang Maring shrieked, wailing: "I saw him, I saw him, I saw him, I saw him."

"Manong Babe?" I said. "But I just saw him."

"No, I saw him, I saw him," contradicted Maring.

"But I just saw him a few days ago. At the tournament. He took me there and drove me home."

"Ma'am Sol, that is more than one week ago," explained Armando. He started counting: "Día de los Inocentes—'Cember twenty-eight, thirty—eight days ago. After that day, he has disappeared. I also saw him too. When he drove you back: it is the last day of his appearance."

"You haven't been out of your room since then, Sol," my mother said. "You're leaving for college tomorrow. Everyone knows that. You locked yourself in your room since the last day of the tournament. Isn't that right?"

The servants nodded.

"Everyone here has been witness. You never left your room. We have been packing your bags for your departure for America. We have been planning your departure. Everyone knows that, isn't that right? But Manong Babe sadly disappeared. Didn't you know, Sol?"

"No one told me."

"And you know, his name has been in the papers. I wondered about that. Do you know that, Lita?"

Lita shook her head.

"See, no one noticed," my mother said triumphantly, as if that fact meant something. "It doesn't mean anything, maybe," she said hurriedly. "But his name was in the papers yesterday, you know, in that horrid news about the Colonel, God bless his soul. Not that I thought it was Manong Babe, any Chinese person could have the name Co, Ching Moon Co. But you know he's been missing, and it occurred to me, but I knew it must be a typogrammatical error, no one can trust those journalists, they're illiterate. And you know what, inday, I thought I saw the name of your friend, the dark one with the kinky hair? Sally. Sally Soledad. I thought it was her name. It's sad. She's an activist. And who knows who those foolish, crazy devils are who killed the Colonel, God have mercy on his soul, but Manong Babe could not have been part of their plot. Still, it was a sad coincidence, I thought about it just the same. To see his name in the papers. But the police know, sure they do. They'll get to the bottom of it."

"But I saw Manong Babe—," I said. I heard myself, sounding strangely croaked, a tone in my voice like a keening. Could it be possible? I felt a dry, slow whiplash in my chest.

Maring began shaking again.

My mother was impatient. "And you say it was Babe, Maria?" she asked.

"They found him in the Pasig," Manang Maring sobbed. "I saw him, I saw him."

"I saw him, I saw him," I repeated.

The maids were looking at me. I was horrified to hear the strange feeble groaning: I was bleating like Manang Maring.

7

I AM A SICK woman, my memory certifiably unreliable. It's all in a document, clinical. Anyone will tell you that. But I remember that on the last day of the tournament Uncle Gianni called for me.

"D'you see him?" Uncle Gianni asked me. He was strolling around the soccer area, an anxious host. "Did he arrive yet? Go look around for him, Sol."

I could tell in the tight movement of his lips that he was annoyed about something, either angry or nervous, and it was betrayed only in brief expressions and that taut nerve on his temple.

A lot of people sought Uncle Gianni at the games, old and young women, housemaids and businessmen, all of whom he charmed and flattered with his eagle attention, and I was sent to look for his prey, Colonel Grier, who had promised to attend the tournament.

Jed strolled to the car with the bags while I went off to look. I took a turn around both sides of the field, down to the far reaches where some men rested in the shade, watching Belgium, those extraneous Italians, thrash Team Malta. And though many of the stalwarts of the tournament, fleshy, grinning men, had a counterfeit haunch or profile, or simulated the Colonel's bald gravitas, none of them had the upright, scary posture I'd recognize with clairvoyance now, I could spot him in my sleep.

There was no Colonel Grier. I reported to Uncle Gianni.

"That son of a bitch," he said.

I stood before him, letting it pass. I held a hand out before my face to shield myself from the sun's glare.

"The shit. He's been playing with us for too long. He thinks he calls the shots. We'll see. He'll see who's boss."

I cleared my throat.

"Uh, Uncle Gianni. I'm going now. I'll be back tomorrow," I said.

"It's all your fault, Sol." But Uncle Gianni was grinning at me.

"What?"

"I heard about it—the little escapade at the Colonel's house. Very funny. I told your Pa it couldn't have been you—maybe it was your evil twin. You never drink coffee in the afternoon."

"What are you talking about?"

"Don't worry about it, Sol. It was a lousy trick—but the guy's an ass. A chump. Frankie fixed it."

"What did Pa do?"

"He said you were ill. D'you see Spain kick the Philippines? Wasn't that too bad. I was rooting for those kids. That was too bad. I should have rigged the teams a bit more."

"But that's cheating," I said.

"Sol, it's my tournament."

"I know," I said.

Then I kissed him on his thin, hot cheeks.

"Oh yes," he said. "The young man is here. Well, take care of yourself, kid. I like that boy. Jared, his name is? Mariano's boy."

"No. His name's—well, anyway, bye, Uncle."

"Oh all right. You won't talk about him, but I'll find out. You'll see. Ciao. Be good now!"

B Y THE CAR, I saw Manong Babe. He wore his usual pressed outfit, a man of dignified order amid the naked slovenliness of the event. He met me with that wide smile, his mole folding into his flesh like a buried volcano, his eyes squinting against the sun.

"Ma'am Sol, you didn't wait for me," he said, his hand shielding his eyes. "Did sir Jed play?"

"Uh, well, no, but Jed is here. Jed!"

Manong Babe and I walked toward him. A little heart of dust had formed on Manong Babe's wingtips. He noticed it and stooped to wipe it off.

"Oh, Manong Babe," I said, "when will I ever see you in slippers, or even sneakers? You're such a neatnik."

"Never, Ma'am Sol," he said, grinning, "God willing."

Jed came up to us.

"So you played, sir?" Manong Babe said, pointing to Jed's bag. "I did not see you in the tournament."

Jed swung the bag behind him, as if trying to hide its bulk. "No, no, not this time, Manong," he said. "How are you?"

"Good, sir, good."

Manong Babe, it occurred to me, might be as infatuated with Jed as any silly girl. Whenever Jed was around, he spoke only to him.

"Can you take Sol home today, Manong?"

"Of course, sir."

"Be sure she gets there safely now."

"Of course, sir! I always do that."

"Salamat, Manong," Jed said. "And how's your son these days? Did he like his present?"

"He plays with the basketball everyday, thank you, sir. My eldest, Chitong, is back from Jeddah for Christmas."

"You must be very happy. And your girl Nene?" Jed asked.

"She's on the honor roll again, sir. She says thank you for the books."

"Good," said Jed. "And your wife?"

"She's still sick in bed. But all her children are home to help. I'm a lucky man, sir, with friends like you. And Ma'am Sol, too. Thank you so much, sir."

Jed strode to his car, leaving me behind. He was trying to open up the trunk while he held on to his heavy burden, when Manong Babe came over to help him, lifting the bag.

"No, no, Manong," Jed said. "Don't bother."

"It's heavy, sir, let me take it."

"No, no," said Jed.

Manong Babe patted the bag, its hard bulges.

"More Christmas gifts, sir?" he asked, smiling.

Jed heaved the bag into the trunk. "Yes," he smiled, "more gifts."

"But Christmas is over, sir."

"I know," said Jed. And Jed smiled at him, while Manong Babe beamed back. "They're gifts of the magi," Jed said, grinning.

"More surprises for people, sir?" Manong Babe asked. "You're a good man."

Of COURSE, I could dwell on the conversation, as if it were exactly as I record it—as if life really did have foreshadowing, as if it could be lived backwards. And now the scenes are tainted with the suspect vision of foreknowledge. Little counterfeit shivers of premonition.

I could find an ironic moment in the statement "But Christmas is over." I could witness a gleam in Manong Babe's eye. I could make the conversation a puzzle, an ambiguous dialogue, teasing me with the knowledge Manong Babe may have had. I could turn on the words "gifts of the magi"—a password that escaped me? A symbolic code? Gold, myrrh and frankincense, the Feast of Ephiphany: January 6. What secrets were between them, lost to me?

But it does not convince me. Manong Babe took me home, as I said, though I protested. It was no great incident. I do remember my short, heated argument with Jed—a jealous fit in the raging sun. It was muggy, and the crowd was in some uproar—a tied game.

Nothing was resolved that day.

Jed went on his way, and I returned home. Manong Babe delivered me safe and sound. It's true: that was the last I saw of Manong Babe.

I know that never in his life would he give up his car or allow someone else to drive it; a decoy theft, a faked carnapping? No: Manong Babe would not have allowed it. And the car abandoned on the side of the road by the so-called getaway men? Manong Babe would never have abandoned his car.

In fact, the news had already cleared my suspicions—the abandoned car, in all subsequent reports, was a basic-blue Toyota, a beat-up Corona stolen from an expatriate in Makati.

I do not imagine they will ever find the white limousine.

The fact is, these last conversations I remember were small, passing moments, not worthy even of a chronological place in my report; and if I had had any suspicion then of Jed's duplicity, of our own twin trap, that in effect we were leading Manong Babe to danger like one of those peasant teenagers I once saw dead in a funeral chapel with Soli, many months ago, those five young corpses in their biers whose faces remain buried in my blind brain, I didn't think of it at the time. I never believed that Manong Babe could have been part, actively, of the plot.

I heard instead, and this is what I remember clearly, the gentleness in Jed's voice when he said, "Salamat, Manong." And how Manong Babe looked happy, beaming with gratitude over Jed's gratitude. I remember that moment because it struck me at the time—it struck me how easily Manong Babe learned to love.

What I do not accept is the accusation the events leveled against Jed when Manong Babe's body was found in the Pasig—miserably naked. They had taken away his modest undershirt. Only his mole identified him. They'd stripped him even of his shoes.

I was bleating in the kitchen, lowing like a calf. It was then that I knew it, the irrevocable, vast burden—and I would never cast it off. It remains with me, my knowledge, with the flow of my blood. It was then that I realized, with a whole heart splitting, a soft, mewling disintegration—that yes: we had killed a man.

8

"I saw him. I saw him."

Everyone in the kitchen was staring at me.

My mother looked stricken by Manang Maring's report and was giving instructions to the staff.

"I will visit Babe's family," my mother was saying. "If anyone wishes to come with me, you may come. We'll get to the bottom of this. Do you want to come with us, Sol?"

But I was already on the way to my room. Soli, I thought. Soli. They had found something out about Manong Babe. I thought about it, a flash of panic: What were those names, those clues again? What was that my mother had said?

Had I been looking in the wrong direction, my heart praying for the wrong name?

"Your friend, the dark one, Sally Soledad."

Had she ever met Soli? Why don't I remember?

I ran up the stairs to my room.

I whispered Soli's name as I searched for the clues. *Sosolosolo-sol.* I hunted for the back copies of the papers. I needed to look at each of the lists of names. There were four morning newspapers carrying the event; in addition, a women's magazine had started a foldout special on expatriate lives, with a centerpiece on the American colonel and his family, lifestyle, and passions. A photo spread, all blurred and furry in the cheap newsprint, included a snapshot of a plumpish blonde with a baby—they sat at a swimming pool's edge, the newsprint water behind them; the same lady, but pregnant, wearing a mini skirt and high heels and holding on to her husband at an airport (the ovoid woman in an awkward pose was waving, but the Colonel would have nothing of her joy and stood scowling at the sun, ramrod-straight, grim even on vacation); the smiling exonumist in a flowered shirt, showing off a glass case of valuable Roman stamps (no one ever got things right); and one more rendition of the shattered car, glass and newsprint-blood on the street, a dark swimming-pool puddle: in the background one could distinguish a brief, gray flash of tropical plants—an ordinary path cleaned regularly by Metro aides and favored with civic street gardens.

I tore through the magazines and papers and impatiently read through the text until I arrived at what I wanted. I looked at the lists of names, I read and examined them. Sure enough, there seemed to be a rhythmic pattern.

A crafty interchange of names. Soleado Soldado in one. Soltera Soleado in another. Even in error, a chiasmus. In yet another, Solidaridad M. Tangere was incriminated; and in a one-off tabloid insert on the scandal, a name was reported as an alias, "aka Fili Solidaridad." And was it a calculated mishap, these epistrophic shifts? Sally Soliman. Sandy Soledad. The way syncopes abounded. Alias Victoire in one, alias Victor in another. In the first day's reports, she had been nonexistent, not part of the event. But already, slowly there began in small, creeping increments, in tiny, restrained clauses I had barely noted, an emerging portrait of a rebel. Teenage Terrorist. Sparrow Queen. Ridiculous labels. Brief, sensational possibilities for glib caption writers and alliterative pens.

In any case, none of the lists ever got the names right. Perhaps they were waiting for the last report. I checked the date: it was the only paper I hadn't read, the one I had left behind that morning. The morning's news. Solidaridad "Soli" Soledad.

"Soli," she had introduced herself. "As in the revolution. You know."

I read the morning's report. It was almost expansive: a little *talambuhay*. She was Visayan, it said. From Leyte. A brief toccata on a provincial life. Academic record. Salutatorian, Philippine Science. Coconut federation scholar. Campus activist. Tragically misled. Seventeen years old. *Kinse—kinse anyos—*. Possibly a liaison or a lookout. Objects found in her possession: *Mao for Beginners*. The triteness almost makes one laugh. *The Little Red Book* (in a hoard of coins, a rattling box). Full-time in the underground. A full-scale launch for her arrest. Bounty on her head. Missing.

I read it again.

Missing.

I knew exactly when I had seen her last.

Missing.

I looked at my organized, ransacked room. I checked—I moved quickly to a drawer. I searched everywhere for the rattling can. The tin container of Fox's Glacier candy, with the pamphlets in it. *The Little Red Book*. Cartoon Mao. *Society and Revolution*. Small change you could find in Popular Bookstore: all you needed to do was stroll in and look. I looked for the coins, the copper centavos. Copper. For smelting.

It was strange not to have seen the irony all along. There was I, a gun dealer's daughter, scrounging around for copper coins. Copper five-centavo coins, with the ancient smelter, Panday Pira, on the obverse, and on the reverse the seal of the Philippine Republic. These were the only copper coins in circulation in the country—the only coins you could smelt into bullets. And I, the gun dealers' daughter, kept collecting my redundant hoard.

I found a tidy layer of notes—unaccountably well arranged, my diary, sheaves of paper. The tin container was gone, or maybe it was that I didn't look hard enough; at this point, it's hard to tell. I lay on my bed, on the morning's newspaper sheets.

I looked at the line of names. It was odd. Slowly, as the news progressed, there turned out to be no trace of him, none of him at all. Jared Margaux, Joaquin River, Jet Migra de Bel Vedere. His name slowly disappeared. In its place were other priorities, all unknown to me: who knows how they picked up names. Not so randomly, I knew. There had to be a name to present to the public, after all. Habeas corpse: rescue me, over someone else's dead body.

9

WHEN A BODY is missing in a city like Manila, there are known
avenues of retrieval. Countryside sections of the southern coast-
line, jungle areas near the North Luzon Expressway, goat-ridden
ramparts off of busy decrepit roads. In the old days, they might have
been havens for native bandits, escapees from the *polo,* or righteous
tax-evaders: now they were spaces forsaken by townspeople and forgotten by law. Nature is not the least subversive of the elements in
the countryside. Lastly, of course, there is the accommodating river
Pasig, so intimate with death as it weaves through the miserable,
littoral municipalities of Metro Manila that it holds sway in our
dreams: the last witness of the ever-loyal city's grief.

"It is better to die in the water," the gardener Armando was saying to the maids as I came down the stairs. "You do not see what
happens to the body. Everything is erased."

The girls did not look convinced.

Is there, really, comfort in effacement? Mutilation, electrocu-
tion, unthinkably refined savage acts—can the river hide it?

"Well, are you coming with us, Sol?"

It was then I looked at my mother.

She had been sharp and impatient with me throughout the furor. She was lucid and alert. For weeks, I understood her presence in the bustle of the maids around me. My father was gone again on one of his trips—was it around the country? To Indonesia? Another rushed visit to some dismantled air base in Europe? Now my mother wore her matriarchal demeanor, her hair teased up, her high heels like steel. She stood with her faithful flock, the household staff gathered around her.

"We're all going to Babe's house in Punta, Sol. Are you coming?"

And I asked my mother from my perch on the stairs: "What did you do to Manong Babe, Ma?"

She had moved amid the crowd so that now she was distinguishable mainly by a nest of hair.

"What are you talking about?" came her reply. She walked closer, away from the servants, her voice coming near.

"You knew who was part of the group, Ma, the group who stole your guns—you knew all about it. You knew who was going after the Colonel."

My speech sounded silly. It sounded only like a madwoman's digression, a wild guess, in this hubbub of grief. It came out of me in a splatting croak, like soprano gibberish. The servants stopped moving. The maids, carrying their food hampers and Tupperware trays, the water jugs and cookies, heading for an ever-more-sumptuous wake as the car was loaded with pastry, dregs of a pig's head, leftovers of leche flan—the parade of busy mourners stopped. My mother moved toward me, her arms in the air, and the laden servants followed, atomized and distracted.

My mother's eyes were wide, in shock or rage, it didn't matter.

"What is the matter with you, Sol?"

She waved her hand at me as she came forward, the other gesturing toward the maids as if she were puzzled, asking them to
explain my words. It's as if they all had been put on mute. A girl in
a corner began shaking without words, and now even the gardener
looked wan, at a loss. Reina Elena strode up to the stairs where I
stood; as she came close, she looked as if she were going to hit me,
her arm raised and face taut, her hair about my face. Instead, she
hissed at me, whispering, her eyes flashing dangerously: "Servants
are with us, Sol: are you mad?"

"That's why I speak. Let someone hear!"

I was horrified by my mother's question.

"You know who stole the guns from your warehouse, Ma. You
know who took the guns away to New Manila. You know it wasn't
Manong Babe. He had nothing to do with it. Do you hear me,
Manang Lita? Manong Armando? What did you do to Manong
Babe, Ma? What did you do to him?"

I heard my voice sing horridly, a wild, vague pitch. I have never
been good at confrontations.

"Leave her!" my mother announced to everyone. "She's having
a fit again. She's going crazy again. It's her old sickness. Call Doc-
tora Varona, Lita. Armando, you tell Sergio to drive everyone to
Babe's house. I will follow. I have to call the doctor. Go, go, all of
you. I'll deal with Sol. She needs her medicine. I'll deal with her."

Some kept standing around, but Armando herded them out.

"Go!" said my mother. They scuttled out of the doorway except
for Lita.

"You know who did it, Ma," I wailed, my tears streaming. "You know who stole your guns. You know who killed the Colonel. They're blaming all the wrong people, Ma."

My mother slapped me in the face.

"*Ingrata!*"

I hobbled under her attack, and it was she who held me up. She shook me and I cowered as she moved again to strike my face. I stumbled on the staircase, almost falling against her as I did.

"Silence, Sol, silence! What will I do with you? Shut up! Idiot! *Ingrata!* After all we do for you, this is what I get? We work hard all our lives for you—and this is what we get? Lita! What are you staring at? Get away from here! I told you to get the doctor—get away!"

Lita looked frightened. She hurried from the room.

I watched Manang Lita retreat.

Now the massive Chinese vase alone witnessed our intentions.

I took a step down and in doing so tripped against my mother. She held me to her.

"Inday"—I heard her in my ear—"you have to leave us."

My mother's mascara had dribbled onto her cheek and on her shoulder. I felt on my arms her damp flesh and smelled the rich, enfeebling scent of her perfume. Her brittle hair brushed against me: a soft, scented scratch.

She was whispering, a wet, hot wind in my ear: "It's the only way, Sol; you are safe right now. That's what Pa says. But you have to leave us. They are looking. They have to go after them."

"Who?"

"They have to go after the murderers. Your father knows most of the men in the investigation. I mean, he knows their bosses. Thank God for that. The Secretary is in charge. He knows you could not have been a part: he knows you had nothing to do with

it. You did not go near the Colonel. Everyone in the house is a witness: you stayed in your room. You never went out. Everyone is a
witness. But justice is needed, the Secretary says. The Colonel—
he's an important man, inday, you have no idea who he was. A
Vietnam vet. An American hero. A P.O.W. The Americans need
justice. That's what the Secretary says. You have to leave. You are
all packed away. Uncle Gianni knows where to go. Uncle Gianni
will take you."

"What did you do to Manong Babe?"

"If he became a witness against you, heaven forbid—if they
ever got hold of him and he could say where you had been—"

"What did you do to Manong Babe?"

My mother looked like a child, a child hurt in the mud, her
mascara clinging to her lips. "He told Pa everything. I don't know—
he told Pa."

"When?"

"I don't know."

"When?"

"When we learned the guns were gone!"

"But how did you know?"

My mother looked confused.

"I don't know. Ask Pa. Manong Babe told him. He told Pa
everything he knew."

"He didn't know anything," I cried. "You know he didn't know
anything. He knew nothing, Ma. If you knew the guns were stolen,
why didn't you stop us? If Manong Babe told you about us, why did
you let us do it? Why did you let us do it if you knew?"

She said, her eyes suddenly gleaming, as if the information
would give her more credit in my eyes: "It was your Uncle Gianni—"

"What?"

"He said, he said—"

"What?" I felt a low, bunched fever in my gut: a keening in my womb.

"Why, the Colonel had to go, of course," my mother exclaimed. "One way or the other, Gianni said, he had to go. He was not following the plan."

I stared dumbly at my mother.

"He had to go. He was bad for business, Gianni said. He had to go."

I looked at her.

"You used us," I said. "You knew about us all along."

"No, inday. No. I did not know. I did not know what you were doing."

"Pa knew?"

"When I learned what had happened—I did not know what to do. Gianni knew. Gianni knew what we should do."

"So who picked up Manong Babe?"

"I don't know, inday. Events were so quick—"

"Who picked him up?"

"He knew too much. He told Pa everything when Pa confronted."

"No, he didn't. He knew nothing."

"Pa said. He could be picked up—he'd give everyone's name—the Americans could get hold of him—Gianni said—Pa said. You know Babe always followed you, everywhere you went. That was his job. And Babe—Babe told Pa everything he knew. Events moved so fast—inday, they had to decide—they did not know if they should let him go or make him—"

"But he was innocent."

"I know."

One can imagine how one weeps, keening and choking and rocking—like the wild, old river itself—against my mother, who held me to her, as in the old days, my gangly body in her lap.

"I want to know what happened to Soli, Ma. Find Soli, Ma. She's missing."

My mother was crying, holding me tight in her arms, rocking me back and forth, whispering, sobbing: "I didn't know what to do, Sol. I really didn't understand. I kept thinking, night and day, every day, ever since it happened: we have to find a way. I thought I should go mad." She whispered: "They found her at the scene of the crime, Sol."

"No they didn't, Ma."

"She was there. She was part of the plot. She was with Jed."

"She didn't know where they were, Ma. I gave her the wrong address."

My mother hugged me, softly moaning.

"You know where she is, Ma. You know what happened to Soli."

My mother whispered: "They have picked her up in Cubao. She has papers on her, incriminating evidence. She is a ringleader of the Urban Sparrows. She has books, everything. Notebooks and money. She is full-time in the underground. They have found out all the clues."

"In a rattling can."

"They have evidence. She is part of the plot."

"No she isn't, Ma, you know she isn't, Ma."

"They also know about Jed."

"What happened to Jed?"

"Don Mariano took him away. Don't worry. He's safe. He's gone away. His father made him go."

"Jed is gone?"

"He wanted to go to jail, you know—he was going to turn himself in, the fool—but Don Mariano organized everything. Thank God for Don Mariano. He knew exactly what to do. He acted fast, before they could come for Jed. You have to go. They could get you, too, even though they are not looking for you. They know you were not a part."

"But Soli?"

She rocked me on the stairway, and faintly on the green sheen of the Chinese vase I could see our vague, rustling reflections, an inextricable pattern of faint, moving shadows.

"They need justice," said my mother, murmuring. "They need suspects. They need Soli. She's so obvious. So perfect. Don't you see? Because even the police—even the police are confused. Because, inday," she whispered, as if she could barely speak it, "even the police keep confusing your names."

10

WORDS HEAP UP, descriptions. Rumor.
Vicious terrible news.

A shootout. A hunt for the killers, the Sparrow Queen. Found dead in an ambush. In a hideout among cadres in the countryside. All part of the plot. Jubilation in the papers: The suspects all accounted for. The missing found.

But what were the rumors?

The city whispered in the event's wake.

Examination of suspect's body revealed——. Rubber, paper, grass, glass——. A ruptured womb. Metallic trash——.

Stop.

Hand-to-mouth rumor was all we had, impoverished, garbled stories. An inexperienced hangman. Newly trained recruits. Counterinsurgency gangs. What were they called? Alsa Masa? Bantay Bayan? Rough, untutored hands. As if that explained horror. The glutinous grays of the newspaper photographs. Gnarled narra hands, the color of mahogany. Soiled wrapper of dead fish. Rumors, like a drug, roaming with all the openness of strangers, of people who didn't know her. Details wandered, like bad dreams, by word of mouth, striking listeners pale, inducing insomnia, miscarriages, despair.

My mother crying in the green glaze, the sobs that shattered a porcelain vase.

Stop.

HULLABALLOO IN THE hallway. A stampede of servants. The knives were sharp, but they had no feeling. They did not hurt, and I watched the blood ooze, a dark batik dye, and I was surprised. Hang yourself, you will regret it. I slashed it again to feel the pain. I felt none. I cut my flesh. Again and again. There was nothing. Nothing I could feel.

11

UNCLE GIANNI MET the girl at Nice Airport. A cold day: early January. He held her hand as light bulbs flashed. Revise that: not hand. By the sleeve. He held her by the sleeve, gently. On closer inspection, one might note her slightly discordant figure. Something awkward about her arms. Bandaged, gauzed lump of hands. The girl does not raise her head.

A cordon held curious onlookers at bay, and a film crew, Gallic and impervious, skinny, tilting men in black, strode about the cleared path. The girl, dark and gawky, a lanky adolescent, moved along the cleared-up space of this orchestrated welcome, following the straight line of a utility rope. A blond gaffer on his knees, a gofer pulling tape from the floor. "A commercial," Uncle Gianni muttered. She shivered as a door blew open. A lightbulb blinded her. A murmured rush toward something behind—a lady walking a dog, or a lame man with a parasol? Her myopic eyes distinguished someone's fleshy elbows; or was that a leash? Uncle Gianni tightened his grip and, almost dragging her by an armpit, moved quickly along. And in a cutting room somewhere, freeze-framed, on the margins of a black-clad crowd posing to sell condoms or perfume, the girl's stricken face looks down, denying evidence of its arrival, gaunt-cheeked and hollow-eyed.

No questions asked, no thoughts pursued. Olive groves are medicinal. I walked the wharf, noting names and origins, boats from Guernsey and Oporto. One was a namesake: blue and sunless *Sol*. Evenings we walked around the town, up the Haut Castelet, where a writer had pursued a novel in exile. It was my second escape. I wished to live.

In those endless hours, we waited for news of final reprieve, waited for some nameless storm to pass, an impasse beyond my grasp—and the daily spell of the light of France followed our false steps. By a town's rocky, leisurely ramparts we caught the Mediterranean, true and changing and pensively woven by the sun that favored it. The light of Antibes. It lay at the corner, it lies in my eye—at the end of a tunnel, it beckons. It was at the end of my walk down the cobbled streets, dog shit mingling with the sea breath of mussels and the vagrant malingering herbs; and at the end, the ancient light welcomed us, the harrowing, gentle hue of France. Beauty for its own sake is said to be terrible: and I strode under it, its blind-eyed benediction, its luminous and golden myrrh.

12

'M THE SAME size I was when I was a teenager; I take after my
mother in that way. Downstairs, they are installing a new gym—
hauling out the trash in the basement, dismantling the ancient
bowling alley. A thing I slightly regret. But my mom says, you need
a new gym, inday. Endorphins. Exercise. She has a new guru, a
yogini, from Canberra or Katmandu. One day, I think I would like
to jog to the river. I would like to volunteer as a docent at the local
museum. I have stopped playing soccer. My doctors say my body is
healthy, aerobic, but my mind—it has a mumbling sense of time.
Even now I fancy taking courses, maybe special topics in art history,
some day. One day I hope to pursue a degree—but something in me
fails. I have a fickle brain. Infrequent bursts of interest—in obscure,
petty corners of history, in languages, in numismatics, in entomology. I have a string of names on my tongue. Pigafetta. Elagabalus.
Magellan. I have many bits of knowledge, like little red ants up my
sleeve. But my mind turns. I lose interest, my attention dribbles. I
get headaches. Anyhow, it doesn't matter.

Sometimes, I dream. My dreams are innocuous. Nothing fancy.

He sits at a table, drinking coffee. Or I see his figure walking toward me, that detached gaze. In one dream, we talk about gazebos.

OTHERWISE, I KEEP to myself. I write things down when I get news. Despite the lack of change in my looks, people who have known me might stare. They might not be able to place me even though I look the same.

I keep to myself in the room with the oriel window. It has a view of the glittering river. The river is framed by stucco pomegranates against a marble ledge. I keep in a pile the drafts of the past, copies and revisions. I am still looking. I still search for it, the rattling can of memory.

I keep asking them, my doctors: how can it be anterograde amnesia when I have recalled with words everything—absolutely everything that has happened, including the terms for herbs and the shine of someone's shoes?

The senile doctor looks down, for his misplaced shoe (he's taken it off, as he does when he pretends to listen, and I can see it peeking under the Persian carpet's tassels, but I do not bother to help). He looks up at me, bringing a hand to his mouth as he clears his throat.

Uhum, he says. Uhuh.

His throat hoards phlegm, his entire body is a miserable sac of endless sputum, and I watch him, his throat-clearing and his shoe-hunting, the geriatric maneuvers of his jerky limbs.

Repetition—he repeats—casting his blind foot about— repetition—

Yes, doctor, I know. Repetition is the site of trauma.

Your memory, he coughs—and his foot at last finds his target, in tandem with one tremendous spume.

He completely loses it, spazzing into his papers.

I wait patiently as he settles back into his sedate wingback chair, pretending nothing has happened.

Uhum, he croaks.

I twiddle my thumbs. I watch a pale moth in the room, the color of a croissant, resting on a notepad, like a parchment shadow.

"You have a great memory for the past, Sol," the doctor says. "But remember, it is the present tense we are working on. For years, you have fully elaborated your past in your work with me, telling your story in so many words; but I hope you have finished, I am glad you have put that story in a box after all these years. You have been working on a long-ago six-month period—a traumatic episode consisting of one hundred ninety days—and you have persisted, quite valiantly I must say, remembering what is obviously painful to recall. But you perseverate. You circle around a sore, the same incidents, the same scenes, the same details. You hover around your scars. We have gone through this before. Your amnesia, as you know, is of the anterograde type. You recall only trauma. It is a mental self-punishment. You do not exist productively in the present."

I am looking at my thumbs. My clasped hands cradle them against my chest. They are going around and around, chasing each other and not touching, around and around against my chest.

"Sol! Are you listening?"

The moth on the notepad, crouching, does not stir.

"Language, for instance, Sol—you found a way to tell your story—with all those words—but do you see? It has mired you in your trauma. Your story is a poison pill—do you understand? And you keep eating it up—your toxic trauma. It is true, Sol, that language is all we have to tell our story. That may be so. But you can see where the tragedy lies. It is a paradox at the heart of our human mystery perhaps. Words are all we have to save us, but at the same time, they are not enough to make us whole."

My thumbs are stuck. The right, moving clockwise, is now raised above the left, moving counterclockwise, and each is in its frozen current, waiting for the signal.

"Sol! Do you hear me? You must try to move forward, instead of backward, in time. Your present tense is uncomplicated, lacking in intuition and insight. You do not relate to yourself or to others in the present. Only the past has meaning. Which is sad. You must try harder, Sol, to find peace."

And the doctor drags out the rest of his hiding shoe, puts his foot into it, then snaps his notebook shut.

The moth flies away, and my thumbs rest.

Lᴇᴛ ᴍᴇ ᴛᴇʟʟ you. I have the fortune to receive some news.

My old acquaintance, Sally Vega, has found me. She is a famous artist. She wrote me some weeks ago, and then she telephoned. She is in Manhattan, she said, for a show.

I tell Eremita my news calmly.

I am taking a train to the city, I say.

Inocentes, the wise one, shakes his head at the thought.

"Ma'am Sol," he says, "are you sure?"

"You are a dwarf, Inocentes: that is why the city scares you. I am not the same as you. My health has returned. I am well now, you know."

The stunted man, his beard always stubbly in the morning, beams and raises his thumb, for victory.

Eremita's shoulders are shaking, and she hides her face from me.

"What's so funny, Victoria? You are always giggling like that."

Inocentes stares innocently at both of us.

"What's so funny?" I repeat. "Are you laughing at me again, Victoria?"

"Ma'am Sol, no. No, I am not. It is just that you are calling him Inocentes again. His name, ma'am—his name is *Pete*!"

One of the nurses, a wiry Dominican, volunteers to take me. I let her. Anyhow, I do not drive. We drive to the station, toward the river. I am surprised to find it is there: the silver river from my picture window. I am happy, I am shaken by its generous welcome, by the way the water beckons to me.

I sit crying by the river's brown bank.

The nurse takes me by the hand.

There, there, she said. It's just the Hudson. You've seen it before.

Pretty, isn't it? I love this train ride—a view of beauty, just for us, all the way into Manhattan.

I nod.

A man leaves the newspaper when he gets out.

That's when I point to the picture.

Who's that?

The nurse starts giggling in her seat, she cannot stop.

"Oh, Miss Sol," she says finally, sobering up. "That's the president. That is President Barack Obama. Don't you remember we watched his inauguration?"

But he's black, I say.

Isn't that great? Change has happened in America.

But he should be careful, I say, concerned. He could be lynched.

Again, the nurse starts rocking in her seat, sputtering as if she cannot stop.

"Oh, Miss Sol. You are so funny."

A wasp is flying right next to me, by my shoulder against the glass, its wings parallel to the Hudson. I watch its shadow buzz. Buzz buzz buzz, buzzing right beside me. My shoulders are stiff and alert, all the way into the city. Buzz buzz buzz. It keeps buzzing at me, its hairy haunches stuck on the glass.

WHEN WE GET to the city, I am confused, frightened. I feel dizzy. It is full of people. The nurse steers me to a waiting taxi, and we slam the door so I can sit in my darkness. I close my eyes against the city. I cannot breathe.

We go to the park. It is where we shall meet, Sally Vega and I. At the park by the carousel, she said.

I know it, says the nurse. First you pass the Balto dog, then you go through a tunnel, then you see a big playground, recently fixed. If you turn right, you will miss it, and you will be among the skaters.

But we will find it, she says confidently. I always visit with my niece.

If only it did not have any people, this park could be pretty.

I watch the city with my eyes half-closed, watchful of rising trees, tiring flowers, horrifying gigantic rocks. Is there nothing that this park does not shelter? Badminton games, naked women, squat squirrels and greedy chipmunks, random ducks and rolling dancers, an entire softball game on its moors? I stop in my tracks.

What is it, dear?

It is Jed. He is smoking a cigarette, striking a soccer ball against a rock.

Should I go up to meet him?

He turns to me and to my relief I am mistaken. It is just a tall Asian, with an odd birthmark on his cheek.

This is a roundabout way of finding a friend, I say, wandering about in a musical park.

A man in the tunnel plays a saxophone. He stares at me, wishing I were dead.

Here it is, the nurse clucks. See? I told you I would find it. You can tell the merry-go-round by the songs.

Sᴀʟʟʏ ᴠᴇɢᴀ sᴀɪᴅ she had found my address in a complicated way—but she had not intended to, she wrote. She said she thought of me occasionally, but she had not been looking for me.

"I'm amazed at what occurs through coincidence," Sally had said on the phone.

Look for a big woman in the park in a furry pink coat, she warned.

When one meets people one once knew, it is tempting to imagine oneself in their eyes.

Sally, all in pink in a furry boa, stares at me, looking dubious.

She is sitting on the bench, watching children clamber up the painted horses.

She looks surprised to see me.

And so when I hold out my hands to Sally, I hide them, my browned, burnt wounds, tucked under my sleeves: my wrists' keloidal stars.

No one must know about them, even the scurrying squirrels.

But Sally refuses to take my sleeve at all. She stands and hugs me to her tightly.

I am scared by this wild-looking fat brown woman in a pink boa coat. I look around for the nurse.

And we do the *chica-chica*, cheek to cheek.

Sally is a celebrated woman. She is a photographer. She is chatty. She looks like Gertrude Stein in that portrait, the one painted by Picasso. Like me, she is still the same size, and we recognize each other.

Sally talks and talks. She confides everything that has happened through the years, and I let her go on and on, surprised by my lack of interest. I get distracted by all the insects. The ladybug, the moth. Her art, her awards, her past. Her widowed father, the government minister. Her mother, the famous adulteress, now dead. I swear it is a cicada, gobbling a piece of lint. Dates and events and incidents. Rebellions, presidents, elections. I cannot follow. I have a headache. The entomology is overwhelming.

I look for the nurse, but I see she has gone to throw bread crumbs into a duck pond, feeding some lame ducks.

The music of that carousel would drive anyone nuts.

"I met one of my parents' old friends in Germany, of all places,"

Sally is saying. "I was in Berlin for an arts festival. Postrevolutionary stuff—lots of East Europeans. I was the lone Asian, since a Cambodian guy, the one who makes collages of genocide victims, stayed home on a hunger strike. My parents' friend was Mrs. Grimes? Miss Grapes?"

"Mrs. Grier," I say automatically.

"Hey, right! You have a good memory. You were always the one for detail, Sol. I always thought you and Soli were so bright. Brighter than all of us. Twins! Now this woman had figured in that tragedy, you know, the assassination of the American."

"Colonel Arthur Grier."

"Yes. Good one, Sol! Remember how you used to talk about the smallest details of ancient history, as if they had happened only yesterday? So sharp! Anyway, it was sad. Her late husband. What a fate. I remember she and her husband went to parties with my dad when he was in government, and she introduced herself. A platinum blonde, interested in Asian art. She lives in Germany now. She asked me who I was, where I lived. She asked me about obsolete places in Manila. I told her of the changes—the malls of Fort Bonifacio, the public bidding to sell the LOTUS grounds in New Manila, now that the American bases are gone. She is married to a consul now; they live in Berlin. She asked about this and that, about people she knew. She knew your parents. Frankie and Queenie. She wanted to know about them, and Bumbum Esdrújula, et cetera. She's a resilient woman, you have to say that for Mrs. Graves. Anyhow, I told her all about my parents, and about your parents, too. About all the new palaces being built in Alabang. Quite the showcase. How happy your parents are now: just about the cream of the crop, in the new regime under the new

president. Your mother had joined the streets for justice and recon-
ciliation after all—years and years ago. She gave a lot of money to
the democracy movement, the yellow ribbon crowd. Mrs. Grimes
was enthusiastic, she said, about the new, wonderful order in the
Philippines. Not so wonderful really, I said. It's a goddamned mess
now, decades after 1986."

"What happened in 1986?"

"Oh, Sol, you're so funny."

"I remember when John Lennon died. Even the commies
cried."

"Wow. That was way before. Way before the rebellion that
kicked out the dictator in 1986. We were babies when John Lennon
died."

"He died on December 7, 1980. Manila time," I said. "We were
seventeen."

"That's what I mean. We were babies! Anyway, I said to Mrs.
Green: that's so nice of you to think kindly of the Philippines, after
your husband's death. I thought it might be safe to mention, after all
these years. But she kind of teared up. I think. I felt bad that I mentioned it. Anyway, guess what? I got your mother's phone number
from her, the one I called, here in New York." And there was a delicate lift in her eyes: or was that the sun's glare. "And then, can you
believe it, I saw Jed."

"What?"

"You know, that fat-faced guy with glasses?"

"Jed was tall, lean, light-haired."

"Well, then it wasn't him. I remember his name was Jed."

"Ed," I say. "Edwin Cardozo."

"Yeah, him. Now that guy is doing very well for himself."

"Really?"

I am faintly interested. I am trying to keep up with an ant, clambering down the bench to a glazed nut, right by the tongue of my silver shoe.

"I saw him in Berlin. He procures things. For his boss. He's a consultant for Secretary Esdrújula."

"So he is still around."

"She. Secretary Bumbum Esdrújula. The newly appointed head of the Department of Culture."

"Ah. The Secretary's wife."

"The Senator's," she says. "He's a presidential candidate, you know. And who knows? He certainly has enough money to win."

"So," I murmur.

"So I saw Jed. Ed. He procures things."

"Munitions," I guess.

"No. Museum pieces. He came to Germany for some Rizaliana, in Heidelberg. He was looking for a statue the hero had described in one of his letters. He's a scholar. Educated at Cornell. Something like that. He's a learned man. Isn't that a scream? He used to be this creepy guy in a dirty ponytail, always hitting me up for money for his causes. Now he's a government consultant. I guess it's only fair— it's happening everywhere—the recurrence of the past in odd ways. We talked briefly, in the crowd. He was leaving for America that afternoon, he said. I gave him your number in New York. And then guess what?"

"What?"

"He sent me your address: see? You had given it to him a long time ago, he said. More than twenty years ago. And he kept it. Just in case. That's what I have to tell you. Weird, huh. So did he come? Have you seen him?"

"No."

"Anyway, I had both your phone number and your address, from two different people. I thought it was fate, so I got in touch. Isn't that strange?"

"Not really," I say. "You know there is something amateurish about reality."

The little ant has found its goal. It is laboriously shouldering its sticky prize.

"Let's go," she says suddenly. "Let's take a picture of us on the carousel!"

My head is so dizzy just looking at the crazy horses, I clutch the pole, my scars cold against the metal. I have to shut my eyes. She takes my picture on one of the musical painted horses, going around and around.

IN A LETTER to me, Sally types: "You're right. I was wrong. It wasn't Jed in Berlin; it was Ed. He gave a lecture the other day, at a new bookstore in Makati. We did the chitchat, the reminiscence of old times. We had coffee. He gave a run-through of where they were. Item: Vita Tupas, remember her? I called her Miss FQS. She's married with five children, to a banker in Pasig. She works with a woman's cooperative, fundraising. Five children: can you believe? Item: Esmeraldo, the Fourth Ism, is still in the hills. Ka Noli, he used to be called. He never surrendered. The last Maoist in the world. Maybe I'll go out and try to photograph him, too: for my new series,

Geishas and Guerrillas, contrasting portraits of socialites and rebels. An analysis of the present through the past, or vice versa. Edwin only laughed at me. Item: Buddyboy Wong, the skinny, hyperactive basketball player, is now a skinny, hyperactive chef—owner of the best Chinese restaurant in Caloocan. He's expanding into the north, Edwin says—he's just waiting for the roads to improve. They see each other often, he says, at karaoke bars—you know Ed. He was a Beatlemaniac. Item: Kiko de Quirico. Remember, Francis 'Kiko' Not-Coppola? He's a stocks analyst. Very rich. He's still a geek, though—spends his money funding indie films that never get an audience. Movies about debt collectors and cockfight wardens. Lowlifes who come to sad ends. Too depressing for Filipinos. But you should see them—they're moving. Sometimes they are at the MOMA. Item: Jed, that war freak, the adventurist? The one they said had been a lookout for the assassins. The driver or the messenger, something like that? He wanted to make his name as a hero for the revolution. Soli's old boyfriend. They said he did it for her. He wanted to kill the American to impress Soli. Red freak. Well, he's alive and well in Mexico or Texas, Ed is not sure. As he puts it, somewhere out there, in a town between E and X. And as for Soli: we both felt sad, we had a moment of silence, when we remembered Soli. Some new details have surfaced. Do you know? A guilty soldier came out of the woodwork. What a story. He went to her family home a few years ago. He told them where to find her body. Somewhere in Batangas. Buried, not gunned down. There had been no shoot-out. The rumors were right. She was mutilated, tortured, as the rumors always said. He could confirm it, the man confessed, because it was he—he was a torturer. A CAFGU soldier. He wanted to come out in public with the truth, he said, because it was the right thing to do. Can you believe? How many stories like this will be coming out of the woodwork from those times?

"Her face, the soldier said, it haunted him every day.

"I cannot fathom, I cannot imagine. It is still incredible to me, her story harrows the soul, does it not? Ed and I both agreed: she could not have been the Sparrow Queen. It is a lie. But it is one of those things. No one will ever know. No one will tell. There have been no more confessions. It's horrible how we forget the past, just like that—we forget how war has killed the best of us. People barely remember her name, the names of those who fell to the dictatorship. The best among us have died. And it is the cockroaches who survive. I told Ed: somehow, it seems to me, we are all guilty of a failure of memory. Ed agreed.

"And then there's us: U.F. Useful fools: that's what we were, you and I, Sol. U.F. That was the term Pablo had for me—my erstwhile guerrilla love. I told Ed all about you, about our meeting in Central Park. How you looked exactly as you were all those years ago. You looked exactly the same. It's a wonder how we all survived the eighties! Ed was happy to learn: he says hello."

ACKNOWLEDGMENTS

This novel is for Arne, the book's first reader.

I'd also like to thank the George Bennett Fellowship of Phillips Exeter Academy, where I first worked on this novel's draft; and the Civitella Ranieri Fellowship, which gave me space to write in the hills of Umbria, leading me to return to this book. I'd like to thank Charlie Pratt of Exeter and Dana Prescott of Civitella Ranieri, artists who support artists.

Twelve years span the novel's beginning to its completion. I owe a lot. First of all, to the Tangherlinis: Frank and Jane, and Tim, Dan, Niels, and their families; Sam and Sandra Heath and their family: Aymara, Santiago, Mimi and Awaya; the Berrol-Youngs: Lisa, Skeff, Maya (the book's first student reader) and Cedar; Ubaldo, Elisabetta and Brenda Stecconi; David Errington; Eric Gamalinda; and Lara Stapleton, for her faith always. I'm grateful to so many: Karina Bolasco and the people of Anvil; all my great colleagues at the Masters School who sustained me for twelve years; Caroline Dumaine, who gave advice, Darren Wood, an early reader whose intelligence never fails, David Dunbar, for his vast generosity and passion, and Pam Clarke; all of the students I have taught in Manila and the U.S.; my Filipino writer friends in New York, whose dedication to art is as steadfast as it is joyful; and my fellow artists at Civitella Ranieri, especially Michael Dumanis and Dora Malech, from either of whom I stole a phrase for this book.

Above all, my gratitude and love to my sisters Marie and Carol, and my brothers William, Tito and Dean, and their families; my aunt Tita Lully and uncle Tio Diony, last of a clan; and my cousins, especially Daryll, a beautiful writer and reader, and Beng, whose home is always open.

None of my books would have been written without my sister Marie, who taught me how to read.

In preparing this book for publication, I trusted absolutely in the fabulous good taste of my editor, Denise Scarfi, and the wisdom of Kirby Kim.

And to Ken: for your patience and love, this book is not enough; and last but never the least, to Nastasia: loveliest reader of the tower of Babel, here's another.

GUN DEALERS' DAUGHTER

Gina Apostol

DISCUSSION QUESTIONS

Thematic questions:

1. Think back to the opening passage of *Gun Dealers' Daughter* (p. 3):

   > *Uncle Gianni met the girl at Nice Airport. He held her by the hand as lightbulbs flashed. Revise that: not hand. By the sleeve. He held me by the sleeve, gently. There was something awkward about my arrival.*
   >
   > *My stooped, discordant figure—my bandaged, gauzed lump of hands.*
   >
   > *A cordon held curious onlookers at bay, and a film crew, Gallic and impervious, skinny, tilting men in black, strode about my cleared path.*

   When you began the novel, what was your impression of the scene, of the narrator, and of the characters? What did you make of the author's switching between third- and first-person point of view? What about the narrator's instruction to "revise that"?

2. At what point in reading the novel did you begin to understand what was actually transpiring in that opening scene? Were you several pages in, at some point in the middle, or near the end? Can you recall the specific passage or scene that led to your understanding?

3. In the novel's first chapter, Sol, the narrator, is recounting her arrival in Europe. She mentions several suicide attempts. What was

Sol so desperate to escape through suicide? Remorse? Humiliation? Speculate on the psychological factors at play here.

4. During Sol's first encounter with Colonel Grier, the American, she confesses that her understanding of history is composed of "obscure little things. Useless knowledge" (p. 36). What role do these "obscure little things" play in the novel's style? In the novel's depiction of Filipino history?

5. How does Sol's faulty memory—or her outright amnesia—shape the narrative? Does it add to or detract from your enjoyment of the novel?

6. Explain the importance of "high culture" (art, classical music, literature) in the novel.

7. Sol spends her early university days in love with Jed, the "millionaire who dressed like Saint Francis and acted like Saint Jerome" (p. 53). How do her descriptions of Jed as a "privileged anarchist" (p. 51) and as "grumpy and worthless . . . a beautiful creature wrapped up in vague martyrdoms" (p. 53) indicate the passing of time and her own change in perspective? Do you have any sense of what would have attracted the young Sol to such a person? Does Sol see herself in Jed?

8. Describe the significance of Sol's friendship with Soli. Can you think of any reasons the author might use so many versions of "sol" in naming the novel's characters (Soli, Soledad Soliman)?

9. What have you been able to glean about Uncle Gianni? How is he similar to—or different from—Sol's mother and father?

10. Why do you think Sol's Marxist group chooses to attack Colonel Grier? What of his attributes and behaviors are most odious to the group? Does he seem like an appropriate "target" for a socialist group? What about for Sol personally? Why or why not?

11. What connections does the novel draw between economics, poli-